Cold War

The Richard Jackson Saga, Volume 9

Ed Nelson

Published by Ed Nelson, 2024.

Table of Contents

Other books by Ed Nelson

The Richard Jackson Saga
Book 1: The Beginning
Book 2: Schooldays
Book 3: Hollywood
Book 4: In the Movies
Book 5: Star to Deckhand
Book 6: Surfing Dude
Book 7: Third Time is a Charm
Book 8: Oxford University
Book 9: Cold War
Book 10: Taking Care of Business
Book 11: Interesting Times
Book 12: Escape from Siberia
Book 13: Regicide
Book 14: What's Under, Down Under?
Book 15: The Lunar Kingdom
Book 16: First Steps
In the Richard Jackson World
Mary, Mary
Stand-Alone Story
Ever and Always
The Cast in Time series
Book 1: Baron
Book 2: Baron of the Middle Counties
Book 3: Count
Book 4: Earl
Book 5: Earl of the Marches

Dedication

This is dedicated to my wife Carol for her support and help as the first reader and editor.

Also, the BHS class of 1962 just because.
Professionally edited by Janet E. Rupert

Quotation

That is exactly how it happened, give or take a lie or two.

James Garner as Wyatt Earp describing the gunfight at the OK Corral in the movie *Sunset*.

Copyright © 2019

ISBN 979-8-89434-014-2
Library of Congress Control Number: 2022911369

Chapter 1

On the last several flights I had been introspective. Not this one. I didn't have the time or the inclination. The flight started well...at least until I got to my seat. A young lady with a baby was sitting in the window seat. The baby was obviously in discomfort from the way it cried. Some baby cries mean they are hungry or need a diaper change.

This cry said I'm sick, Mummy; make me better!

The mother was rocking the baby, who was about two months old. It wasn't working. She then opened the diaper bag to get something out. Her bag was a huge model, and she was having trouble opening it while holding the baby. In a moment of insanity, I offered to hold the child.

Big mistake! The handover wasn't even complete, and the baby threw up all down the front of my suit, tie, and shirt. I have no idea how such a small kid could hold so much puke.

This got the flight attendant's attention, who brought me a wet towel. This entire time, people were boarding the aircraft and squeezing past. I didn't mind the dirty looks, as I thought I deserved them. I did mind the smell. The plane had been sitting in the sun on this warm day.

They hadn't turned on the air in the plane yet, so it was very warm inside. The smell got worse and worse. Now, I only had a kit bag with me as I had clothes waiting at the other end, so I had no replacement shirt or t-shirt.

After handing the baby back to a mortified mother, I made a trip to the loo. There, I removed my shirt and t-shirt and washed up; after that, I brushed my suit jacket off. Fortunately, the puke hadn't penetrated that deep into the fabric, so most of it brushed off.

Coming out of the loo, I wore my suit coat buttoned up, so I only looked semi-weird. I gave the shirts and tie to the stewardess to put in their trash. There was no way I was going to haul them around with me.

The tie was no great loss as it had the Lifeguard regimental stripe. I was with the RAF, so I thought it was a fitting end.

Mummy was now breastfeeding baby, who, of course, was hungry now that nasty stuff was out of his tummy. I sat back down, closed my eyes, and wished the flight were over. I was able to sleep for most of the trip or read a light novel.

Mummy apologized over and over. I finally told her all was forgiven, and kindly please leave me alone. She told me she would be glad to but had a delicate question for me. I nodded my head to get her to go ahead.

"Would you hold my baby so I can go to the water closet?"

Shoot me, shoot me now.

"Of course, I will."

The baby, who was asleep at this time, didn't wake until Mummy closed the door of the loo. Then he woke up and must have realized I wasn't Mummy. He let loose with a screaming fit.

Mummy's trip to the loo was more than a quick pee. I ended up walking the baby up and down the aisle of the airplane for over ten minutes. The cowardly stewardesses were not to be found. How does one hide in a long aluminum tube?

I just thought I was getting dirty looks at boarding. People were trying to sleep, and the one thing we didn't have to worry about was the baby's lungs. Someone must have recognized me because they pulled out a flash camera and took a picture.

Just go ahead and shoot me.

Finally, Mum got back, and the baby settled down for the rest of the flight.

Thankfully, the rest of the flight was uneventful. The cowardly stewardess, Abigail, finally showed up after I managed to clean myself as much as possible to offer me a drink.

The young mother, whose name was Emily May, apologized once more. On impulse, I autographed a photo of her and her son Mark.

"For a flight I will never forget."

A car and driver were waiting for me at LAX. I think the traffic was getting worse day by day in LA. The smog made it impossible to see the mountains. What had been a paradise was now becoming a hell hole. The trip seemed like it took forever, so I was glad to get home.

A large sign at the guardhouse stated, "Welcome home, Sir Richard, winner of the 1960 US Open." That was nice. Even better was that my whole family was waiting in the courtyard to welcome me. The driver must have called ahead. The car had one of those new telephones that could call from the car. It was set up in the front and with the window closed; I didn't know he had used it.

I got out to hugs, kisses, and handshakes. You can figure out who did what.

I was overwhelmed and had to wipe a tear out of my eye: maybe there was more than one.

Until I got home, I hadn't realized how much I had missed my family.

Mum was the first to notice my dress or lack of a shirt.

"There must be a story here."

I gave a quick explanation of what had happened. The boys thought it was neat that a baby could eat so much and throw it up. Mark May would grow up to be a strong kid.

We went into the house, where I took a quick shower and changed into California casual. England was seldom warm enough to wear a golf shirt.

My siblings had wandered off to whatever they had been doing as Mum, Dad, and I sat down for a conversation in the library. Rather than face an interrogation I gave them a synopsis of my time since winning the golf tournament.

They had questions about being dubbed a knight and my rescuing Miss Bardot. Dad thought it was good that I had saved the Mona Lisa from damage even though he never understood the big deal made over the painting. She was only a woman, and they were all mysteries.

I started to open my mouth to object that she demonstrated the quintessential mystery of women when I saw him grin. He had got me. It was good to be home.

"Rick, one more thing; we didn't have time to celebrate your golfing victory as you had to leave right away. We are holding a party in your honor this Saturday."

"How big of a party is it?"

"Big, all the people involved in your journey to victory, a select group from Hollywood, business leaders you have dealt with, and some old friends."

"I guess I have to cancel my date then."

"You have a date Saturday night, with whom?"

It was my turn to grin.

"It's nice to have you home, Rick."

Dad told me, "Rick, you may not have heard, but *Over the Ohio* is being released the week after next, so you will need a date for the premiere or let the studio send a starlet they wish to publicize."

"I will try to get a date since every starlet I meet is too desperate to make fame and fortune, and I seem like an easy route for them."

Who can I ask? As it is relatively short notice to obtain a dress and everything that goes with it.

Mum asked me, "Rick, if you don't have anyone in mind, could you take Mary? She is in the movie and wants to go. Your dad was going to be her escort, but it would work out better for both of you to go together. That takes the burden off you and Dad."

I looked at Dad, who mouthed, "Please."

I guess Dad didn't want to walk on the red carpet. I don't blame him; all the noise and shouted questions are bothersome.

Mum followed up with, "Please ask Mary. We haven't told her yet that she can go."

"Okay, I will do it right away. Where is she anyway?"

"She is up on the tower with several friends. They had a sleepover, and it is still going on. I'm afraid that they may never go home."

I took the elevator up, thinking as it went about the last time I had come up here and discovered Mary and her five-year-old friends sunbathing topless. What a mess.

At the top, the warning sign wasn't out, but I yelled anyway, asking if it was safe for me to come up the last set of stairs. Not many things frightened me, but little girls were high on my list.

"Come on up, Ricky," my little sister yelled.

Mary and her friends were all dressed in shorts and t-shirts, so my fears weren't realized. Still, I will always check first.

"Mary, are you planning to go to the premiere of *Over the Ohio*?"

"I haven't asked yet because it will be past my bedtime before it is over. I would like to go, and I'm hoping Daddy will be my escort."

"Mary, I have a problem. I don't have a date, and it is too late for me to ask a girl who would have to find a dress and everything. Even if I paid for it, she wouldn't have the time to get ready."

"That's right, Ricky. That is poor planning on your part."

"Would you go with me?"

"So, I'm chopped liver? You are concerned about other girls having enough time but think I can be ready at a moment's notice?"

The other little girls were watching us avidly. Their heads moved back and forth like a tennis match. For them, it was either a sport or a learning experience.

"What were you going to do if Daddy said he would take you?"

"Uh, I would, uh, okay, you got me. I would wear a dress and its accoutrements from my new fall collection. I'm still not allowed to wear makeup, but I would have to have my hair done."

Where did my little six-year-old sister learn a word like accoutrements?

"Well, would you go with me if I asked Mum and Dad for permission?"

"Yes, I would. It will be good for my image to be seen with a hunk like you."

Who is this monster?

"I will check, but I think it will be okay with them."

"Okay, I'm counting on you. Now I have to call my clothing people to get what I want to be shipped immediately."

"I thought they were sending you one of everything in every color?"

"They were, but the collection has expanded so much I would need several of our basements to store them."

I gave her a stern look. Has she given up the secret of our sub-basement?

"I tried to get Daddy to dig down for more room, but he wouldn't do it. Then I asked if I could have your workshop space since you are never here. They told me no since you paid for it. Would you sell it to me?"

"Squirt, that addition cost almost ten thousand dollars."

"I will pay you fifteen."

Some battles you can't win; some should never be fought in the first place.

"I will think about it. What are you doing with all the clothes as you grow out of them?"

"I have an arrangement with the Salvation Army. It gives me a decent tax deduction and favorable publicity. Susan Wallace helped me set it up."

In other battles, you just run like hell from the field. I told the other girls it was nice to see them and retreated from the tower.

When I related my conversation with Mary to Mum and Dad, they both chuckled.

"We have to keep a tight rein on her, Rick; she is growing up too fast. There is nothing bad, just out of balance with other children her age. We are scared to death that she may end up like other child stars.

"On the brighter side, of course, she can go with you to the premiere. Just make sure you protect her from the press and the paparazzi."

"I think they would need protection from her."

"Well, there is that, but you know what I mean."

"Yes, Mum."

Thinking of clothes, I checked in my closet to make certain I had a tux here to wear to the opening. I had shipped so much back and forth across the Atlantic I couldn't remember what was where. It was a good thing I did check because, apparently, my tuxedo was in England.

It was still early enough I was able to call The Meadows and ask Mr. Hamilton to ship it to me by air. He wondered if I should just rent one here or have another made. That took me aback for a moment. It had never occurred to me. I told him not to bother to ship one; I would have a new one made up. It sure is nice to have money.

Not wanting to leave it to chance, I called a tailor on Rodeo Drive, who had been there forever. His shop was next to a hair salon from which I had bought gift certificates for my office ladies last Christmas, so I knew exactly how to get there. I would visit them first thing in the morning.

I got up on British time on Wednesday. It was barely daylight. It was a pleasure to take my run on the soft paths of the nature reserve. After my exercises, I had a hearty breakfast and was good for the day.

I did stop for a few words with Ben at the stable and fed an apple to George.

I then headed out to the tailor. Mum let me borrow her Morgan. I must be in good standing! It was fun driving the Morgan in and out of traffic as fast as I could. If I had got a ticket, it wouldn't have been so much fun, not so much from the fine but Mum.

As I got out of the car, I heard a loud "Stop thief!"

A full-grown man was running down the sidewalk with a purse in his hands. He was looking back. Further away, a young lady was the one yelling. It didn't take rocket science to figure out he was a purse snatcher.

I was in a perfect position. I just held my arm out and let him clothesline himself.

He hit hard and went down. It took no effort on my part other than that I would have a sore arm tomorrow. I leaned down and rolled him onto his stomach and then knelt on his back. It was right in front of the tailor shop, so the tailor came to his door to see what all the commotion was about.

I asked him to call the police, and after that, I would like to be measured for a new tuxedo. The young lady ran up and grabbed her purse. She thanked me for saving it for her.

She let out all at once that she had just arrived in town to try to break into the movies, and all of her life savings were in her purse, and I was her hero, and she didn't know what she would have done if I hadn't stopped the bandit. This all came out without a breath. From the way she could yell, I think she had a future of some sort.

The police didn't take long to arrive and cuff the man after a quick explanation. They separated all the witnesses and took our stories. The event was so simple that all of us told the same basic story. He grabbed her purse and ran. I stuck my arm out and brought him down then sat on him until the police arrived. Pretty cut and dried.

The aspiring actress Lily Tomlin, who appeared to be in her early twenties, thanked me and left.

She never asked my name, so I avoided the dreaded, "Could you introduce me?"

I'm certain that she would be found and find a place out here. If nothing else the snort she gave when she laughed would make her stand out.

Since this was Hollywood, people with cameras came out of the woodwork. At least no reporters wanted an interview.

After that, it took an hour to get my measurements taken and a new tuxedo promised by next Tuesday, in plenty of time for the premiere. He would provide everything, including shoes.

By that time, the adrenaline high dropped, and I needed sugar. Welcome back to America, Rick!

Chapter 2

After leaving the tailor, I stopped by my office to see how things were going. Jim let me know everything was in order without going into detail and the money was still pouring in. We did set up a formal business review for next Wednesday. He would contact everyone who needed to be there.

I did pay for the visit as I was roped into signing cards for employees and friends. There were several news clippings of special events held or won by people I knew. I took the time and wrote a short note of congratulations to each of them.

What I thought would be a short visit took until quitting time. I left with a sore hand from all the writing. It was well worth it because all those people had earned recognition for their efforts.

One of them was neat. A girl Mary's age had formed a fan club for Mary. The club had a sale where they sold all their outgrown clothes from the Mary Collection. They then used the money to feed puppies and kittens in the local pound.

I had to show this to Mary because she needed to give them some recognition.

That was the first thing I did when I got home. Mary knew nothing about her fan club and their actions. She agreed that she needed to do something. I suggested she talk to Mum and Susan Wallace about this and also find out if she had other fan clubs.

If nothing else, she should have a clipping service. I only received the news about her fan club because she was identified as the sister of actor Ricky Jackson. She left at a run as was usual for her to find Mum and to get something started. Oh, to have the energy of a six-year-old. I know, I know, I'm only sixteen, but you should see her go.

I spent the rest of the afternoon precisely doing nothing of any value. It was great. Well, I did push the elevator button to the tower.

Does that count? Until I stopped, I didn't realize how hectic my life had gotten since I started at Oxford.

I didn't even read before falling asleep.

Thursday morning, I was up early and felt refreshed. I did my run and exercises and then on an impulse, took George out for a ride. He hadn't got out much lately, and he was frisky. Not in a bad way; he just wanted to get out and move, so I let him.

We rode to the Forest Service airbase over the new bridge. The back gate was unlocked, so I had no problem getting on base. The last time I was here, I was stopped and had to identify myself. I was at ease when a Jeep came roaring up to me and slid to a stop.

A man in a uniform unfamiliar to me told me, "Get off that horse and get your hands in the air, or I will shoot."

Since he had pulled a .38 revolver out and was holding it FBI-style with his finger on the trigger, I did so without argument.

"Now turn around, get down on your knees, and put your hands behind your head."

This guy is crazy! Crazy or not, he had the weapon, not me.

I followed his instructions slowly. This wasn't fast enough for him as he came up to force me down. This was a mistake on his part because my unarmed combat training covered this possibility.

When his left hand touched my shoulder, I turned and ducked to my left. By natural inclination, he followed me in turning left. This also brought his right arm off, so the gun wasn't pointing at me.

I then used the momentum to force both of us to the ground with me on top. I then rolled him onto his stomach and used the handcuffs on his belt to cuff him.

After retrieving his pistol and removing the shells, I had him stand up and get in his Jeep. Since there was a coil of rope in the back, I used that to tie him in place. Then it was a simple matter of tying George's reins to the rear bumper and driving slowly to the Forest Service Headquarters building.

I will not repeat any of the language used during the short trip.

When I arrived at the building, a couple of Forest Rangers in uniform took one look and started laughing. I wasn't sure what was funny, but it seemed to make their day.

"Does this guy belong to you?"

"Not really, he is a rent-a-cop hired to patrol the grounds. There have been some teenagers sneaking in at night. I think they sent him here because he is such an idiot, they didn't know where else to send him. He had been giving all of us grief, but we weren't allowed to do anything."

"What do you want me to do with him? No matter what, he doesn't get his gun back."

This set the guy off again.

As was my practice, I had saddlebags on George. I opened them, pulled out my US marshal's ID, and showed it to them.

"Now, who is in charge here?"

The Forest Service people took me inside, leaving the so-called cop tied up. The chief ranger, or whatever his title was, recognized me from previous trips. When I explained what had happened, he just shook his head.

"I knew something like this would happen. I tried to get rid of him, but he is related to some congressman, and we can't touch him."

"Please tell the people you report to that I don't want him within ten miles of my family."

I then laid the pistol on the desk sans bullets. The guy would probably get the pistol back, but not while I was around.

"The congressman won't like that."

"Tell the congressman who I am and what I have donated here. If he has any questions, please have him call me."

That proved to be a mistake, as I didn't understand how shameless some congressmen could be. He called and tried to get me to donate to his campaign. Not only did I turn him down. I made a point of donating to his opponent.

It didn't help, as the congressman got reelected by a large margin. Maybe when I'm old enough, I will run against him.

Returning home after that exciting look at how it pays to be related to a politician, I spent time brushing down George. I had to do something to calm down a little.

After that, I cleaned up and drove to the studio to see what was happening. Mr. Monroe wasn't in. I stopped at the schoolhouse, but a class was in session. All the stuntmen were busy working. I watched them setting up for a jump from a three-story building, but it was tedious work as this had been done many times.

I was so desperate that I checked in to see if there was any need for extras. There weren't, at least none of my description. If I had been short and fat, I could have had two different jobs.

I did have lunch at the commissary. The usual mélange of costumes was present. I won't say it was boring, but it didn't leave me feeling excited as it did at one time. I was jaded at sixteen!

After lunch, I drove down to the beach, but it wasn't a good day to surf. I thought about renting a plane and flying, but it was too late in the day. I was so bored I even thought about going to Disneyland, but quickly set that aside.

I then drove out to the Riviera Country Club and hit a few buckets of balls at the driving range. At least I was able to get into a zone with my practice. I did have to sign autographs, but at least people didn't interrupt me on the tee box.

Returning home, I ran into Mum in the kitchen. The kitchen is where the cookies hang out, you know. She asked what I had been doing all day. I related how nothing seemed to work out other than finding out that nepotism is not a good thing. I sort of knew that, but that guy at the Forest Service base brought it home.

"Rick, some relatives can do a good job. It goes bad when a worthless person is given the job. There is a difference, you know. Your dad had you work on houses in Bellefontaine, and that was a form of nepotism, so you have to be careful how you think of it."

"I guess you are right, but that guy was a loser, and thinking of him being armed is scary."

"There are always people like that; it is the way of the world. Just be careful that you don't put someone in a position they are unsuited for."

After those words of wisdom, I put myself in a position that I wasn't suited for, promptly losing six games of eight ball to Denny. At least it was fun.

He updated me on his work at the photography studio. It was going very well. He appeared to have a lock on the local market for beauty pageant portfolios. He had even picked up some work with aspiring actors and actresses.

Sam Nielsen was even talking about opening another studio in Santa Anna, and Denny could make appointments there. He and I played around with that thought for a while. We wondered if it would be profitable to start a chain of franchise studios.

It would appear under his name as the photographer of the stars. We decided that he didn't have enough name recognition yet. If one of his actors or actresses made it in the movies, he would have something to work with.

I asked to see the pictures that he had taken so far. He had copies in an album. Most of them were average. There was one young lady who stood out. Her name was Goldie Hawn. We just couldn't figure out how to help her get a breakthrough.

I thought about using my influence at the studio but decided against it as I knew nothing about her. She would probably end up as one of those who would tell her grandchildren that she could have been a star if she had gotten a break. That is sad, but that is how most of the aspiring actors and actresses turned out. How lucky I had been!

We promptly forgot about the proposed project and went to dinner.

At dinner, Mary was excited about the upcoming movie showing, and that was all she could talk about. It was all so exciting. Mum was even going to let her use fingernail polish for the first time. She tried for lipstick but got nowhere with that one.

She even was going to have her hair done. The studio was sending a stylist over to do her hair just before we left. Her best girlfriends were coming over to watch her get ready. I asked if Patty would be one of them, but they were on the outs again.

More immediate to me was getting information on the party they were holding in my honor on Saturday. At least I could get away with a polo shirt and sports coat for the event.

We have had so many large catered events at Jackson House that it was getting to be old hat to us. On average, Mum and Dad sponsor a charity event every month. That meant catering, parking, and extra staff were all on Mum's Rolodex.

It was going to be less than formal as the weather promised to be good, so it was going to be hamburgers and hot dogs rather than a rubber chicken meal. That sounded good to me. Mum was even trying out a new group with a portable pizza oven, and they would make them onsite.

I was most interested in the plans for dessert. There would be an ice cream bar where you could fix your sundae. This was my kind of party. There would be an open bar for a limited time. That didn't interest me. She also had a band lined up, The Beach Boys.

They agreed to play for a reduced fee but had a condition. I had to sing "Rock and Roll Cowboy" with them. I'm going to kill Brian.

Chapter 3

I stayed out of the caterer's way on Saturday morning as they arrived to set up. The affair was going to be in the field behind the garages. They set up large tents. The largest would have a stage and dance floor.

There were several food service tents with barbeque setups. A whole hog had been roasting overnight in a fire pit. There would be hamburgers, hot dogs, barbequed beef, and hog. Then, chickens by the dozen. All the help was dressed in Western style. There were children's rides and games.

A miniature golf course had been erected. A driving range was also set up on the other side of the fence in the park. Buckets of balls and clubs were available from an attendant. I wondered if the park people were aware of what we were going to be doing.

I asked Dad and he told me they had received permission after posting a bond that the woods would be cleared tomorrow. Somehow, I doubted it would be cleared, as I had seen how some golfers hit the ball. Maybe that was why the head of the park commission had been invited.

After seeing all this activity, I decided it would be a good day to go to the beach. That was the plan, anyway. I ended up being a runner for Mum. It seems everybody thought someone else was bringing the, well, you name it. I didn't know how many items were needed for an event like this.

I even had to help put up the signs congratulating me on winning the US Open. That felt a little weird. Especially since the guys I was helping didn't recognize me. They talked about how I must be a snobbish big shot. I asked them if they had ever seen Rick Jackson before. Neither of them had. It was a beautiful and embarrassing moment for them when I introduced myself.

They both stumbled over themselves, apologizing. I laughed it off and told them they now had a story for their girlfriends and grandchildren. That eased the moment, and we finished up the large signs and then helped others erect tents, haul ice and drinks for the coolers, and worked our butts off.

As things came together and our general labor was finished, I asked them how much they were being paid for the day. It wasn't much since they were from a pickup labor agency, so I gave them a healthy tip. They gave more thanks and much laughter about how things had started.

After that, I boldly left the area. Well, it was more like a slunk out of Mum's sight so I could shower and get dressed for the afternoon festivities. I had been told that I would have to make a short speech, and yes, I would sing "Rock and Roll Cowboy."

As I got dressed, I rehearsed a short speech, thanking everyone for coming, all those who had helped my golf career, the American way of life, and apple pie.

I decided since it was a Western theme, I would go all the way and wear my total Sir Nicklaus on a cattle drive outfit. This included a Stetson and my six-shooters. I double-checked they weren't loaded but had live rounds in the belt loops. I remembered our last big party and a machine gun.

I'm glad to say nothing negative happened at the party if you didn't count a shanked drive hitting a deer that was passing through. I didn't see it, but I guess the deer jumped and took off.

I managed to get through both speech and song without embarrassing myself or my parents. I was fortunate that I was upstaged while singing. Mary and her friends got up on the stage and jitterbugged. They were good, and it took the attention off me.

Mum wasn't thrilled when Brian asked if Mary could tour with them.

I think he was kidding.

I spent most of my afternoon shaking hands and accepting congratulations. They even had a photo setup for me to pose with people. For this, I had to hurry to change into golfing attire. My face started to ache from smiling. I don't know how models can do that day after day.

That and sign autographs. There were pictures available for me to sign. It was of me accepting the US Open trophy.

There were a couple of guys there from the PGA tour. They tried talking me into turning pro. They thought my public face would help attract people to the game. Also, think about the money I could make. With the right sponsors, I might make half a million dollars a year!

I let them down gently, saying nothing about a pay cut. I told them my education was the most important thing on my mind right now. They were gentlemen about it, but I knew this wasn't the end of things.

I did get to see and talk a little with my friends in the movie industry. The whole stuntman contingent had shown up. I doubt the free drinks had anything to do with it.

Mr. Monroe wanted to know if I would relent on making another movie shortly. I told him no, which he thought was a shame because the soon-to-be-released *Over the Ohio* would make me a big name at the box office. At least he knew that for me, it wasn't the money.

I asked how Nina was doing. He told me she was becoming like the European crowd she hung out with, and he wasn't happy about her new attitude. He requested that if I were in Switzerland, I would talk to her and see if it was getting as bad as he thought.

I told him I would but that I had no plans to be there shortly. Mentally, I made a note to fly over after getting back to England.

Putting up a large party takes a long time. Breaking it down isn't as much. Within two hours of the last guest leaving, all the equipment was cleared and tents were down. The area was raked clean.

The only thing left was golf ball retrieval. Eddie's Scout troop would be doing that the next morning. During the day, there were various contests, largest and longest hook or slice and weirdest shank.

When these occurred, they marked them with stakes. A cone was also established for hooks and slices. Two pairs of stakes did this with a ten-foot rope between them. One stake was never moved. The other stake on each side of the range was spread out as a new "record" was established. This made a cone that would be gone over by the Scouts.

It was around nine o'clock when things had settled down. Mum, Dad, and I were having coffee in the library.

Mum asked, "Rick, do you have any plans for the coming week?"

"Nothing that couldn't be changed. Do you have anything in mind?"

"Not really."

"I was thinking of going to Bellefontaine for a couple of days. I want to catch up with everything that has happened in the last year."

"Just remember you have a movie opening this Saturday."

"I would fly out on Monday and be back on Thursday, so that should work out."

"It will, but remember, Susan Wallace will probably need you for interviews on Saturday morning and definitely on Sunday after the showing."

Dad then reminded me that I had to have a full business review before returning to England.

"That shouldn't be a problem. Michaelmas, the next term, doesn't start until September 28. I would like to return in mid-August to do some sightseeing around Europe."

"Then how about I set up a board meeting and business review for two weeks from now? "

"That would work Dad. Thanks for taking care of this. I know I technically own these businesses but have no illusion that I'm running them."

"We've had this conversation before. It is the rare founder that can scale up with the growing business. Most fail when they try to do things they aren't capable of."

"I know, Dad, but it seems weird that I'm getting all this money when others are doing all the work."

"But you had the idea and the drive to turn it into reality. Besides, if you were running it, it would consume all your time. Do you want that?"

I replied, "Not at all."

Mum then butted in, "Rick, take the money and quit whinging."

"Yes, ma'am," was the only thing I could say.

That ended the discussion. I still felt like I was getting one heck of a deal out of it and that I had better take care of all my people.

Sunday was a day of rest for the Jackson family. We all slept in late. I made it until 6 a.m. A good run and workout set me up for a leisurely day. I watched the Scouts collect golf balls for a while.

I could only stand that for a while. A bunch of twelve-year-olds in the woods can do some strange stuff. Was I like that? Thinking back, I was probably worse. At least none of them were trying to cook an egg up in a tree.

I chatted a bit with the Scoutmaster, but from the conversation, I knew that my active Scouting days were over. He tried to get me to sign up as an Assistant Scoutmaster when I turned eighteen. It would only take a few hours a month. I've heard that song before.

After that, I drove down to the beach for a long walk in the surf. It was a mindless exercise, and I thought I needed it. I had been living at a fast and furious pace for a long time now. Hmm, fast and furious.

That had a good ring to it. It would be a good title for a song or movie.

On Monday, I called and made reservations to fly to Dayton, Ohio on Tuesday morning. I also had to line up a car and driver since I was too young to rent a car. Well, I called Susan Wallace, who took care of these things for me. She would call our travel agent. I confirmed my availability for interviews on Saturday and Sunday.

I packed light for the trip as there were no events, just a visit.

On Tuesday, our driver dropped me off at LAX, where I was escorted to the Ambassador Club. A cup of coffee later, I was taken by a back hallway to the plane. I mentioned to my escort that this service seemed over the top and that I wasn't that famous.

"We have found that any famous person will attract attention. People will want autographs and slow things down."

"That is nice that you are thinking of us."

"We aren't. We have had too many flight delays because of that."

That put me in my place. It also made me feel better for some odd reason.

The flight to St. Louis and then on to Dayton was uneventful. I signed a few autographs on the flight, but it had become routine for me. As usual, I tried to be nice to everyone as they were paying to see my movies.

One person asked me to sign a scandal sheet. It was the one with inquiring minds. There was a picture of me holding a baby on the front page. It was titled Ricky's love child.

I wrote, "No," and signed it. From the look of the baby, Mark May, he was going to be a big guy. If his dad was like that, I hope he didn't hunt me up.

We landed in Dayton on time, and my car and driver were waiting as planned. We drove up to Bellefontaine. He took the new section of I-75 and then Route 33 into Bellefontaine. It was a little

longer but a much nicer road than going through Springfield and
Urbana.

Since it was after dark, the time zones were working against me,
so we checked into our rooms at the Fountain Lodge. My room was
neat and clean, but a little block of nothing. When I thought of my
rooms at the Plaza in London, I had a hint of how much my life had
changed.

Wednesday morning, I had the driver take me out to the
roadside area near the airbase and let me out for my run. I was getting
to be such a wimp. I didn't want to run up the hill on Sandusky
Street.

After that, I cleaned up. Since school wasn't in session, I took
a walk downtown. The stores were all the same. Looking in the
windows, I found the fashions looked a little dated. The stores
themselves needed a good up-dating. They were shabby around the
edges.

I ran into a few people I recognized, and they said hello, but
none of my classmates were around. Most of them probably had
summer jobs.

I knew where some of the kids would be and had the driver
take me to the Summit Drive swimming pool. The only person I
recognized was Tom Humphries, who was working as a lifeguard. I
didn't feel like talking to him, so I had the driver take me out to the
country club.

There, I talked to the pro, who wanted to know all about the US
Open. I was able to say hello to Dr. Costin, who was about to tee off.
Other than that, there was nothing there for me. Now, looking out
over the golf course, which at one time looked like the epitome of
class. It now seemed like a little cow pasture.

From there, I was driven up to the high school. The doors were
unlocked, so I went in the entrance to the Trophy Room. My

trophies were still on display. I was standing there and remembering the events which led up to them.

One of the janitors who had been there many years came up to me. He asked if he could help me. I told him no, I was just remembering past events.

He smiled and said, "I have seen many kids come and go. Some go to good things, some go to bad, and most to what I consider a normal life, but the one thing you all have in common is you can't come home. Time passes, and things change. You can't go back, and would you want to?"

"I guess not."

"Richard, just because you can't come back doesn't mean we don't remember you or aren't proud of you. Heck, I have even bragged to my granddaughter who thinks you are the bee's knees that I had you picking up trash for me."

Bee's knees—he can't be that old, can he?

I laughed and pulled out one of my ever-available publicity photos to sign a personal autograph to his granddaughter Janet.

After that, I had the driver take us back to Dayton, where I rented a room for the night and took the first flight out in the morning. It was sad, but I learned you can't come home again. Well, not true; I was on my way home.

Chapter 4

I goofed off Friday morning. At breakfast, Dad asked me what I planned to do with the rest of my vacation. I hadn't given it a lot of thought, but off the top of my head, I told him I would like to visit different cities in the US.

"How would you do that?"

"I suppose I could rent a plane or fly commercial."

"How about using the new Cessna 320 sitting over at the Forest Service?"

"What!"

"Mum and I knew you would need or at least want an aircraft in the US, so we went ahead and ordered one last year while you were at Oxford."

"Wow, you bought me an airplane!"

My brothers and sister were sitting at the table, and you could see the wheels turning. Mary's were whirling like a slot machine.

"We ordered you an aircraft. Your company paid for it."

Just like that, the wheels stopped, except for Mary.

"Daddy, does that mean my company can buy me an airplane?"

Have I ever mentioned that Mary can be wickedly sweet at times? Most people would say sickly sweet, but with her, it was wicked. Dad was a Mary veteran, so he never hesitated.

"Certainly, dear, as soon as you have your pilot's license."

"Can't I hire a pilot?"

"You know you are not allowed to ride with strangers."

"But I would be flying and could take a bodyguard along."

"I suppose so. Go ahead and draw up a budget and present it to your mother."

I don't know if Dad is a coward or just plain brilliant. I'm going with brilliant yellow. This took the wind out of Mary's sails. She thought she had him cornered.

Meanwhile, I was scarfing down the last of my breakfast so I could go see my new plane.

I was in a hurry, so I drove the Jeep over. It was a new addition to our growing fleet of cars but was the best choice for the back way to the Forest Service airport.

Unlike the last time I was there, the only welcome I received was a wave from one of the rangers I had met on my last trip. The idiot with a gun was gone. I guess that left me as the only idiot with a gun. At least I didn't throw the weight of my badge and pistol around. Still, I'm an idiot, at least around girls.

My hangar doors were closed. I say my hangar because the whole building had been painted in British racing green with my coat of arms on the large door. Going through the normal-sized man door, I turned on the lights.

There sat a beautiful brand-new Cessna 320 with the same paint job as the one in England. The inside of the hangar had been done up, and there was a complete setup for the minor maintenance required. Anything major, it would go into the Cessna service center at the dealership.

I had to get inside and check everything out. It was identical to my British aircraft. I thought about taking it up for a flight but realized that I didn't have time at the moment.

Returning home, I thanked my parents profusely for thinking of buying the plane. Once more, I thought it was nice to have money.

We talked about my proposed trip around the US and what cities I would visit. The list covered every major city and a lot of the minor ones in the entire country. It would take several years to visit all of them. I decided that I would do a southern route, with the last stop being in Philadelphia, before heading home.

I would fly from LA to San Antonio, followed by New Orleans, Miami, Savannah, Washington DC, and then Philadelphia. There would be fuel stops between some of the cities. I would have to plan those out.

As all this conversation was occurring, Susan Wallace walked in. She was there to talk to Mary and me about the premiere. When she caught up with what we were talking about, she suggested. "As you visit each city, you could invite your local fans to a special showing of *Over the Ohio*. I can take care of getting it all set up. That would help the ticket sales. Also, it is time you made the news again; plus, the whole trip could be charged off as a tax deduction.

I had never given much thought to tax deductions until I got involved with my businesses. Now, I realized the impact that not having them would have on my income. I didn't mind paying the legal amounts but didn't want to pay any more than that. I think I got that from Dad.

Then Dad brought up the fly in the ointment.

"How are you going to get around in each of those cities? You can't rent a car."

We considered the options. I could just drive the trip. That would take too long. I could rent a limo and driver at each stop. I could have the company buy me a car for each town. That was the most far-out suggestion.

While these ideas were being bandied about, the question of security came up. While I wasn't wild about the thought, I knew that if I were going to appear in a large crowd, I would need security.

For the film showings, we would hire a local firm with multiple personnel for crowd control or, if available, off-duty policemen. The off-duty was what I wanted; it gave the men in blue a chance at extra income. They certainly deserved it.

Mum insisted I have even closer protection, even if it was just one man. I had the bright idea of hiring an off-duty US marshal. I thought of it as I was wearing a sports coat with my shoulder rig, and it was starting to chafe a little. It had become part of my clothing as much as wearing shoes and socks.

So, it was settled on a hired car and driver, local police off-duty for the showings, and a US marshal at all times. This didn't include the advance party of one of Susan's employees to have everyone at the right time and place, advertising, arranging the film showings, and hotel rooms.

I was reminded that the local newspapers and TV people would want interviews, and the school would be out if the politicians got involved.

I began to have second thoughts about the trip. We continued to talk about the logistics of the trip through lunch. What had started as me on a sightseeing tour had turned into a full publicity blitz.

After many phone calls over the next couple of days and multiple conversations, it worked out that I would visit the cities I listed. Susan Wallace would have a car waiting for me. It would be rented in the company name, and I would be listed as a driver.

The studio would arrange for the publicity of a special showing in each city for my "fan club". I did have a small club in each city. At least the studio had a written record from someone in each town saying they were the president of my club.

In every incident, it was a young teenage girl. There wasn't any real idea of how many members there were in each club. When the studio contacted them, it turned out the largest had seven girls and the smallest, two. That was good for my ego.

This wasn't new territory for the studio publicity people. They had radio announcements and newspaper ads about how my fan club was getting a free special showing on a given date. It is surprising how many people of various ages joined the clubs for a free movie.

Hotel reservations were made for me under the company name. I certainly understood why after that debacle in New York. Each city had a map with spots shown that I would like to see, such as the Alamo in San Antonio.

Mum looked at the map and went hmm, but didn't say anything about Bourbon Street in New Orleans. I suspect she put it in the same class as hitchhiking across the country or working as a deckhand. In other words, a learning experience.

When Dad looked at it, he just winked at me. I'm not sure what he meant by that, and I wasn't going to ask. I just grinned and got out of there as fast as I could.

I had to be at each theater two hours early to sign autographs. After the movie, there would be a meeting of the original fan club members. There would also be a dozen or so people from the audience, who would be invited as they were exiting by the studio people present.

The combined group would be interviewed on what they thought of the movie. It would be a combination of written and oral questions. They called it a focus group. The results of the questions would give them an idea of the perceived strengths and weaknesses of the movie so they could refine the advertising.

This would normally not be done for most movies, but the studio felt like it would be in theaters for an extended run. I wasn't sure I agreed with them but went along with it, as the movie would make me a ton of money, and if it played enough times, the studio would even make a profit.

These meetings would be at a hotel, which Susan would chaperone. They would have refreshments set up. The whole event would be done in two hours. My previous experiences told me that there would be uninvited guests who couldn't be turned away and that I would be lucky if it was less than four hours.

The receptions, as I thought of them, weren't at the hotel I was staying at, another lesson learned.

I will say here that Warner Brothers handled me with kid gloves throughout this process. I think they, at least Mr. Monroe, realized they had pushed me too far and that their legal position wasn't the best.

I was way past being mad about how I was forced into the movie after making my intentions clear, but it was too late to change things. One change I made was to have an agreement drawn up with the Shawnee Tribe that half my profits from my movie would go to an educational fund for children of the tribe.

This was good from a tax point of view and more importantly, helped the people who got the short end of the stick in real life. I was going to do it quietly, but the Shawnee, to my surprise, wanted to make a big public deal about it.

A stop at the Shawnee reservation was to be made on my way home from my tour. I was told they wanted to do a presentation for my aid to the tribe and also to publicize their charities. I couldn't argue with that as I was on a publicity tour.

Saturday morning was hectic around the house. Mary and I had interviews after lunch. All I had to do was to put on clothes, which ones didn't matter. I kept on the jeans and shirt I put on after my workout and shower. No need to dress up as it was at our home.

The hectic part was Mary. What dress should she wear? Did these shoes match? Should she wear any jewelry? How about makeup? Mum finally had to put her foot down. An at-home type of dress, a small bracelet, and absolutely no make-up.

That set off another round. We had a diva in the making. Dad settled it with a swat across her butt. Just enough to get her attention. That settled that. I can remember those. They never really hurt, but they sure did send a message.

Mum had told us of her father taking off his Sam Brown military belt and setting it on the table. He never had to use it. Just the threat was enough. After I saw one in a museum, I could understand why.

Mary was calm until lunch when she spilled tomato soup on her dress. You would have thought her puppy, parents, and family had died. She and Mum retreated upstairs to select another dress. Mary was sobbing all the way.

About half an hour later, she came back down in a nice frock. I noticed she had a hint of color on her lips. I wonder.

The reporter and cameraman for the first interview showed up on time. I have heard the saying attributed to W.C. Fields, "Never appear with kids or pets, as they will upstage you every time." Those aren't the exact words, but they are so true.

I was asked two questions: did you enjoy working with Mary? And is Mary ready for larger parts?

Other than that, it was all Mary. I must say she came across as a professional young actress. Butter wouldn't melt in her mouth. She was calm, cool, and collected.

"I did enjoy working with Ricky. He knows how to bring out the best in me. Other than I had to stand on a box in one scene to talk to him, he does well with the camera."

Sororicide—I didn't think I would be convicted.

I love the little brat, but I can't wait till she grows up and I can get revenge. Now, it just would look like I was picking on her. Now that is a good idea. I could always fall back on tickling her until she pees.

The second set of interviews went better from my point of view. They had some questions for me. It is a shame I couldn't give a straight answer. The word was out on the street that the movie had a twist.

My honest answer was yes, it might be perceived as a twist. Buy a ticket and find out.

On a more serious note, I explained that we had tried to show all sides of the story rather than stereotypes. That in itself was a twist to most modern storytelling, especially when it involved American Indians.

I was asked if it was true that I owned a major portion of the movie. I sidestepped that a little, saying I was invested but not how it had come about. I had contributed the basic plot and screenplay. Fortunately, they didn't follow up.

Mary was less self-centered in her replies this time. I think she and Mum had a conversation. I also noted that she had no gloss on her lips. I pity her first real boyfriends.

Chapter 5

After breakfast, a reporter for *Variety* showed up. This interview was different from yesterday. First of all, Mary was not present. The reporter had been at an advanced screening of the movie and had questions specifically for me.

Susan Wallace was going to be there but had a family matter to address, so I told her not to worry. I could handle it. I had done dozens of these.

The first one was simple, "Is your song going to be released?"

"Yes, it is. It will go out on Monday. The movie should give it a boost." I didn't mention the opposite. If we had released it first and it bombed, it might have hurt the movie. Someday, people will realize that I can't sing.

"Rick, how did you feel about playing a character that proves to be a psychopathic killer?"

"Just remember it is a role, not me. We did it this way to show how history can change the way events are viewed. Most of the literature out today makes Lew Wetzel out to be a hero. Both sides of the story needed to be told. We tried to keep that theme throughout the movie at the government, tribal, and individual levels. There were a great many wrongs committed by all involved. Yet few were bad people.

"Many of them were ignorant of the effects of their decisions or had no idea of the possible ramifications. Somehow, I don't think the British would have chosen the path they did if they realized they would lose all the colonies.

"The only inevitable part was the Indians losing their territories and, ultimately, their way of life. It was the clash of the farmer versus the hunter-gatherer. The farmer always wins."

"Rick, I understand you had a major role in creating the storyline."

"I did. It was based on my Ohio history courses in Bellefontaine plus my reading of the newspapers of the day. That and conversations with Chief Redfoot of the Shawnee Tribe. It gave me a better perspective on what occurred. I thought it was worth telling rather than the Cowboy and Indian stereotypes we see today. It certainly makes a more powerful story to tell."

"That it did. It is amazing that the budget for a B-movie can result in a possible Oscar contender."

"Let's don't go there. This movie was made to make money. The audience will judge that, while my peers in the industry will judge the artistic merit. Too often, the two are confused. Frankly, I would rather have the money."

"Rick, you do realize that statement is the kiss of death for an Oscar contention."

"I don't see why. The movie should stand on its own merits."

"You don't act your true age very often, but I'm afraid you are a bit naïve about the way the artistic community works."

"That is probably true, so I won't be considered one of them. Their loss, not mine."

I realized at that moment I had forgotten the rule of the hole. When you realize you are in one, stop digging.

"I know I just came off sounding aggressively stupid, but I want to say that I realize two different standards are being used to judge the movie. As you pointed out, a B-movie's main goal is to entertain and, through that entertainment, make money. It never occurred to me that anyone would consider it a work of art."

"May I quote you on the last?"

"Please do."

Oh, Lord, please do.

After that, a few questions were asked about working on the set and how it was working with my little sister.

"It was fun."

At this point, I wanted nothing more in the world than to finish with this almost disaster of an interview. Of course, I wasn't out of the woods yet.

As he was wrapping up, I thanked the reporter for the interview.

"Rick, I was young once and stuck my foot in my mouth. A kind gentleman didn't punish me for it. I'm passing that kindness along. I realize that you weren't trying to make a statement about the artistic side of the industry but just got tangled up in the words."

"I can't thank you enough, Holl. Do you think this has a chance at an Oscar?"

"Stranger things have happened."

After he left, I went for another run in the woods. Here, I thought I was getting to be a smooth talker and understanding the industry. I had just about blown it. I needed to run off some of the stress.

Thinking back on how I told Susan Wallace not to worry, I thought, *how wrong could I be?* It seems even we experienced pros could get off on the wrong foot. Maybe I wasn't as experienced as I thought.

Now, all I had to do was hope that Holl was a man of his word. I will know by tomorrow morning when the interview appears.

After my run, it was time to get ready to go to the premiere of *Over the Ohio.*

Fortunately, my new tux arrived yesterday, with everything to go with it here. Getting ready probably took me ten minutes longer than normal as I had to put the studs in my shirt. My braces were in a tangle, but they weren't hard to get on. I thought the braces were much nicer than suspenders.

My cummerbund would hide them, so it didn't matter which ones I used. The braces felt more stable. I had a vision of the pants fabric slipping out of the suspender clamps and my pants falling. I bet that is why so many old guys wore belts and suspenders.

Now, Mary getting ready was a different story. I'm proud to announce to all females of the world that my little sister was ready to join the ranks. It was time to go, and she was still dithering about which necklace to wear.

Mum didn't help when at the last minute, she brought out a real tiara for Mary to wear. Real, as in they were real diamonds. I must say she looked like the perfect little princess.

At last, all was acceptable. Not perfect but acceptable. Mum brushed the last little bit of lint off my shoulder and hugged me. She and the rest of the family would meet Mary and me at the theater.

We had our motorcade leaving the house, Mary and me in our limo, the family in theirs, and guards in vehicles front and back. It got wild when we drove out the front gate.

The sheriff had sent two patrol cars to escort us to the theater. Lights flashing, we went down the hill. It was cool; the only thing missing were flags on the front bumpers of the limousines. I would have to ask about that. We could use two sets, one each of my and Mum's coat of arms.

Well, maybe that would be a little ostentatious.

We arrived at Grauman's Chinese theater in a lightning storm of flashbulbs. Mary and I descended from the limo, with her taking my arm. I told her in the car not to worry, that I would take care of her. She had been very quiet during the trip. I could tell she was nervous.

Those nerves lasted until we got out of the car. She put on a million-dollar smile and waved at everyone.

I whispered to her that she was doing well.

"Of course I am. I'm scared to death. I'm just acting like I'm comfortable with this."

If anyone deserves an Oscar, it is my sister.

We posed for pictures and gave brief statements prepared by the studio. They called them sound bites.

Eventually, we made it inside, and once we were settled, the movie started. The audience was made up of reviewers and people who had been involved in making the movie.

There was also a cross-section of people who would make up what the studio thought the typical audience would be. These people would be questioned after the movie to see how it would be received.

As anyone who has made a movie knows, until you see the finished product, you don't know what it will be like. In the making, you did bits and pieces at a time, and many of the bits and pieces were left on the cutting room floor. I could have attended an early showing but elected not to. I wanted to be in a real audience rather than the biased one at an early showing.

The way people got into my song told me it would make the charts when it was released tomorrow. In the barn dance and people scenes, I came across as a happy-go-lucky guy. You had to wonder why I was even in the movie.

That is until I was shown to be Death Wind. It was startling how evil I came across. There were actual gasps in the theater when the audience realized it was me, the happy, go-lucky guy.

Afterward, there was a press interview. It was a circus. The main train of questioning was, "How could you do this? It will change your image forever. This is the dark side of the American Hero. Should it be shown?"

"Yes, it should. It is consistent with the rest of the movie about the dichotomies of the times. It wasn't a black-and-white time in American history."

Chief Redfoot was with me. He broke in and stated how all the Indian Tribes would agree with the portrayal of the wars in the Ohio territory. He went on to comment that until very recently, Indians identified themselves by tribes. Today, they were now Indians who belonged to tribes. A new national identity had been created.

As such, they would be more of a voting bloc than before.

While all this was true, the entertainment reporters weren't that interested in the political dynamics; they cared about the image that had been created. The consensus of the reporters seemed to be that I had damaged my image and that my normal fan base would reject it. Furthermore, no one else would care to see it.

Those were the critics' opinions. The exit interviews told a different story. The audience loved it. As one of my fans put it, "It makes Ricky a more real person. No one is as good as he has been presented." Interesting, I thought I was the goody-two-shoes. Would this let me get away with more? Thinking of Mum and Dad, there was no way. Nice thought, though.

What was interesting was the reaction of those who weren't considered my fan base. The reaction was that it was a thoughtful piece that was exciting and showed all sides of a complex issue. One guy said it should be required viewing in all schools.

Mary had her moment in the sun and performed as expected. She even had an opportunity to plead for funds for Feed the Puppies and announce her latest dress fashion release for the discerning young lady. Her words, not mine.

We went from the theater to the Beverly Hills Hotel and Bungalows. They are okay if you like pink. This was the opening party. The final shoot party had been held some time ago. I was in England then, so I missed out on the better party, at least a more enjoyable one. This was more of a political event than a celebration.

This is where aspiring actors and actresses looked for future parts. Agents looked for parts and talent. Producers looked for investment in their projects and directors looked for work. Writers peddled their screenplays. Everyone wanted something from me. This included the waiters and waitresses, who were all aspiring actors.

Mr. Monroe was there, and he kept close to me to help fend off those trying to get near me. By taking major points in the movie,

I was now a target of everyone looking for money. It was also becoming well-known that I had money beyond the movie industry.

I did the glad-handing as needed and talked to a few nice people. But on the whole, I would rather have been anywhere else. I was so jealous when Mum and Dad took all the kids and left. It was past Mary's bedtime, you know. Ratfinks.

I had several invitations to go with individuals or groups to their bungalow after the party. This had become a common occurrence. I turned them all down as gracefully as I could. One guy got snotty, but I didn't respond, turning away.

It wasn't as though I wasn't interested in sex; I was very interested, just not with that crowd. Early in my career several of the stuntmen took me aside and explained some of the realities of life in Hollywood. The badger game being part of it. There were several variations to watch for. The best way to avoid them was not to get involved.

I suspect Mum, Dad, or Mr. Monroe were behind my education.

To top it all off, I found out who made those VD training movies for the armed forces as I had to sit through every one of them. It lent credence to the punchline of an old joke, "The good news is it will shrivel up and fall off."

The main reason I didn't want to go with anyone was that I thought it would be better if I had my encounters with someone I knew and liked. At least I should be able to trust them. I didn't feel saintly about it, just able to control my urges.

To me, this public party was not a party. It was a torture Rick device.

The strain must have shown on my face as Mr. Monroe took me aside and told me, "Go home, Rick. You've done your duty."

I gratefully slipped out a side door. Of course, my escape wasn't clean. A reporter I had met before was standing outside enjoying a cigarette. He politely asked if he could ask me a question. Feeling trapped, I agreed.

"Rick, you look like you are running away from something."

"I am. This party is not my thing."

"What don't you like about it?"

I told him the entire story about people wanting to use me in every manner possible."

"It's a shame you have gotten so cynical so young."

"Am I wrong?"

"That's the really sad part, you aren't. I have seen more in my twenty years in this job than you can imagine. My only advice is to run away from it whenever you can."

"That's what I'm trying to do right now."

"Do you mind if I mention in my column how you have seen through this world and are on your guard?"

"That would be fine. Maybe it will make some people understand that they are wasting their time and back off."

"Dream on and enjoy the rest of your evening."

At that, I bailed out and headed home to bed. I had two good encounters with reporters recently. Maybe they weren't as bad as I thought. Maybe more of them were like George Weaver.

Chapter 6

Monday morning was the start of a hectic day at Jackson House. At breakfast, we were all engrossed in reading the movie reviews. We had six different newspapers and all of them raved about the movie.

The comments ranged from historically accurate to a stellar performance in a new role by Richard Jackson. Then, of course, there was that new rising star, Mary Jackson. Entertaining, thrilling, action-packed, and romantic were just a few of the adjectives used.

Now the only thing left was for people to go to the movie.

While we were eating, reading, and commenting, Mrs. Hernandez turned up the radio. A new song by Rick Jackson was playing. I liked it; it didn't sound like me. It was a catchy, upbeat tune with a little twist at the end. What's not to like? Did I mention it didn't sound like me?

The phone kept ringing all this time with requests for interviews and comments. Mary would answer the phone with, "No comment at this time. Buy a ticket to the movie."

Susan Wallace, who had brought the newspapers to us, was about to pull her hair out. Dad was encouraging Mary to say something more outrageous, but fortunately, Mum stepped in and settled everyone down.

Mary still answered the phone with a more sedate, "Jackson House, there is no comment at this time."

Susan told us that Mary's antics on the telephone were getting known in the industry and that it was a badge of honor to have had a rude answer from her. Boy, those people needed to get a life. My sister had been rude to me all my life, and I never felt like it was a badge of honor. More like a pain in the neck.

While all this was going on the last-minute details of my trip were being discussed. I had already been to the ranger station, loaded my luggage for the trip, and ensured the plane was fueled.

I finished with last-minute instructions on where to meet my first car and driver in San Antonio, along with a written itinerary of hotels, theaters, times, and places. Finally, I was ready to leave. There were hugs and kisses all around, even with the little sister monster I loved.

I made a promise to call when I was safely in, and I was off. Dad drove me over to the Forest Service airport. I swear, every time I went there, they made it nicer. New barracks were being put up. These would be for aircrew rest in between dumping water and retardant on fires.

Well, I was off after making sure that the wings hadn't fallen off overnight, no water in the fuel, etc. San Antonio, here I come.

I was under visual flight rules as there was no control tower in use at this time. The current tower was being refurbished and would be manned during fire season, so I was taking off under "see and avoid" rules, looking around for other aircraft on the ground and in the air, and trying not to hit anyone.

I got into the air without any near misses. I would have had to work at it since there were no other aircraft in sight. It was nice having a remote airport so close to our house.

I double-checked my compass settings and followed the relatively new Interstate 10 to Phoenix. The flight was only a few hours, but I took an hour's break while fueling and eating lunch at Sky Harbor Airport.

I was in line to take off behind Bonanza and Frontier planes when a Medevac plane flew by. Air Evac jumped the line. The tower put us on hold while it took off. Mr. McGarry would have been proud of them. I suspect a retired fighter pilot was flying that aircraft.

After that bit of excitement, I was off to El Paso for my next fuel stop. It was a rather boring flight. It all looked like the southwestern desert from up here. The mountains and dry rivers were interesting for the first one hundred miles or so. After that, I channel-hopped on the radio to listen to other aircraft to keep me awake.

Again, it was I-10 all the way. I had my time and compass settings written down, but I was following the highway most of the way. I saw why pilots joked that IFR meant "I follow roads" instead of "Instrument Flight Rules," which was not much of a joke.

There were several big curves and zigzags that I could cut across to cut down on distance, but not that much.

For a while, I think in New Mexico there was a train track with an actual train going east. It would not have been legal for me to swoop down on it and pretend I was strafing it, so I won't tell you about it.

El Paso was interesting as I saw some different aircraft operating and several old planes in the bone pile from airlines I had never heard of. I wonder what happened to Standard Airlines and Varney Speed Lines.

Continental was flying DC-6s, which I had never been on. There were also some Convair 240 and 340 craft. A Vickers Viscount turboprop jet came in while I was waiting to take off. Now, that was one nice aircraft. If I owned a jet, that might be it. I had heard they had almost no vibration and were very quiet inside.

From El Paso, I was to follow the yellow brick road, or in this case, continue on I-10 to San Antonio.

Eight hours after leaving home, I touched down at Stinson Municipal Airport in San Antonio, Texas. Named after the aviation-pioneering Stinson family, it was the oldest airport west of the Mississippi. I knew this courtesy of Mr. McGarry, who learned to fly at the Stinson Flying School before World War II.

After my plane was fueled and tied down, I went to the private terminal. A man was waiting for me who recognized me because he had one of my publicity pictures in hand. He identified himself as my escort for the fan club meeting and film presentation.

He presented his credentials. Off-duty US Deputy Marshal Elliot had an agency car that would be loaned to me after his escort duties were finished. I don't know what strings had been pulled to make that happen, but I knew I had better take care of Uncle Sam's car.

Marshal Elliot drove me to the Hotel Contessa to check in. It was right on the famous Riverwalk. There was a boat dock right at the downstairs exit to the hotel, so it would be very easy to get around. You could also walk the entire path if you so desired.

On the way to the hotel, the marshal and I discussed how I was viewed within the Marshal's Service. It had become common knowledge that I carried a deputy marshal badge. Some approved, but most didn't. The reason I had been made a deputy was never made clear to the rank and file, so they had good reason to question it.

I had never been told that I couldn't share that information. I briefly told him my story about my run-ins with the KGB. My first encounter was in Cuba, where I found critical information about the Soviets building missile launching pads.

I was very vague about the incident at the airbase. It made sense not to spread how we almost got into World War III. For Mary's kidnapping, I gave a graphic description of how the family reacted. You could see him cringe at the beheadings.

Then, there was the counter-surveillance training where a Soviet spy ring was exposed. This was followed up by a KGB trap led by an FBI traitor. Finally, there was the most recent attempt at the dry-cleaning store.

I explained that I had never been told not to share these stories, but he probably should keep them within the Marshal Service if he chose to share them and that I would appreciate it if he would do that across channels rather than up to his superiors.

I would probably catch hell about this down the line, but I would rather ask forgiveness than permission. I had to deal with the marshals for the entire trip, and those questioning my validity could endanger me.

That was all a worry for later. I unpacked at the hotel. I didn't have any commitments until the following day. I was to be at the Majestic Theater after lunch. I would be in the lobby an hour and a half before showtime, signing autographs.

It was ironic that the Majestic had been picked. It was well past its glory days and now only had B-movies. This is what *Over the Ohio* was initially budgeted as. Well, it did come in within budget, so I guess it technically was still a B-movie. You couldn't tell it from all the reviews.

You had to be a member of my fan club to get in free. My understanding was that the few real members I had were sent membership cards with a free ticket attached. These were also sent to all the parks with summer recreation programs and youth centers in town.

Since I was free for the evening, I walked around the Riverwalk. It was a pleasant evening, not too hot. It seemed like there was an enticing restaurant every inch of the way. Roving bands of musicians kept the crowds in a happy mood. There were bridges every couple of hundred feet so you could easily cross to stores and restaurants on the other side.

The boats, really little barges, chugged along the river every several minutes. The Riverwalk was truly a continuous festival. I was able to get into a program called "Fiesta Noche del Rio" at the Arneson River Theater. It had upbeat music and dancing, all with a Southwestern or Mexican heritage. I was well aware that you had to be careful not to call a Tejano a Mexican. These were people of Mexican heritage who were in Texas before the revolution. They fought for freedom alongside Houston, Bowie, and Crockett. They were proud of their heritage, and rightly so.

They were the true founding families of Texas and, to this day, had great influence. Their music and food had even been diverging from Mexico. The food was now called Tex-Mex. To say it was spicy was an understatement. I think I know why their young ladies were said to have fire in their blood. Not that I would know. One could only hope.

I had thought I had dressed appropriately for the evening. I wore jeans, boots, and a rodeo belt buckle, along with my white cowboy hat. I was just about the only cowpoke there. There were many young men with their dates, all in their suits and ties.

The evening was cool enough that I wore a light denim jacket. This allowed me to wear my shoulder holster. I had my US marshal badge and ID with me. Since I was in Texas, I also wore my Honorary Texas Ranger badge on the outside of my jacket.

From the looks and whispered comments, I must have been over the top. Oh well. I wondered how many of them had been caught in a cattle stampede or tangled with rustlers.

I had even been in a showdown on Main Street. Oh, right, that was in a movie. Let's not get carried away, Rick.

Even though I stood out, no one made an issue of it. Several people recognized me, but they didn't make a big deal of it. I had pictures with me and autographed them, handing them out with free tickets for tomorrow. I was afraid I might get swamped, but it was all done quietly and quickly in three separate incidents.

The most exciting thing I saw was four frat boys. At least they had fraternity t-shirts on, running, or more like staggering down the center of the river. The water was only three or four feet deep. They would stumble and come back up and keep moving. Two policemen were on each side of the path waiting for them to come ashore.

It looked like a night in the drunk tank for them.

That is until one of them pulled a gun out and pointed it at an officer across the river. The two policemen on my side were out of position to do anything. Since he was only three feet away from me and faced the other way, I jumped on his back and took him down.

He did not fight me as I stood him up. He still had his six-shooter in hand. Once I got a look at it, I realized he had gotten the paper roll of caps wet, so we were in no danger.

I brought the kid to the edge where he was seized by the police. The other guys sobered up quickly and surrendered at once. I felt silly for not realizing it was a toy gun, but the sergeant in charge assured me that it was better to be safe than sorry. The guy was lucky they hadn't shot him. The police were drawing their arms when I jumped him. I probably saved his life.

I was wet from my waist down, but luckily, my weapon didn't get wet. My Texas Ranger badge was recognized as being the real deal, so I was questioned about it. I ended up showing my US marshal ID and badge to show that I was allowed to carry a concealed weapon.

As far as they were concerned, I could have tied a hog leg to my hip, and it would have been okay. This was Texas.

The hoorah had collected a crowd, and a crowd had collected a reporter. The police told me that they weren't authorized to give interviews; it was all mine. I might have believed the sergeant if the reporter didn't know him by name.

I did the "Ah Shucks" routine, but the reporter didn't buy it. He knew who I was and my national reputation, so it became another Ricky Saves the Day story. Well, I was on a publicity tour. At least Susan would be happy.

I squished my way back to my room in a very wet pair of boots. It would take days to dry them out, and they would never look the same.

It wasn't that late when I got back, so I called Susan and let her know about my latest adventure. She made sure she had the reporter's name and newspaper correct. She would call him for all the details and make certain the story had wide dissemination.

Chapter 7

The next morning, Tuesday, I met Marshal Elliot for breakfast. I had gone for my run around the Riverwalk. It looked different with no people or entertainment. It was pretty, but it seemed like it missed the excitement.

He had driven by the Majestic on the way to the hotel. There was already a line forming to get in. That led to an immediate change of plans. I had dressed in my California casual for the day: chino, polo shirt, and dark blue blazer with the Oxford emblem on it.

Taking a box of the autographed pictures along with me, I arrived at 10 a.m. instead of the scheduled 12:30. That would have been an hour and a half before the 2 p.m. showing.

The ones who were in line early were my true fans. It didn't take long to figure out that the time we had allowed would not have worked out. There were over a hundred kids in line when we got there.

Mr. Elliot went far beyond his duty as a bodyguard for the day. There was no table or chair set up, though they would be in the lobby later. He took one look around and then asked the two young ladies at the front of the line if they would help him. They looked thrilled and said yes.

It probably helped that he had dressed for the part today. He looked every inch of a US marshal with his badge on display, gun on his hip, Stetson on his head, and his big drooping white mustache. I just thought I looked like a cowboy when in costume.

He asked them to go to the furniture store across the street and ask the owner or manager to join us. It didn't take long for an overweight gentleman to join us. After introductions and a handshake, two workers soon carried a table and chair over to us.

They also brought a sign for the table with the store's name and a handwritten addendum of "Provided by". That, and I posed for a picture with the owner. I told him he could display it in his store but not use it in print ads. He was fine with that.

He told me the table and chair wouldn't be sold as his granddaughter, who was in line, wanted them for her room. That explained the girly chintz covering the chair. Granddad was no dummy.

He brought her up for a special signing and picture-taking. I could see we missed a bet on having pictures taken.

I could see we hadn't taken several things into account. A quick discussion with Mr. Elliot resulted in the flagging down of a passing police car. They had been going by with an increasing frequency as the crowd grew.

I explained to the corporal that things had grown quickly. I realized that we should have a permit for this gathering. Who should we contact?

Also, could he recommend a photographer we could hire for the day? Plus, did he know where we could rent some portable toilets?

He didn't know anyone who could get toilets here quickly. My new friend the store owner stepped up and volunteered the use of those in his store. I think he saw a line of future customers. Things were already falling into place when the theater manager showed up.

I asked if the people in line could use his toilets, but he didn't want them in the theater before time. There were some bad experiences from prior events.

He and the store owner knew each other, so very quickly brass poles with red velvet rope were carried across the street to keep things in the store orderly.

The policeman who had been on his car radio told me that a man from city hall was on his way with the paperwork for a permit; it would be twenty dollars for the day. It would also have another cost. The mayor and two city councilmen were on their way to get in on the publicity.

While things were falling into place, I had struck up a conversation with those in the front of the line. Nothing great or earth-shattering was said. I told them this mess they saw ongoing was my life in action. They wanted to know what it was like having Mary as a sister.

"Tiring."

They collectively thought that I should be appearing in more pictures. One young man asked me about my golf plans, or did I have any? I told him it was a hobby for me, and I had no intention of going pro.

Shortly thereafter, the mayor and other politicians showed up. I posed for pictures and told them that this was not to be construed as an endorsement. They took that in stride but had their kids brought to the front of the line for more picture-taking.

I asked the mayor what his favorite charity was. It turned out to be the Salvation Army. I suggested we include them in the day, and he borrowed the phone inside the theater. I had learned a few things from the event in New York.

At my suggestion, the theater manager wheeled out a popcorn machine. We negotiated a fee of one hundred dollars, and he had an usher start popping corn—free for the line.

These things were happening quickly. I hadn't been there for forty-five minutes yet. The people in the front of the line were happy as they could see and hear all that was taking place. Those further out were getting restless.

A man from the Salvation Army showed up around the same time as a photographer from a local studio. I took them aside and explained what we had done in New York. They agreed for the photographer to take pictures, the Salvation Army to cover his cost plus a fee, and the rest would go to the "Blood and Fire" group. I loved their motto. They would do the record-keeping so the pictures would go to the right person.

The store owner had another table and chairs brought over for them.

I would have to be hopping back and forth for the signings and pictures, but it was doable.

In the meantime, street vendors descended on us like vultures settling in for a meal. I was glad that a soft drink and water peddler was amongst them. I had just thought about that need.

My new best friend, the store owner of Feldman's Furniture, suggested that he call a local radio station that broadcasts from his store on Saturdays. They had a mobile setup and played music from his store.

I told him that would be great. It would give the kids something to do for the next several hours while waiting. It took an hour, but by noon, they were in place and playing.

Marshal Elliot, who had experience with crowd control, suggested that we write a number on each picture handed out so that the first people in line were allowed in the theater.

It turned out easier than that. The theater manager had a stamp with the Majestic on it. He quickly stamped it on five hundred pictures, well stamped it a lot faster than I could have written it. The marshal also suggested we hire a couple of off-duty police to let people in. That would reduce the arguments at the front door.

Things evened out then. By noon, people were getting their autographs on a stamped publicity picture of me. About every third one, I had to pose for a picture so that wasn't too bad.

The radio DJ managed a quick interview with me. I don't remember his questions or my answers, but they must have been okay because I didn't hear anything else.

Around one o'clock, a local TV station showed up. They thought they could just barge in and interrupt everything for their story. I kindly explained that we had a crowd to get through and that I would talk to them when I could.

They didn't like it but backed off. I think it was Marshal Elliot's scowl more than my words that convinced them they should take their turn. By two o'clock, I had signed the last of the stamped pictures.

A street party was well underway. The fire department had shown up and blocked the street off with equipment at first, then taped between the sawhorse-type barricades. More off-duty police showed up to direct traffic. The mayor let me know about this and that it would cost the city overtime money.

Being able to take a hint, I handed him a business card and told him to send me the bill. I would forward that bill to the studio to charge against the movie.

Finally, it was time for the movie. I got up in front of the curtain and said a few words, like glad to be here and hope you enjoy the movie.

The movie opened differently than had become the norm. It had an Indian family running for their lives and losing. The blood and gore occurred off-camera, but there was no doubt that bloody murder had been done.

That took the first five minutes, and then the movie title and credits rolled.

The crowd, which was restless at first, settled in quietly as they realized that this was not something to cheer about. The background music was dominated by tom-tom drums. There was no question but that a war was coming.

After the credits rolled, there were scenes from Europe where decisions were made that would make the situation worse. They would talk of treaties made with Indian tribes which covered areas that did not belong to the tribes. Error upon error compounded into an untenable situation.

After the quick high-level policymaking, we saw the people who were to be affected. They were the settlers and the natives. For the most part, they were shown to be good people, but the bad was epitomized by Lew Wetzel, who did everything possible to make a bad situation worse. The Indians called him Death Wind.

Whenever I was in a scene, the audience would cheer. On an impulse, when Death Wind appeared the first time, I booed. That was picked up on. When Mary would be in a scene, it was, "Ah."

When it came time for me to play the fiddle and sing my song, the audience clapped along with the sprightly tune.

Most of the time, the audience was engrossed in the movie. Simon Girty was not a crowd favorite. They loved George Washington even though it was a small part. When it was time for Simon Kenton to run the gauntlet, there were groans and cheers. At one point, he fell but managed to get back up. You could feel the audience straining to get him to stand and continue.

Then came the big ending where it was revealed the cheerful beloved fiddle player, me, was Lew Wetzel, Death Wind. You could have heard a pin drop in the theater.

When it ended and the audience filed out, it was a very quiet group of people. Their worldview had been shaken. I followed them out and tried to hear what was being said. The main comment was, "I don't believe all that I saw and heard. I have to see it again."

We had a hit.

The local reporter who had been with us most of the day asked me for a comment about my change, no longer the pure hero as typecast.

"We all have to grow up sometime."

That simple quote became part and parcel of the movie.

Marshal Elliot took me back to the hotel. I thought he would drop me off and leave. Instead, he came in with me.

"There is someone I would like you to meet."

He took me to the seating area in the lobby. A woman and a young lady in a wheelchair were waiting there. He introduced me to his wife, Sara, and ten-year-old daughter, Georgia.

Georgia was a fan but couldn't take the commotion of crowds. She had polio, and while she could walk a little, in public she used her chair. We sat and talked. I thought I was exhausted, but when I saw how this young lady had to struggle, I had the time for her.

We talked for an hour, and I invited them to have dinner with me. There we spent another pleasant two hours. There were the obligatory pictures taken. This was the best part of my day for me. The crowds and applause were fun, but this was real human interaction. I didn't have it on this level very often.

Sara was a Mary fan. I told them about some of Mary's antics, and they thought it was a hoot. The story about me and the sunbathing five-year-olds had them laughing till tears came.

Both Sara and Georgia thought it must be a wonderful life we lived in Hollywood. Marshal looked at me with an obvious question. "Why don't you share that tomorrow? Tonight is too much fun."

They didn't need to know the grim side of things. I hope he shared an edited version.

Georgia let me know she was a Mary fan, too. She loved her line of clothes and feeding puppies and her acting. She even watched out for the public service announcements that Mary made.

Our hotel had a feature that I had never seen before. They could bring a telephone to your table and plug it in for you to use. I asked for a telephone. I then dialed our home number. With the time difference, Mary would still be up. Mum answered the phone.

I told her all was okay and that one of Mary's most ardent fans would like to talk to her. Mary was brought to the phone, and I told her that one of her fans by the name of Georgia would like to talk to her. I then handed the phone to an open-mouthed girl.

At least she didn't squeal.

The girls talked for a good half hour. In the meantime, Elliot and I casually talked about the events of the day. I made notes as we talked. I would have to call Susan Wallace in the morning and make the events like this for every stop.

There was a soft pop outside. Small Roman candles had been lit off. We turned to the large picture window and saw that a wedding had just taken place on what I learned was Marriage Island. There were hundreds of weddings held there every year.

The evening came to an end, and I realized it had been a long and tiring day. I profusely thanked Mr. Elliot for his assistance and retired for the night.

I slept like a log. I woke up in the same position as I fell asleep in. Normally, I would roll around the bed all night long. I was as apt to wake up with my head at the foot of the bed as anything.

The next day, after exercising, running, cleaning up, and breakfast, I walked to the Alamo. It was like going into a church. It was hallowed ground. I left a hefty donation in the box set out for that purpose. To think what those men did in the name of freedom.

I know they didn't set out to die, but they did so in a manner that would continue to reverberate down the years. Their story would make a strong movie one of these days.

I then went to the La Villita part of old San Antonio. It was now an artist village. I found the southwestern jewelry to be beautiful. I bought Mum and Mary bracelets made from turquoise and silver. Dad and the boys each got a black cowboy hat with a hatband of the same materials.

If I bought them something at every stop on my trip, I would be overweight coming home.

I toured Jack Hays House. John Coffin Hays was one of the first Texas Rangers. They had his badge on display. The house was a normal house of the day, nothing special. That badge spoke of grit and bravery. I thought the story of the one-eyed Texas Ranger might make another great movie. I could see John Wayne in both of them. I would have to talk to him about them.

That evening, I ate at the Little Rhein Steakhouse, another landmark of the area.

The next morning, after a lengthy phone call with Susan Wallace about what happened in San Antonio, I was ready to continue, next stop, New Orleans. Susan would revise the event in New Orleans based on the lessons learned at this event.

Chapter 8

It was only a two-hour flight from San Antonio to New Orleans, with no need for an intermediate fuel stop. This gave Susan two days to change the event plan for New Orleans.

She was thrilled with the way things were working out. The word on the street was that my movie was an absolute must-see. Some people had already been to two or even three showings.

As far as the event in San Antonio went, she told me I was an absolute genius. I didn't see it that way; I just used the lessons learned in New York. That event was absolutely a genius recovery by me because I had let people know where I was staying, so maybe she had something.

I was met at the plane by US Deputy Marshal David Hennessy. He was a very quiet person. He did keep a close eye on everything going on around us. It was almost as if it were all new to him.

He dropped me off at the Hotel Monteleone. It was an old mainstay of the French Quarter. It had been redone recently and was very classy. There was a wonderful old grandfather clock in the lobby. It must have been having a problem as an old guy was working on it.

I commented on that at the check-in desk. They gave me a funny look. I looked around, but the guy was gone. He must have gone on break.

My suite was as nice as most of them I had stayed at. I wondered if I was getting spoiled. I hung up my clothes and went for a walk around the French Quarter. It was still early afternoon, but there were drunken tourists all over the place.

Being staggering drunk was one thing, throwing up on the street corner was another. I left the foul-smelling area and cut over to Canal Street. Here, instead of dives and strip joints, there were fancy shops. I spent the afternoon browsing.

The only thing I bought was for me, a page from an old atlas. It had the states of Maryland and Delaware. Being printed in 1850, it had the census of Washington, DC. It listed white people, slaves, and freemen of color. It was cool.

Another feature of the map was that it showed that the state of Delaware was laid out by Mason & Dixon, and they had surveyed all sides of the state. So, Delaware was south of, north of, east of, and west of the Mason-Dixon line. Stick that in your ear, US History Bellefontaine.

I then walked down to Jackson Square and toured St. Louis Cathedral. It rivaled many of those I had seen in Europe. I paid my respects to Andrew Jackson, rearing back on his horse. The horse he rode at the Battle of New Orleans was named Duke, but the horse used as the model for the statue was Olympus.

This was a horse owned by the artist who cast the statue. Funny, I can remember the horse's names but not the guy who did the statue.

After that, I played a game of chess with one of several guys set up around the square. All three charged a dollar a game. It didn't take me long to be roundly defeated. I thought I was fairly good, but this guy was a professional.

I quizzed him about it. It turned out that he belonged to the United States Chess Federation and was rated a Grand Master. He played in the tournaments that led to the world championship.

He thought that I would rate at the Expert level if I played often. This was one step below Master, so I didn't feel too bad. One of the other guys on the square was a rated International Grand Master.

He not only would have beaten me, but the defeat would also have been pitiful. He had been known to play ten people at once, blindfolded, winning all ten games.

I returned to the hotel and had an early dinner in the Hunt Room. The hotel had an ambiance. In one corner of the lobby were two guys singing jazz music a capella. I listened to their rendition of "Summertime." It was fabulous.

I told the maître d' that they should be the main show somewhere. He snorted and told me they had been trying to get them to be headliners for a long time, but they were very shy.

After dinner, I went up to my room on the fourteenth floor. I noticed that there was no thirteen, so I was on that floor. It seemed strange that people could be that superstitious.

I almost tripped over a little kid when the elevator door opened. He tore down the hall like he was being chased. I wondered where his parents were when a woman called, "Maurice! Get back here!"

Mum was on the job.

There was a lot of giggling like there were a whole bunch of children, but I didn't see any others. Shrugging, I went to my room and made my obligatory call home.

I was on my own for the day. The movie opening would be tomorrow, so I had the day free to sightsee. I decided to see what Bourbon Street was like early in the morning.

It was hot, sweaty, and stank like I couldn't believe it. The restaurant garbage had been set out when they closed the night before. It had already started to decay. It was so bad I took my exercise elsewhere.

I ran for miles, admiring the architecture of the old city. I was able to go through two major cemeteries, St. Louis and Metairie.

St. Louis was almost fun. As I came in a side gate, a parade was coming through the main gate. It was a funeral procession in New Orleans style. The marchers were flamboyant in both costumes and music. A funeral hearse, a flower coach that was overflowing, followed. Then there was the limo with the close family. After that, there must have been over a hundred cars. I don't know who died, but they certainly had a large following.

Metairie was interesting. The rich people were buried there, at least from the size and complexity of the tombs. Since much of New Orleans is below sea level, people aren't buried in the ground. The bodies are placed in above-ground crypts.

These were pretty fancy. I saw one that reminded me of an old castle ruin I had seen in Ireland on a weekend flying trip. Another was a pyramid with a sphinx guarding it.

A little boy was sitting on the sphinx as though riding a pony. I thought the gate was closed on the pyramid, but a lady came out of it and scooped him up.

"I told you not to play out here in the daytime!"

I was running past the tomb when I heard this and turned to see what was going on, but they were gone when I looked. Oh well, it was a graveyard, after all; one could expect strange occurrences. Not really, but it's fun to think of.

After my morning run, I returned to the hotel. The grandfather clock had been repaired or at least the old guy was not there. No one was singing in the lobby, but you wouldn't expect it early in the day.

Kids came running down the hallway on the fourteenth floor right after I closed the door. They were a noisy bunch but seemed to be having a good time.

After cleaning up, I had breakfast at Le Café, a coffee shop inside the hotel. I had learned that one had to be careful calling a restaurant a coffee shop as it had several different connotations in New Orleans, like several places I had been to in Europe.

I don't mean I had been to them to use them; I just had it explained what they were in Amsterdam.

I then joined a walking tour of the old town. It was ten in the morning, and Bourbon Street was already in full swing. Our tour guide had us peek into several different strip joints. I was afraid I might get a disease just from looking in the doorway. Those places were dirty.

At each place, bouncers or strippers were trying to get us to come in. One very attractive lady was very insistent with me. I almost went in with her when I realized she was a he. I couldn't get out of there fast enough. That was the end of Bourbon Street for me.

Well, except for some college kid puking on my shoes. I returned to the hotel and changed shoes, setting the nasty ones out in the hallway so they would be picked up and cleaned. How was I to know that it was only a leftover tradition at high-class European hotels? Someone did pick up my shoes, but I never saw them again.

From there, I went on my tour. I went into the P.G.T. Beauregard-Keys House. I had read about him in American history. I think the Civil War might have ended differently if he had gotten along with Jeff Davis.

I'm not sure about his stance on negros. I think he wanted them as a voting bloc rather than any true beliefs. I did admire him as an inventor.

I went into Jean Lafitte's Blacksmith Shop, but of course, I was too young to drink. Not that I would have.

From there, I caught a streetcar named Museum, which took me to the Botanical Gardens. I'm not a big fan of those, but I read a sign about the dueling fields, so I went there. It was disappointing as they were now tennis courts.

They did have plaques about famous duels. The one I loved best was when a very peaceful man was challenged to a duel for his remarks about a political stance.

The man, James Humble, a blacksmith by trade, was almost seven feet tall. He was challenged by Bernard Marigny, who was a master swordsman and a crack shot with a pistol.

Mr. Humble knew nothing of dueling but knew he could not turn it down. But since he had the choice of locations and weapons, he chose Lake Pontchartrain in six feet of water with sledgehammers.

Mr. Marigny could have stood on a box but decided that a blacksmith with a sledgehammer was too formidable for him.

Mr. Marigny wisely chose to apologize, and they ended up becoming friends.

I later took a sidewheel boat ride on the Mississippi. It was a tourist type of ride. I found the huge engine and the piston rods to be impressive. I spent my trip below decks talking to the engine crew.

It wasn't coal-fired like the old boats. It had an oil burner. The boat itself was metal-hull construction to meet Coast Guard rules. This was a good thing.

I went past the Saenger Theater, where the showing was to be. It was originally scheduled for the Orpheum, but that theater wasn't big enough. We (the studio) ended up paying for the day at the Orpheum as we had backed out at the last minute.

The Saenger would seat four thousand people. I didn't think we would fill it.

I was proved wrong the next morning when I arrived at the theater at 8 a.m., accompanied by the taciturn Mr. Hennessy.

I bet he didn't say more than ten words. I know a cowboy I would like to introduce him to. I would love to hear a non-conversation between him and Bob.

People were lined up already. This time, we were ready for them. My table was set up in the air-conditioned lobby. Another table with a photographer in place was there. The charity was the Daughters of Charity, a Catholic group. I noticed no one gave the nuns any grief the entire day. That may have something to do with the wooden ruler prominently displayed.

There had been plenty of stories about my role in the movie. I was questioned time after time. The guys thought it was cool. The girls thought I shouldn't be a meany.

Well, I wasn't a meany in the movie. I was a psychopathic murderer. I didn't tell them that.

The movie was received the same way it had been in San Antonio. This time I didn't have to boo when Death Wind showed up. As Lew Wetzel, I got cheers, and Mary had her "Oohs and aws".

The people had been allowed into the theater as they arrived; a band was on stage, and they danced in the aisles. The popcorn and drinks were free. The politicians were there for the photo op. All in all, it was business as usual.

Marshal Hennessy dropped me off. As he drove away, I realized I had never thanked him. I had the local marshal's office number, so I called them to leave a message. They questioned me at length. They wondered why I hadn't contacted them. They had no deputy by the name of Hennessy.

The only Hennessy in law enforcement that they could think of was David Hennessy, the New Orleans police chief in the 1880s who was assassinated.

That was just plain weird. Maybe I should have visited the Voodoo Museum to find out what happened in New Orleans. Not that I believed in ghosts or had any contact with them.

Chapter 9

After filing a flight plan, I refueled and checked that there were no flat tires and the wings hadn't fallen off—not to make light of the preflight checkoff inspection. Strange things have been known to happen. Once a truck clipped a wing with no apparent damage until the wing fell off as they took off. The crew and passengers would have died if they had made it into the air.

I took off for Miami with a fuel stop in Tallahassee. I could have cut across the Gulf of Mexico and made the trip a lot faster. That was another thing you didn't push. Storms came up quickly over the gulf, so there was no sense in crossing it in a light aircraft if you didn't need to. Why risk your life to save an hour?

I made it to Tallahassee in the predicted two hours. It wasn't lunchtime, so I took off for Miami after a quick pit stop. Not being in any hurry, I flew down the west coast of Florida. I was hungry about the time I came across Tampa Bay. I landed at a small airport across from Tampa International Airport. The name, St. Petersburg-Clearwater International Airport, was almost longer than their runways.

A plaque at the airport told how this area was the birthplace of commercial aviation. In 1913, Tony Jannus flew two paying passengers across the bay to Tampa. The maximum speed was 75 miles an hour, and they reached an altitude of 50 feet. That would have been some flight.

On the recommendation of a fellow pilot, I took a taxi to a little restaurant just north of the airport. They were on a bayou and had fresh fish delivered to their dock. I had a grouper sandwich that was out of this world.

I took off again and headed south. Flying along the beach, I came across the most brightly colored building I had ever seen. It was huge, a hotel, I guessed. It was a brilliant pink!

Another interesting thing about flying along the coast was that I could see schools of sharks and other large fish in the shallower waters. I wondered how safe it would be to swim there.

After reaching Sarasota, I turned east, following a two-lane highway across the state. The area below looked swampy. The map called it Alligator Alley. I decided I wouldn't try to land there.

Seven hours after leaving New Orleans, I landed in Miami. Four hours of flying time, the rest for fuel and food stops.

Waiting in Miami for me was US Deputy Marshal Raylan Givens. He seemed pretty nice. His accent wasn't South Florida; I guessed Kentucky, and I was right on. He liked working in this area but wouldn't mind getting stationed back in his home territory someday.

As per our arrangement, I dropped him off at the Federal Building. He would meet me at the Hotel Fontainebleau in two days to escort me to the film event. I had two days to explore Miami.

When I checked into the Fontainebleau, or the Blue as it was called locally, they treated me like a big-shot actor. There was a huge suite with a basket of fruit. No champagne.

It was too early for dinner and too late to go downtown, so I went to the pool instead. I put in some laps and then worked on my tan. It had faded since the canceled movie.

I ended up having a nice nap but was awakened by a young lady, not so young, mid-twenties or so. I had been lying on my stomach for a while and was starting to turn pink. She didn't think I should go beyond medium-rare.

I appreciated the wake-up, but the way she looked at me when she talked about steak scared the heck out of me. The first thing I thought of was a Russian honeypot. What a bummer. A teenage boy shouldn't have to worry about such things.

After thanking her and having a drink for her and her two friends put on my tab, I bailed for my room. It was now late enough that I showered and put on fresh clothes to go to Little Havana to find a good restaurant.

I took a taxi as I didn't know the area and parking would be a problem. I was dropped off at Calle Ocho, where it met with the Tamiami Trail. From there, I walked the boulevard towards town. I don't know if it was a boulevard by name, but it looked like one.

There were restaurants, bars, and stores galore. They cheerfully overlapped the sidewalk and, in some cases, the road. It was colorful and with no sense of coordination between stores. It was like they had moved Havana, Cuba to Miami.

There were people all over the place. A few tourists spoke the only English I heard. Spanish was the language of the day. The accent wasn't as soft as mine, and they talked about ten times faster. I could follow okay, just like I could follow someone from New York. I just couldn't speak that fast myself.

There was one little café that attracted me. They had food and drink. Domino players took up half the tables outside. I had noticed this before. If you were from one of the Caribbean Islands, you played the game with a passion.

Each table would have players and watchers. I noticed a few bills changing hands. I can play the game, but not with these sharks.

My waitress asked for my order in English. I gave it in Spanish. I swear this got me better service. I had a leisurely meal and a cup of Cuban coffee afterward. If you have never had it, it has a kick like a horse. You drink it in a small cup and don't be shy about the cream.

I listened to those talking around me. They were all excited about the invasion force that was training to retake Cuba from Castro. They were training down in Nicaragua. These guys were talking openly about the 1400-armed soldiers and the B-26 Bombers, which would be painted as belonging to the Cuban Air Force.

They spoke about how the US Air Force would provide fighter support for the bombers.

If this was true, there was an intelligence leak of mammoth proportions. I decided to call someone in Washington first thing in the morning.

After my meal, I walked down the boulevard several blocks and had another cup of coffee. Not only did I pick up the same information, I heard a name I was familiar with. One of the CIA trainers was supposedly Rip Robertson. He was the guy who was going to teach me how to spot a tail.

I had to call DC. It sounded like this operation was doomed before it started.

I took a taxi back to the hotel. This was one of the few nights where I didn't have a good night's sleep. I was awake at first light, so I went for a run on the beach. It was a wonderful time to be out. Others were taking a stroll, and a few, like me, were running full bore.

I kept on the hard-packed sand next to the water. After putting in five miles, I returned to the hotel and used their exercise equipment. It was a little lightweight compared to what I was used to, but it did the trick.

After cleaning up and having a hearty breakfast, I called the White House. Not messing around, I went straight to the top. The president wasn't available, but I did get to talk to his chief of staff. I felt I had better back channel this some other way, as he didn't appear to take me seriously.

I asked to be returned to the White House switchboard but got "lost" in the transfer. I called back and asked to be connected with Mr. Gerry Droller of the CIA.

I was put on hold for a few minutes, probably to see if it was okay for me to be transferred. I was finally put through. I found out that it had taken so long because he was in Paris.

He remembered me and my connections so he gave me the courtesy of hearing me out. He told me that he wasn't read in on that operation, but they had a big problem if what I told him was factual. He would take it from there. The whole thing might be a disinformation ploy, so please don't rock the boat.

I told him I wouldn't. This didn't mean I wouldn't call Mum in a few hours after she had her morning tea. Like most women, Mum was an angel, but if you broke her wings, she would still fly on her broomstick. Talking before morning tea was breaking wings. She could rock the boat.

When I talked to Mum, she told me that I had done all I could. Try to do more and I would be causing myself problems with the different government agencies involved. They had to know from many sources that their operation was completely compromised.

She would let MI 6 know, but she was certain they would also be on top of it. The whole thing made me wonder what the real plan was. No one could be so stupid to think that Castro wouldn't be prepared with the information flowing so freely.

The whole thing must be a disinformation plan like *The Man Who Never Was*.

While I was thinking this through, my phone rang. It was Mr. Droller calling me from Paris. He was calling me back after a quick conference with the powers that be.

They didn't want me to take things any further. They knew that I had high-level contacts all over the world. They were working according to a plan. Maybe not the best, but it was what it was.

They had to count on an uprising of the Cuban people to support the initial troops after establishing a beachhead. They couldn't land an army to counter Castro, so had to raise it once they landed. The only way they could do that was to let everyone know they were coming.

The only real secret was where they would land. The landing group would be accompanied by supply ships which would be loaded with weapons for the local population.

I promised that I would back off and not do anything else. What could go wrong with that plan? They were depending on locals to know when and where to show up while keeping it secret. They were assuming that when and if locals showed up, they would be willing and able to fight.

I wouldn't be surprised if the weapons they were providing were still packed in cosmoline. None of them would have been sighted in. Would the new soldiers even know how to load it or where the safety was? The ammunition was probably shipped in spam cans so it would be needed to be fed into clips. Nah, it would all work out.

Deciding to clear my head with some beach time, I went back downstairs. A guy on the elevator looked very familiar, but I couldn't place him. It became clear when the door opened, and a famous redhead ran up and hugged him.

I thought about asking for autographs but knew how I felt about it when I was trying to lead a normal life.

I did nod good morning to Jackie Gleason when I passed his table. Wait! That's Jackie Gleason. I had to get his autograph. When I turned, Lucille Ball and Desi Arnaz were approaching the table. Well, in for a penny in for a pound.

I asked them each for an autograph. None of them had pens or pictures, so I provided both. Once they saw my publicity picture, Lucy knew who I was. Mr. Gleason had no idea, and it had to be explained that I had a movie that had just been released.

They further mentioned that I was the one who had saved the Queen of England. That brought it together for him. He invited me to join them at their table. I did and promptly shut up and listened.

It seems that Lucy and Desi were big boosters of Miami. They were trying to talk Mr. Gleason into moving his show out of New York and to Miami. After they made their pitch, he turned to me.

"What do you think?"

"I live in California, and you should do your show from there. Just kidding!"

I had to add that quickly as it looked as though Lucy was going to hit me.

"I think Miami would be cool. It is a casual, upscale kind of place. I can see the opening credits running with a large moon overhead while the orchestra plays 'Moon over Miami.'"

"I like that."

We continued the conversation for another hour. I was quizzed on my show business credits. That's what counted with these people. When I told them I was thinking about stepping down from movies while I was at Oxford, they piled on.

Lucy said it best, "How soon they forget. You have to ride the wave while you can."

I took it very seriously since these people had an untold number of years in the business. I would have a long talk with Mr. Monroe when I got home.

I did invite them to my opening tomorrow, but they begged off because of other commitments. I did notice from the side of my eye that Mr. Gleason gave the others a wink. I don't know what that was about and probably didn't want to know.

I had dinner at the Gotham Steak House that night. I was minding my own business when I heard a "Ricky."

It was my old singing pal Frank Sinatra. He joined me for a few minutes. He was in town on a follow-up to his movie, *A Hole in the Head*.

We talked for a few. I told him about meeting Jackie Gleason and Lucy and Desi. He thought that was cool, as he was a fan of all three. He said he was going to check to see if they were still staying at the hotel. Maybe he could get together with them for drinks.

He took off. His stopping at my table had consequences. From being an unknown enjoying his meal, I was a guy who Sinatra knew.

I spent the rest of the meal signing my ever-present publicity photos. This being a celebrity was fun, but at times I would like to slink away. It might have been more enjoyable if there had been girls my age. After that, I retired for the night.

Chapter 10

I was at the Olympia Theater early in the morning. Marshal Givens had breakfast with me and was along for the day. I liked him a lot but didn't think I would ever want to cross him. He looked deadly, and I don't know why. I think he would only act if it were justified, but it would be decisive if he did.

I had learned from my previous sessions that kids would line up early. I was correct in my thinking. Some of them had been there since last night. A couple of them were entrepreneurial and were holding places in line to sell. I wondered how that would work out. I avoided getting involved.

Instead, I worked the line. I started with the first arrivals, chatted with each of them for a few minutes, and worked my way back. The marshal accompanied me. I switched back and forth from English to Spanish and accents from British to American just to keep it mixed up.

I gave autographs as we went down the line. I hoped to reach the back of the line before the doors opened. By eleven o'clock, we made it. There must have been a thousand people in line already.

After reaching the end of the line, I moved back inside the theater to the picture setup. It was another Catholic charity. Again, nuns in robes kept order. I looked for rulers but didn't see any. That didn't mean they weren't handy.

We had the head of the line move to the picture set. After their picture was taken with me, if they wanted one, that is, they went inside. As before, local bands were playing. These were Rock and Roll or Cuban. Plenty of soft drinks and popcorn were available.

The cleaning bill was going to be horrendous as popcorn fights broke out. These fights were all in fun. I deny I was involved in any of it. I don't know how that picture was faked.

After being set up for a fake popcorn fight picture (my story and I'm sticking to it), I went back out to start signing autographs again. Finally, the theater was full. Many people were left on the street. A quick agreement was made by Susan Wallace, who had wised up and flown in for the event, and the bands moved outside to play.

I went into a madhouse, not a riot, but getting close. I ran down the aisle and got up on stage. I wasn't prepared for the television cameras on each side of the stage. It was nice that there was an overhead microphone.

I immediately welcomed the audience. I hadn't finished my statement when Frank Sinatra came out of stage left. He was accompanied by a fiddle player. I knew he was a fiddle player because he had one with him. It didn't take much imagination to see what was going on.

I was right, as Frank, who I was questioning my respect for, told the audience he and I were doing a duet of my released song from the movie. It had come out two days before and was getting good play. People have no taste.

I hate being put on the spot like that, but what can you do? We sang the song. It didn't come out too badly because I was a little hoarse from talking all day.

Frank exited the stage right. From stage left, a redhead came running.

"Oh, Mr. Sinatra, please wait. I need your autograph."

He was out of sight, and Lucy was in the middle of the stage when Desi followed from stage left.

"Lucy, you got some splaining to do," he yelled.

Lucy went off stage to the right, with Desi following. The crowd was hooting and hollering. Desi was just exiting when Reginald Van Gleason made a grand entrance. When he got to me, he did the famous, "And away we go."

By this time, I knew why TV cameras were in place.

I went off stage as the movie started where the gang of scene-stealing, interloping, best people I have ever known stood, waiting for me.

I shook my head with a big grin.

"Thank you, guys; that will put this over the top."

They all told me it was fun and that they had learned long ago that events like this were publicity gold. Jackie Gleason explained this was personal for him as the last time he was on these boards was in the 1930s in vaudeville.

Again, I thanked them profusely. I thought we were done, but they told me I was nuts. I was escorted outside, where the lines were just as long as the early matinee. Susan was there and smirking when she told me we were doing it all again.

And we did.

My fellow actors were all there for the opening and did their stunts again. There was an addition. It seems Jerry Lewis was in town. His publicity people called mine, and the next thing you know, I had The Bellhop helping me off stage to end the opening.

The next day, the national papers picked up on the impromptu event. My tour also got a name, "Ricky Jackson's Circus". When it came to town, you never knew what was going to happen.

My fellow actors all had gone in their separate directions. Susan Wallace was on her way to Savannah to confirm that setup. I wondered how we would top this show. Marshal Givens tipped his hat to me and went his way.

After all that excitement, I returned to Little Havana for a Coke and to crowd-watch to settle down. I settled down in my favorite café at an outside table. I had just sat down and was joined by a Latin man I didn't know. He introduced himself as Jose Cardona.

"I hear you have concerns about our retaking Cuba from that pig Castro."

"A lot of information about the plans appears to be freely available."

"How much do you think is true?"

"I have no idea; I hope very little."

"Little boys should stay out of matters of their elders."

Now, call me many things, but not little boy. I stood up and towered over him.

"Expressing one's concerns is allowed in a free country. Who is the tyrant here?"

He didn't answer me but turned on his heel.

My waiter, who hadn't left the area, said, "He is a powerful man; you should be careful."

Not being completely stupid, and the evening was ruined anyway, I went back to the hotel and flew out early in the morning.

Miami to Savannah was to be a three-hour flight. However, I had to land in Jacksonville for a pee stop. Some pilots brought along a milk bottle for that, but I just couldn't bring myself to do it.

At Jacksonville, I made a phone call to Susan Wallace to see if everything was set up. She felt it was under control. She had been working on continuing the Ricky Jackson Circus. She would fill me in when I got there.

From habit, I checked the payphone coin return. I hit the jackpot. There were two dollars in quarters left behind. Landing at Savannah, I was met by a security guard named Frank Willis. The Marshal's Service was stretched thin for the next week, so they had hired Frank's firm to escort me on show day.

On the way into town to my hotel, the Ballastone Inn, Frank told me I would be his last job in Savannah. His company was transferring him to Washington, DC, to guard a new office and hotel site that was just starting construction. It was named the Watergate. He was enthusiastic about it as it would get him closer to his family. Other than family, it sounded boring.

It was still early after I got checked in, so I went for a walk around the many parks in the area. The parks were all part of General Oglethorpe's city plan. A row of houses surrounded each side of a park. These were all magnificent mansions at one time, though many were showing their age.

Altogether, there were originally twenty-two of the parks. Some of them had been torn down for development over the years. These were called the lost parks. I made a note to let Dad know about this area. Redeveloping this area could make a fortune.

By the time I got to Chippawa Park, I was ready to sit and watch the world go by for a while. This park had a huge statue of General Oglethorpe. A guy in a suit and tie was sitting at the other end of the bench, but he seemed okay, so I sat down.

He started talking to me. He was interesting to a point. He lost me when he told me his mother's saying, "Life is like a box of chocolates. You never know what you're gonna get."

She must have bought cheap chocolates. The ones we had at home had a flier with them that told what each one was, or it was printed on the box.

Shortly thereafter, I got on board a streetcar that stopped in front of us. Nice, the guy was, but enough was enough.

I got off the streetcar at a restaurant called the Pirate House. I decided to eat there. It was an interesting place. It was named in Robert Louis Stevenson's book, *Treasure Island.* It was reputed to be where the pirate Captain Flint stayed when in Savannah.

Furthermore, the local legend was that he had died in a room upstairs and that his ghost still haunted the house. I found that funny, as he was a fictional character. All I can say is that they had a strange way of mixing reality and fiction.

After dinner, continuing my stroll, I passed Club One. A sign outside said the Lady Chablis used to appear there. Whoever Lady

Chablis was, I had never heard of her, or from the picture they had, he, she, or it.

After that discovery, I returned to the Ballastone and turned in.

The next day was another free day, so I continued my walking tour of the city. I saw the Chatham cannon that the city had since the Revolutionary War. They had been taken from the British at the Battle of Yorktown. George Washington had presented them to the city.

They had been buried under the armory during the recent unpleasantness to hide them from Sherman. A guide standing at the public display told me this. It took me a moment to figure out he was talking about the War of Northern Aggression. Conversely, it could be called the War of Southern Rebellion, but when in Rome.

The guide, Stacy Keach, was knowledgeable and was a pleasure to talk to. I didn't identify myself, so I think everything he said was genuine. He told the tour group he was going to Hollywood. He wanted to be in the movies or at least on TV. From his looks and how he handled himself, I thought he might make it.

I took a tour bus out to the Roundhouse. This was a museum under construction. It was the oldest railroad roundhouse in the state and about the only one not destroyed in Sherman's March to the Sea. It would be gone if the city had not surrendered. It was part of the Central Georgia Railway. Since I grew up in a railroad town, they always fascinated me.

Going back into town, I had lunch by the river. I toured Juliette Gordon Low's house and then returned to the hotel. At lunch, someone had left a copy of the *Savannah Morning News*. On the front page was a headline announcing that the Ricky Jackson Circus had come to town. The article wondered what a spectacular follow-up to my Miami and New Orleans visits would be.

Oh, oh. I had better catch up with Susan and see what was set up for tomorrow. She was staying at the same hotel, so I was able to talk to her at dinner. When she told me what she had put together, I was blown away. That she could do this on such short notice was almost a miracle.

Accompanied by Frank Willis, I was at the Savannah Theater early. Everything was set up. I worked the early arrival line, signing autographs as I went. When I got to the back of the line, I moved to the photography setup. We had it down to a routine. I don't know what charity we were working with.

Mayor Mingledorff, a nice guy, showed up for the obligatory picture for the newspaper. He asked me if I could sneak his teenage daughter and two friends in early as he couldn't get them moving this morning. Not being stupid, I escorted them to a side door. This inadvertently gave them an introduction to my surprise guests.

Even Dad was amazed that the Beach Boys would be playing for the crowd and that Paul Anka and Annette would appear. The one that impressed most was Jerry Lee Lewis. He was a hero in the South.

When we did the opening, I thought it poignant that Paul and Annette did a duet of "Puppy Love". The Beach Boys had them dancing in the aisles before the kickoff.

When I asked Susan what this was costing, she told me I didn't want to know. Annette had to leave after the first showing of the movie, but the others stuck around for the second show. We could have done a third as there were so many people outside.

The hit of the performance was Jerry Lee when he and his band played "Dixie". From what I had heard and seen in Savannah, I was glad I hadn't worn my Ohio Volunteer Infantry uniform.

Of course, there was a fiddle player, so I had to sing my song. I think I sang it the best I ever did that night.

When the movie itself played, the audience had their part down well, cheers for Lew Wetzel (me), boos for Death Wind (also me), and aws for Mary. I will never tell her, but her oohs and aws were louder than my cheers. Maybe it's a southern thing.

From the early bookings of the movie, we had a financial winner. The critics were being kind. This was almost unheard of. They hated anything that made a profit. They talked about me showing the real America. I guess I got whatever credit or discredit was given because I had come up with the theme of the movie.

I just hoped the Shawnee didn't scalp me when I stopped by at their request. Maybe they would settle for me running a gauntlet.

I was dead beat when I returned to the hotel. As I was falling asleep, I wondered what Susan would come up with next for the Ricky Jackson Circus.

Chapter 11

I arrived at Baltimore's Friendship Airport around one in the afternoon. Susan insisted on my flying to that airport instead of Washington National. Something was up.

Well, something was up alright, but I don't think it had anything to do with Susan. A US Deputy Marshal, two FBI agents, and two Secret Service agents met me at the airport. They all approached me as I entered the general aviation terminal.

Each of the three groups told me they had been ordered to pick me up and escort me during my stay in Washington.

The deputy was there to provide me with a car and then accompany me on the day of the movie showing. This was a paid overtime job for him. The studio would be picking up the tab.

The FBI told me that their superiors had heard I was going to be in town and were ordered to watch out for me because of my background with the KGB.

The Secret Service had shown up because I was listed as a high-profile person in the White House. Not only that, but I also had a meeting with the president later today.

This was all news to me. Each group heard what the others had to say. The only one that seemed at ease was the marshal; after all, he was getting paid overtime.

We finally settled on me riding with the marshal. The Secret Service would lead the way to the White House, and the FBI would ride drag. When I used that term, the agents looked puzzled. They both chuckled when I explained it was those last in line on a cattle drive and would eat dust all day.

"Sounds like any other day then."

Considering three different government agencies were there, I didn't feel like I was in the middle of a turf war.

We sorted ourselves out and took the B-W Parkway to US 50. When we arrived at the railyard across from the Hecht's store, I saw Susan's surprise, or what I thought her surprise would be.

Sitting there was the Ringling Bros. and Barnum & Bailey circus train, all fifty-plus cars of it. There was no doubt in my mind that the Ricky Jackson Circus would arrive on an elephant's back.

I would have to talk to Susan tonight. We were both staying at Willard House. It was now my regular place to stay while in Washington, and it was an easy walk to the White House from there.

Of course, I wasn't allowed to walk. Our cavalcade drove up to a set of White House gates. We drove right on in; well, the Secret Service stopped and cleared my car. The FBI was halted and not let in. They didn't have prior clearance.

It warmed my heart to see that agency rivalry was alive and well. Those Secret Service agents must have been chuckling about it the whole trip in. That was funny, but I would now be stuck with a couple of FBI agents with their noses out of joint.

After surrendering my weapon and showing identification, I was shown to the Oval Office. The president was there with two people I didn't recognize. They were introduced as Senator John Kennedy and Senate Majority Leader Lyndon Johnson.

We shook hands. I didn't cotton up to Johnson for some reason but liked Kennedy.

Ike explained, "Part of the presidential election process is to bring the opposing candidates up to speed on issues facing the country and major operations that are underway. Normally, we wait until there is a clear candidate. This time, it looks like it will be brokered at the convention, so I elected to have both candidates attend the briefings."

I wondered what that had to do with me.

"Rick, you are probably wondering why you are here. First of all, the timing is convenient for all of us. Second, you don't realize how your Chinese connection has great potential for the country."

"To avoid embarrassing you in front of these gentlemen, I have told them how you possibly averted World War III, had your sister kidnapped by the KGB and the rescue, the several attempts on you and your family's life, plus what steps you took to explain the error of their ways.

"Then there is the matter of Cuba, first the missile crisis and now what you have passed on about the coming invasion. An aside from that is that we are committed, and it looks like it will be a disaster, but we have no choice but to proceed."

"Then, recently, your family rolled up a Soviet spy ring in LA. All in all, interesting things happen around you. On top of that, you are quickly becoming one of the richest people on the planet. This doesn't even count having me and Queen Elizabeth as your godparents. Put all of that together, and I thought it would be in their interest for these gentlemen to meet you."

He then asked them if they had any questions for me. Kennedy didn't; Johnson did.

"I got dragged to your latest movie last night. Why did you sully the reputation of one of America's heroes, Lew Wetzel?"

"If the truth sullies his reputation, one wonders if he was a hero, Senator."

I could tell I would never get along with this man.

The president offered to have my contact information forwarded to them. Senator Kennedy said he would contact me if he had any questions on China. Also, I should feel free to contact his office if anything came up.

Senator Johnson wanted to know if I had directed my company to make any donations. He would be interested in my financial support.

I told him that I left that to my Board of Directors. I made a mental note to have it made official company policy that we didn't make any political donations.

The look on my face must have told my feelings on the issue because it got dropped like a hot potato.

I noticed nothing had been said about my US-deputy-marshal status. That soon came out.

Senator Kennedy asked, "What, if anything, has been done to keep this young man safe?"

The president then explained about my being deputized. Senator Kennedy thought this was a good thing, Senator Johnson not so much.

"Why on God's green earth would you allow a kid to go around armed?"

I edited the senator's words. He was much cruder. Before the president could reply, I butted in.

"The Texas Rangers don't seem to have a problem with it since they've given me a badge too."

I didn't tell him it was honorary.

"What was that for?"

I told him about the rustler ring I had broken up.

If it was good enough for the Rangers, it was good enough for him, as there were no further objections.

Senator Kennedy did ask why I chose Oxford over Harvard and told me it was a shame I hadn't seen the light. He was nice about it, though.

Mr. Johnson surprised me.

"From what you have told us, I would think that Rick's parents would need protection also."

That brought a dry chuckle from the president.

"If anything, it is the other way around. The KGB needs protection from them."

He went on to give a brief synopsis of Mum's war experiences and activities with MI6.

"What about his dad?"

"He is just plain scary."

Now, that surprised me. I knew that there was an untold story about the president and my father, but this seemed to go deeper.

That pretty well wrapped up my meeting. The president asked me to stay for a minute as they were leaving.

"Rick, has everything been going okay for you?"

"Yes, sir, it has."

"I wanted you to meet them. There is a good chance that one of them will be the next president."

"I thought Vice President Nixon had it in the bag?"

"Dick Nixon has several problems, but I think the most dangerous one is he doesn't come across well on television. Don't get me wrong, I support him, but I'm concerned."

That I understood. Some people were photogenic and others were not. Also, you had to have the camera people on your side, or you were toast. I relayed that to Ike, and he promised to talk to Mr. Nixon about that. Much later, I wondered if he ever did.

We talked a little about Cuba and the planned invasion. That was weird, me talking to the president of the United States about invading a foreign country. He told me that when he first approved the plan, it had tighter controls. Now that the CIA had complete control, it was becoming a circus.

Since he winked when he said circus, I got the poor joke. It was funny on the surface, but it would lose all its humor when the guns started firing. Of course, this joke was made by the man who planned and directed D-Day, so maybe it seemed like a little sideshow to him.

His chief of staff came in and moved us along. I exited a different door, so I wouldn't meet the next appointment.

The Secret Service returned my weapon and drove me to the Willard. I noticed my two FBI agents sitting in the lobby. I stopped and told them I would be eating in the hotel restaurant tonight and had a meeting with my publicity agent.

They thanked me for the information. I thought they would be more bent out of shape, but they took it all in stride.

When I checked in, I had a dinner reservation for two made. After cleaning up, I put on a suit and tie. Susan walked into the lobby at the same time I did, so that worked out.

As soon as we sat down, I asked her if I would ride an elephant to the theater. She laughed and told me she thought I would pick up on it as soon as I saw that train.

"Besides the elephant, what else do we have, a calliope?"

"More."

I inquired, "Clowns, lions, tigers?"

"More."

"How much more?" This was like pulling teeth.

"We have the whole circus!"

"What!"

"The studio got a pretty good deal. The circus was going to parade near the convention center the day after. That's where they will perform. By appearing a day early, the studio was able to get permits for them to go downtown, which will give them a lot more publicity. The DC city council wasn't wild about the idea, but an appeal from the White House changed their mind."

Now I know why Ike winked at me!

The next day, I spent time visiting monuments and museums in the city. I had seen most of them before, but it was still neat. The stamp and jewel collections in the Smithsonian were impressive. I had seen many diamonds in Africa, but nothing as glorious as the Hope diamond.

Something about that upside-down airplane on a stamp was awesome. I wondered if they would ever do a release like it as a commemorative. I used to collect stamps but had failed to keep up my collection of US commemoratives in the last few years. The stamps were boring. Other countries had interesting stamps, but not the US.

I took the ride up the elevator to the top of the Washington Memorial. The view was great. The Lincoln Memorial was awe-inspiring.

I took a tour of the FBI building for fun. I wonder what the two agents tailing me at a discreet distance thought. It was juvenile of me, but hey, I'm still considered a kid by most people.

I went for a run before dinner. I circled the National Mall several times. It was interesting to see all the people, especially two FBI agents in suits and ties trying to keep me in sight. If they got desperate enough, they might decide to shoot me.

I know I was being mean, but I hadn't been consulted about their presence, so they would have to take it as it came.

I had mercy on them by grabbing dinner at a small café. After that, I retired for the night. I even approached them in the lobby and let them know I was done for the day. You would think they would have been more appreciative.

After my normal physical activities the following day, I met Susan in the lobby. I noticed the lack of FBI agents. At Susan's suggestion, I wore my Death Wind costume. My part in the movie was now national news so there was no surprise left.

We took a taxi to the train yards where the circus was lining up. I can't begin to tell you how chaotic a circus is when it is forming up. Strangely dressed people everywhere, elephants trumpeting, lions and tigers roaring, and other animal sounds I had never heard before. I just thought the studio looked like a circus. This was a circus.

I was introduced to my mahout; I would sit on the elephant, but he would control and direct it. My elephant was named Jumbo in honor of the original circus elephant. He wasn't as big as the animal, which introduced Jumbo as a size, but he was right up there. At least, it seemed that way when I was sitting on top.

I didn't have that little building they ride in, just a saddle.

Right on time, all the confusion ended, and the circus parade started its march, calliope and all. We marched off with me in the lead, well, with the elephant being directed by the mahout. Lots of radio and TV ads ensured the parade route was lined.

It was fun riding down the street in a swaying motion atop Jumbo. Everything was fine until the halfway point. Did you know that elephants and firecrackers don't mix?

Some kids threw a bundle of Ladyfingers out in the street. Wow, Jumbo can move!

Now, I had been in a stampede, but it was the wildest ride I ever had or could even imagine as we tore down the street. I hate to think what it would have been like if the parade route hadn't been closed off.

I held on with both hands for dear life. The mahout was left far behind. After about five blocks, Jumbo must have realized he was safe from those nasty noises because he slowed to a stop. A fast-thinking motorcycle patrolman had given the mahout a ride to catch up with us, so things were brought back under control rapidly.

By the time the rest of the parade caught up, Jumbo was peacefully eating flowers in a small park next to the road. From there, we marched in formation to the theater. As one would expect, my elephant had run away in front of TV cameras.

When the story appeared, it was labeled, "Ricky's Wild Ride". I wouldn't live that down for a long time. I bet those FBI Agents were glad they had been recalled.

The rest of the day was anticlimactic. Sign autographs, pose for pictures, and sing my song; clowns and jugglers behind and with me on stage. Midway through my little welcome talk, a lady on a trapeze passed over me. You know, just another day at work. The sword swallower was distracting.

The audience cheered, yelled, booed, and awed in all the right places during the movie. The movie had been playing in the DC area for several days, and you could tell that the people present had seen it already. Susan later told me that we were breaking box office records.

I was so glad to be done with that day. I returned to the Willard after the second showing and collapsed.

Chapter 12

By the time I got back to Baltimore from the airport, I was almost to Philadelphia. I had clearance to land before I took off. That was something different and would probably become more prevalent in the future as air traffic picked up. There was no doubt in my mind that it would.

Thinking that over, I decided to invest in the flying industry. Not in airlines because they seemed to come and go, but instead invest in the companies that served airlines: aircraft builders, for one, and there would be a need for maintenance, engines, and catering, to name a few.

Airport infrastructure would need expansion. As the airports got bigger, the walks got longer. I wondered what could be done about that. I had read that in-flight movies were about to be introduced. Watching one of my movies at thirty thousand feet would be neat.

It took longer to do the preflight check than to fly to Philadelphia.

Susan had kept the car I had in Washington and driven it up to Philly. I was to have a marshal accompany me the day of the showing, but other than that, I was on my own. I was staying at the Bellevue Stratford.

The centerpiece of the Ricky Jackson Circus at the Boyd Theater was to be Dick Clark's *American Bandstand* show. The show was going to be on TV, so it had been announced in advance. Susan explained to me that there would be nothing ad hoc about this show. No stampeding elephants allowed!

This was to be a professional presentation, so I only had to show up. Everyone thought what I had made happen to start the tour was wonderful, but they were scared as hell about what I might do next.

Well, there goes my appearance with the Flying Wallendas. Just kidding, I'm not that crazy.

I was interviewed by one of the local TV stations. First of all, they wanted to talk about the stampeding elephant.

"Was I scared?"

"Heck, yes! I would be stupid not to be scared."

What about the other stampede I had been in while doing the movie, *Sir Nickalous*?

"That was a little different. There I was trying to save a life. I was too busy to think about being scared and sitting on Jumbo with nothing to do but hang on gave me time to be scared."

"What would you like to say to those guys who threw the fireworks? They got away."

"Jerks."

"That seems harsh; they were just trying to have fun."

"Fun doesn't put people in danger."

"Aren't you overreacting? No one was hurt."

"This interview is over,"

Maybe that was overreacting, but I didn't have to put up with that nonsense.

The other TV channels in town took them to task for tasteless questions and trying to sensationalize the interview. That channel tried to portray me as a spoiled Hollywood actor.

Susan's only concern was that they got my name right. Publicity, publicity, and more publicity.

After that, my role was limited to having my picture taken for charitable customers. Everyone would be given a signed publicity picture. I would welcome all to the show, sing my song, and turn it over to Dick Clark.

Mr. Clark congratulated me on my new hit song. This was the first I heard it was a hit. I wondered how much it cost the studio. The Payola hearings had just finished, and the scandal was rocking the industry. That didn't mean the industry had rolled over; it had just gone underground. Yeah, puns intended.

Mr. Clark did make a comment that surprised me. He called me a versatile singing talent. Each of my songs was different from the other. I told him not to expect me to sing opera anytime soon.

After that, I sang to a fiddle accompaniment and left the stage. It would undoubtedly be a good show but no fun, at least for me.

It went as advertised. After the movie started, I left the theater and went to Independence Hall. I was recognized in line and ended up signing many of my ever-present publicity photos. It was an awesome feeling when I got into the room where the Declaration of Independence was signed. I was surprised by the history of the Liberty Bell; I thought it had been rung on July 4, 1776.

There were frayed edges at the bottom of the bell. When the bell went on national tours, people chipped off pieces of it. I wondered if any of those pieces were still identified as such or just in someone's junk drawer.

I walked by the Betsy Ross House and Ben Franklin's place. The more I learned about Ben Franklin, the more I admired him. I wonder how he got to be such a ladies' man.

My walk got a little out of hand. I started down Broad Street and ended up in South Philly. I had been warned this area was not completely safe. I had no problems other than being amazed about all the street corner groups singing doo-whop. It was fantastic.

I found myself in a sizable open area with stalls selling produce and other merchandise – somebody told me it was called the Italian Market – and had a Philly cheesesteak at a place called Pat's King of Steaks. I will say it again: it was fantastic.

I was invited to a party that night in a town called Bryn Mawr on the Main Line, whatever that was. I later found out it was the towns and houses on the commuter train line into Philadelphia. The rich lived in this area.

I whined a bit but gave in to Susan. She tried to convince me that I needed to know these people to raise money for my projects. I told her they may need to know me to raise money for theirs.

What sold it was that there would be some disappointed daughters. I never want to disappoint daughters, especially cute teenage ones.

I dressed in California casual. No one told me it was a suit-and-tie affair. Oh well, they would get over it.

Upon arrival, I was taken around and introduced to the movers and shakers. From the questions, it was apparent that they were more aware of my finances than Susan. When the questions got too direct, I pulled the dumb teenager card and hid behind my Board of Directors.

I didn't care what they thought of me and was tired of being hit up for the next sure thing. Unlike in England, no one offered me twenty pounds when they thought I had no money of my own.

The financiers quickly lost interest in me. I was able to escape out onto the patio, where a group of kids my age had formed.

One guy came over to me immediately. He introduced himself as Cadet Rylski 6883. I must have looked confused, so he reminded me of the tabloids and the Bulgarian princess.

I felt discombobulated when he formally introduced himself as King Simeon II of Bulgaria. He laughed at the look on my face.

"Rick, may I call you Rick?"

"Yes, Your Majesty."

"You are to call me Simeon."

"Okay, Simeon."

"I have sorted out what was happening and realize that you were not making fun of Bulgaria. However, there is something I require from you."

"What is that?"

"Could you give me an autographed picture of you for my sister, the Princess Mari-Louisa? She is married and too old for you but enjoyed the articles to no end."

"I would be glad to."

I wrote a note on the picture that it was a shame that time and age made us miss each other, but I had enjoyed our romance in the tabloids. Maybe we could do it again sometime if things got boring.

I signed one of the standby pictures, then had another guy who had his camera with him take pictures of Simeon and me together. We parted on a good note.

I spent some time talking to the girls at the party, but no sparks were struck. They were all going steady, and I had no plans to return this way. It was nice that we were able to talk as a group, and I didn't feel like anyone was out to get me for my fame or fortune.

I guess that is why the well-to-do tend to group.

I later learned this incident between me and King Simeon II gave the communists further reason to hate me. I had read you could judge a man by his enemies. Many countries and several continents hated me. That and twenty-five cents would get me a cup of coffee.

The next morning, I fired up my plane for my trip to Oklahoma to meet with the Shawnee. This was at Chief Redfoot's request. I had asked him what it was about, but he avoided a direct answer. They just wanted to recognize me for my efforts for the Shawnee.

Other than returning Chief Blackhoof's medals, I didn't feel I had done much. Maybe they were putting more stock in the effects of the movie than I was.

I had fuel stops in Indianapolis and Kansas City. I had checked beforehand and found a small landing strip on the reservation, which the chief confirmed, so I flew directly there.

I called the chief from a pay phone in Kansas City and let him know that I would be there in about two hours. There was no money in the coin return. You can't win them all.

When I landed on the reservation, a small group of cars awaited me. The chief was there dressed in jeans and a work shirt. He wore a dusty old straw hat. I rode with him in his ratty old pickup truck. I asked him about it. It was a 1938 Chevy and still going strong. Well, it may have been strong, but it sure was noisy.

I asked him what the agenda was. We hadn't talked about how long I would be there; I thought it was to be a brief layover. I had that wrong.

"We need to get you settled. You will be sleeping on the couch at my house. Tomorrow will be spent in the sweat lodge, the ceremony will be the next morning, then there will be a showing of your movie, a party, and then you can get on your way.

This was getting deeper and deeper.

At his house, we had many visitors. They wanted to meet the man who had played Death Wind and revealed the monster he was to the world. One extremely wrinkled old man told me how his great-great-grandmother had narrowly escaped being killed by Death Wind.

As we talked, I realized it was the little girl we had portrayed in the movie. That made everything real to me. Working on the movie script we used as many historical records as possible. The Draper Manuscripts described the incident with the Indian child.

Now I was in the presence of one of her descendants. I had a shiver go down my spine. The one known as Death Wind had been a fictional character to me until just now. Now he was real, and that meant all his evil actions had occurred.

I began to understand why the Shawnee appreciated my exposing Lew Wetzel for what he was.

The next day was spent in the sweat lodge. I will not say much about it except the name was earned. There was no question that I had been purified. My dirty, sweaty clothes would attest to that.

I had to fast that night. At least I was allowed to take a shower and put on clean clothes. The next day I was inducted into the Shawnee Tribe as a brave. I thought they inducted people as chiefs and gave them fancy headdresses.

I found out they did that to honor politicians and others for publicity. Mine was for defending the Shawnee people. This honor was one of the highest I had ever received. It ranked right up there with my Order of the Garter, maybe even higher. For the Garter, I had saved one person, though granted, the Queen of England was an important person. The simple hawk feather in a headband was for defending a whole people.

I don't think I will share this line of thinking with my godmother. At the ceremony, I announced the forming of the educational fund. I thought Indians were stoic and didn't show emotion. The tears shed by men and women told a different story.

After that, my movie was shown in the community center. There were cheers for the Indians, boos for Lew Wetzel in all appearances, aws for Mary, and cheers for Simon Kenton as he ran the gauntlet. George Washington rated hisses.

King George III of England had them throwing popcorn at the screen. Oliver Spencer got the most cheers as he stood up to Simon Girty. Girty himself was ignored.

All in all, a different take. It was the only time I was booed in a movie and enjoyed it. I booed right along with them.

After the movie, there was a picture-taking and autograph session, the same as everywhere. I slept on the couch again that night. I made a mental note to have a new one delivered to Chief Redfoot. The springs were terrible. Maybe that was why he didn't have a girlfriend.

I kept my mouth shut.

The next morning, I was up early and did my run. A half dozen young braves joined me. They kept up with me with no problems. It was a lot of fun running with boys my age. As we ran, they extolled the virtues of girls in the tribe. I think they were serious about me being a true member of the tribe.

I tried to let them know my path would take me in other directions, but they would always be in my heart. It may sound corny here, but it was from the bottom of my heart.

After that, Chief Redfoot drove me back to my plane. I thought the truck was going to fall apart and even thought about buying him a new one but realized that could be construed as an insult to his beloved *la nàhl we*.

I had no idea what it meant in English, speeding arrow, for all I knew.

From there, I started my trip home to Jackson House.

Chapter 13

I landed at Ontario Airport after fuel stops in Denver and Las Vegas. After the trip, my aircraft was due for some maintenance, so I left it with the Cessna people to wiggle their noses and magically fix my plane or whatever they did.

Dad had arranged for a car and driver to pick me up, so I was able to relax on the short trip home. As I thought over the last month, I had to laugh at myself. I had intended to take a leisurely trip around the country, visiting sites I would like to see.

Instead, the Ricky Jackson Circus hit the road without a dull minute. I was physically and mentally tired. How had I let myself be talked into it? It certainly helped movie attendance. *Over the Ohio* was a box office success and winning the critics' accolades.

On a personal note, I was now considered a serious actor instead of just a movie star. My next role was a matter of great speculation in the industry. Playing a student at Oxford sounded pretty good to me.

The whole family was there to welcome me home. School had just let out for the day. Denny and Eddie hugged me. Mary had brought some friends home from school with her. She insisted on introducing each of them.

As she went on about me, I started to have some suspicions. These were partially confirmed by the smirk Mum was wearing, and Dad was trying to hold back laughter. I asked my sister to join me in the next room for a minute.

She walked in, looking like she was going to her execution.

"How much did you charge them?"

"Nothing!"

"What did they have to do?"

"It wasn't very much, Ricky, I swear. They only had to donate five dollars to Feed the Puppies."

What could you say to that? Puppies need to be fed.

"I'll let you get away with it this time. How much did you raise?

"Sixty dollars."

"There are only five of them there. What about the others?"

"The other five will be here tomorrow; I thought ten would be too many at once. Also, I could charge a premium to be in the first group."

"Okay, you have to match their donations out of your funds, and I will also give a matching amount."

She pouted a little but agreed she had overstepped. Next time, she would ask me.

Maybe I could make another trip around the country, as it might be safer and less tiring.

We rejoined her suckers, I mean her friends. I spent a few minutes talking to each of the girls, asking brilliant questions about the colors they liked and their favorite subjects in school. Mary got her 1940s camera out and took pictures. Denny quoted a price to develop them, and after some haggling, Mary got a ten percent sister discount.

After that, the little girls all went up to the tower. I knew where I would not be going.

Mum, Dad, and I grabbed a cup of coffee and adjourned to Mum's conservatory. First, they told me they were happy with how I had handled Mary. She needed to be taken down a peg or two but not embarrassed in front of her friends.

The latest addition to the house was very nice; all the plants were growing well, and it was very relaxing. They asked about my trip. When it got to the elephant part, I found out about some family history I had never heard. One of my great, great uncles had been in the British Army.

He enlisted as a drummer boy. He ended up as a colonel. This was normally as high as an enlisted man was allowed to advance. He got married when his regiment was stationed in India. The entire regiment lined the streets while he and his bride rode in a howdah. I finally learned the name of that little hut on the elephant.

I asked what happened to him, but no one knew. He and a lot of his men disappeared in trench warfare in World War I. They knew his body was somewhere in no man's land, but it had never been retrieved. What a grim ending.

I told my parents that I felt worn out. They completely understood and suggested I take a week and only do what I felt like. I bought into that so much that an agreement was made to intercept all phone calls and have me call back if I felt like it.

The news of my return was in the daily paper. Thanks, Dad. He said it was his duty and the public's right to know. He laughed and said it sold papers, and that was his job. Unrepentant and unfeeling, yep, that's my Dad.

I understood the fine line between your job and your family, and besides, what harm would it do?

It did none to me because I didn't have to answer the eighty-some phone calls that came through before lunch. Poor Mrs. Hernandez did most of the answering. She only wrote down the ones that she thought I might return, both of them.

One call was from my publicist, and now my movie agent, Susan Wallace. She had been working with Mr. Baxter, and I gathered it was working out. I did call her back.

She wanted to know if I was ready to discuss new movies. I told her to call me back in a week. I would not decide for a while. I had decided but didn't have the energy to argue with her at the moment. Lord, that woman could argue. That was great if she were on your side, but she would go at you until she wore you down if you had something she wanted.

In this case, she wanted a ten percent commission on my next movie. Maybe I could offer her that much to leave me alone while I went back to school. I know, stupid thinking, and that's why there would be no decisions until I get some rest. It was quickly becoming obvious that Susan had to be my publicist or my agent, one or the other, not both.

I had to figure out how to approach this. She was a good person, and I didn't want to destroy our relationship.

To clear my mind, I took a long ride on George. He seemed happy to see me. Ben had been keeping him exercised so he wasn't jumpy, but he sure wanted to get out of the barn. Three hours later, he was ready to return to his stall to eat, and I felt a little more relaxed.

Rubbing him down and putting the saddle and gear away left me sweaty and dirty, so I cleaned up and had dinner with the family for the first time in a long time.

After a good night's sleep, I was ready to face a new day. Exercise, running, and showering made it even better. I called John Jacobs to see if he was available to caddie today. He was, so we agreed to meet at Riveria Country Club. It was presumptuous of me to assume I could get on, but as the winner of the US Open, I thought they would work me in.

I was correct in my thinking. The golf pro asked if I would do him a favor. He had a threesome of some high-profile politicians coming up, and it would look good for him if I would play with them.

They were Richard Kleindienst, H.R. Haldeman, and John Ehrlichman. All I will say is that was the last time I would agree to play with a group like that. What an arrogant group of people! Of course, when I was done with them on the course, they weren't arrogant about their golf.

When they saw how badly I was beating them, they tried to ingratiate themselves with me, but by then, it was too late. That would teach them to complain to the starter about being forced to play with a kid. I guess no one clued them in on me. I had thought the pro was trying to suck up to them; it looked more like getting revenge.

John must have felt the same way because after a quick discussion with the other caddies, my three new "friends" found themselves having to play by the rules of golf. No mulligans, no gimmes, no kicking the ball to a better position. It is surprising what can happen if your caddie announces each infraction.

Perversely, it was fun. I tied the course record, which happened to be mine, and that was after I penalized myself for accidentally moving the ball once.

Afterward, I asked John if he wanted to fly up to Pebble Beach tomorrow and play that course. He thought it was a good idea because I would probably play in the Bing Crosby tournament someday. The club pro was kind enough to call and reserve a tee time. I would get to tee off by myself.

The next day, John came for breakfast at Jackson House. We ate a hearty meal for the day. From there, it was the back way to the Forest Service Station. This was the first time John had seen this setup, and he was impressed.

After loading my clubs and holdall with a change of clothes in the back of the plane, which had had its maintenance done and been flown from Ontario, we headed north. It was a nice trip up the coast. I followed the coastline just far enough offshore to avoid the wind changes as the air changed from water to land.

Did you know that Pebble Beach is one of the nastiest golf courses in the world? They have one water hazard; it's called the Pacific Ocean. That course killed me. Those long open fairways looked like I could carry them. Well, the wind off the tee carried me okay, right into the ocean—not once, not twice, but five times. From my fine golf yesterday, I went to the depths of a golfer's hell. That meant I wouldn't have cut if I had been in a tournament. John assured me that a 78 for my first time on this course was respectable, but I didn't buy it.

At least I didn't throw or break any clubs. I did make a personal vow to defeat this course. John and I flew back and forth for the next three days to play. On Friday, I had a 65 and began to feel like I could play this course.

If nothing else, it took my mind off my month-long road trip. What had started out as a slow, relaxing sightseeing trip turned into a grind promoting my movie. The trip was fun in its way but left me tired to the point of exhaustion. When you wake up tired, you know you have overdone it.

On the way home Friday, I stopped at the small flight center to file my flight plan back down south. I had done these three days in a row. This time, a different guy was at the desk. He looked at me and John and then asked to see my driver's license. I didn't give it a thought and showed it to him.

"That's what I thought; you are too young to carry a passenger. Do you even have a pilot's license?"

I had all my paperwork in my Jeppesen case, so I showed it to him. He was not satisfied.

"This paperwork says you are a pilot in the Royal Air Force and, as such, are to be treated as a full pilot. How do I know if this is real? I have never seen anything like this before?"

"Why don't you call the FAA and ask them."

"I will, smart ass."

He called to what I thought must be the LA FAA flight center. He started by giving my information. Next, he was saying, uh-huh a lot. This continued for a while.

After he hung up, he had one more question.

"Did you land a 707 by yourself?"

"Yes, I did."

"I apologize for questioning your credentials, but I have never seen anything like them before."

"I understand; now understand this. If you ever call me a smart ass again, I will knock your block off."

Childish, I know, but some days you've got to let it out.

After that, the trip was uneventful. I kept looking for overturned sailboats. Who knows? There may be another female star needing rescuing. It was not to be.

Saturday, I spent at the beach. The surf wasn't up, but it was still fun lying in the sun and girl-watching. I loved the new style of bikinis; they were getting smaller all the time.

I strolled over to Katin's to see what was up. The biggest news was that Corky had won a tournament in South Africa. I hadn't talked to him in some months, so I didn't know how the corporate sponsorship was working out. It turned out it was great. Redheaded Nancy Katin told me that just having the Jackson name was opening doors for him. I only mentioned her hair because she must have just dyed it. Man, was it bright!

Before this, he had been sleeping on couches or in rental cars. My sponsorship included hotel rooms. It was a case of them that has, gets. He had invitations at every stop to stay at some very nice homes. He was way under budget for rooms.

Of course, there was a price to pay. Everyone wanted to know his relationship with me in a business sense and if he could help them contact me. I didn't realize that my businesses, especially cargo containers and ocean freight forwarding, were well known.

Sunday was horseback riding and then the beach in the afternoon. At the beach, I met a couple of nice girls who had set their blanket next to mine. We had a pleasant afternoon of small talk. When I left, it occurred to me that they probably had no idea whatsoever who I was.

They were both nice, but I had no desire to get to know either one.

On the way home, I wondered what sort of girl I would be interested in now. Also, I wondered what I was going to do next week. July had been a busy month that tired me out. Now that I had the first week of August as downtime, I was ready to go again.

Oxford didn't start back up until the end of September, but I was thinking of returning to Europe and doing some sightseeing. One thing, though: I wouldn't let the studio or Susan know what I was up to!

Chapter 14

I talked to Mum and Dad at dinner about going back to England earlier than planned. They didn't see anything wrong with it. Mary told me it was okay with her as she didn't have any more friends paying to meet me. How soon they forget!

I thanked Mary for her input. Denny snickered, but a frown shut him up. She was trying to be nice and helpful; he didn't have to make fun of her. Eddie must have felt the same way as he kicked Denny under the table. Mum and Dad took no notice, so Denny knew he had no allies and shut up.

I pitied Mary's boyfriend when she gets older. Though, she did have the right to date anyone she wanted when she was twenty. Dad corrected me with thirty. Mum and Mary said in unison, "Men."

Then Mum added, "Forty."

That broke us all up, even Mary.

Dad reminded me I had a Jackson Enterprises board meeting on Wednesday, so I would have to stay in town for it.

After that, I brought up that I had let a situation develop with Susan Wallace. It was apparent that her job as my agent and publicist created some conflicts for me. As my publicist, she had free rein, and as my agent, she would make a lot of money if I took part in a movie. Thus, she had become a little pushy.

Dad asked what I was going to do about it. I told him I would talk to Susan and let her choose which job she wanted. I would support her either way, as she had been good to me. If needed, I would be a silent partner in her agency to keep it going if I didn't take any further roles.

That led to a discussion about my future in the movies. I was hot and cold about it, one day ready to take advantage of my latest successes and the next wanting to do something different. When asked what I had in mind would be different, I wasn't sure. I wanted to finish school at Oxford as I was enjoying it, but in doing so, I wouldn't have time for movies.

Mum asked if I had heard of Pinewood Studios. I knew the name but nothing about them. She suggested I talk to Mr. Monroe about them, explain what I wanted, and see if there were any possible joint projects between the two studios.

That had never occurred to me. That might work out well. I decided to talk to him in the next couple of days.

After dinner, Mrs. Hernandez asked to speak to me in private. That was out of the blue, and I had no idea whatsoever what she could want. I found out quickly.

"Rick, you know I still have contacts in Cuba."

"I hadn't thought about it, but I can see that."

"I was contacted by a friend who is in the Cuban Defense Department. Not directly but by a mutual friend. Castro is well aware that the CIA is sponsoring an invasion to overthrow him. What I was told is that they know the CIA has provided B-26 aircraft painted in Cuban colors."

"They will shoot them down with their Russian-made Migs. The news is that if the US Air Force joins in, the Russians have fighters and pilots there and will support the Cubans. It will effectively put the US at war with Russia."

"Uh oh."

"I don't know what you can do about it, but I was specifically told to give you this information."

"You can tell your contact that it is being passed on to some very high levels in the US government."

"Thank you, Rick, I will."

Being it was Sunday night, I didn't think I could do much, and it wasn't that urgent. I would make a call first thing in the morning.

After fully awake and following my morning routine, I called from my bedroom to the White House. After identifying myself to the switchboard, I was transferred to an aide, where I gave a set of passwords the president had provided me earlier.

After a fifteen-minute wait, the president came on the line. I passed on the message telling him it came from the Cuban Defense Department through two cutouts.

"Thank you, Rick. Now I would like you to make three other phone calls. Pass the same information onto Nixon, Kennedy, and Johnson."

"Why do you want me to do that?"

"It is so that you will have credibility with the next president of the United States, no matter who is elected."

"That makes sense. I'm not certain why I should have credibility, but I will do it."

Ike sounded a little frustrated when he replied.

"Rick, you have made worldwide contacts. The Cubans and the Chinese have both used you to contact the office of the president. This is mostly due to your worldwide business. I want you to have credibility if anything more of this will occur in the future."

On that note, we thanked each other, and I was transferred back to the switchboard.

I was promptly connected to the vice-president who took my information in stride. He thanked me for the heads up. He would be certain to pass the information on to the president. That surprised me, but I didn't give Ike's game away.

It appears Ike wanted to know who he could trust to pass the information on to him. If they didn't, that gave him some insight into them. Now I see how he was a success in Europe. You had to be able to trust your sources of information and also who would hold back.

Getting through to Senator Kennedy was harder as we didn't have a password setup. I was asked what the call was about; I told him I could only share that with the senator. I had to use the Sir

Richard Jackson card to even get them to accept that I needed to speak to him.

The Majority Leader Mr. Johnson had a more organized office. It helped that I started with Sir Richard. They had me hold while they checked with the White House switchboard to see if I was an approved caller.

I was on the nice list, rather than naughty, as I was put through to the senator in fairly short order. I told him that since we had met and that he might be the next president, I should share this information. Mr. Johnson wanted to know how credible my information was. I told him its origin but could not swear it wasn't disinformation.

He thanked me and transferred me back to his chief of staff, who gave me another phone number to use in the future.

I thought it was significant that the majority leader didn't say anything about sharing this information with the president. Of course, if you thought about it, you could assume I had called the president first. What a tangled web.

Senator Kennedy's office called me back right after I hung up from the speaker's staff.

I was put through to the senator, who was very affable. When I shared my information, its credibility, and why I was calling him, he took it in quickly.

"Have you talked to Ike yet?"

"Yes, he suggested I share it with you."

"Interesting. Is that me or the three candidates?"

I wasn't about to lie.

"It is all three of you."

"Smart man; thank you, Rick. By the way, I have a question for you."

"What's that?"

"I had a background check run on you; we do that to all people who get close to my office. I see that you are a business partner with Anna Romanov."

"I am."

"If possible, I would like to meet her."

For some reason, a conversation on track 61 came to mind.

"I will let her know that you are interested in talking to her."

She is an adult. He gave me a phone number I could use in the future and asked that I please feel free to pass it on to Ms. Romanov.

Somehow, I might forget to pass it on. I liked Anna and didn't want her to get any bad publicity.

By the time I had finished the phone calls, it was lunchtime. Eddie was the only one at the table. It seemed Mary was posing on a fashion shoot for her apparel line. Denny was the photographer. Dad was at the office, and Mum had gone shopping with Ms. Romanov.

Speak of the devil. She-devil? Now that was a thought, down boy.

I got caught up with Eddie and his scouting adventures. Scouting was certainly different in California than in Ohio. In Bellefontaine, we toured Tanger airport. Here, they toured LAX. There it was Hopewell Dairy. Here it was Alta Dena Farms where they had the cows and the dairy where they bottled not only milk but also made ice cream, sour cream, and butter.

He told me about a neat two-and-a-half-gallon plastic container with a spout. The container would sit in your refrigerator, and you could then open the spout and get a glass of milk without having to pick it up and then pour it.

I didn't see where that would catch on. It would be very difficult to have a down-facing spout that wouldn't leak. What a mess.

I asked Eddie what merit badges he had. One that he didn't do was stamp collecting, so we went to my room, and I took him through the requirements.

My pride and joy was a stamp from Nazi Germany. You couldn't tell it until you dipped it in benzene, and a swastika would appear on the back. I loaned it to him as part of what he would share with his patrol. They had a good practice; each boy would show his patrol what he had gathered for his badge. This would give everyone a leg up.

We made up kits that he could share with each boy. The kit had a used US stamp that they could check the watermark on and a small vial of benzene. That along with a perforation gauge, a small ruler, and hinges, and they would be in business. I had enough of the stuff as I had been a merit badge counselor in my old troop.

They would have to obtain and mount other stamps by themselves.

Eddie was delighted with my help. From there, I went out back and saddled George for a ride. It was a great ride, as the day was perfect. What made it even better was that way back on the trail in the park, I came across two very cute girls who were also out for a ride.

We met at a Y in the trail, and we were now heading in the same direction. We introduced ourselves by first name only. It was a perfect day as we rode along and chitchatted, nothing of import or personal. They did talk about that new movie, *Over the Ohio*. They could not believe that Ricky could ever be that evil. And oh, he was so cute.

I watched them carefully, but I don't think they recognized me.

They asked me what I thought of him. I had been speaking normal American. I answered them in my best English.

"I think he's a prat."

They both looked at me like I was crazy, and then it dawned on them who they were riding with. That started the questions.

"What was it like to do a movie?"

"A lot of work?"

"Is Mary that cute?"

"She is cuter."

"What will your next movie be?"

"I don't know if there will be a next."

That last opened the floodgates. I had to explain I was going to school in England and enjoying it and didn't know if I would have time for any movies.

We discussed that in great detail, and they helped me decide on a direction. I wanted it all: school and movies. I would make an appointment with Mr. Monroe and see if it would be possible for me to work with Pinewood Studios.

We parted company at the end of the trail. We didn't exchange any contact information, but it was a pleasant outing, my best in weeks.

After grooming George and cleaning up, I called the studio and made an appointment with Mr. Monroe for the next day, Tuesday.

As I came downstairs, Mum and Ms. Romanov came in the door. They headed to the kitchen for a cup of tea, so I joined them. I was getting partial to Earl Grey.

After they showed me their purchases and described how much they had saved (Woman Logic), I told Ms. Romanov about Senator Kennedy's request.

"He and Bobby, his younger brother, have been chasing me for years. I think they may have a bet going. Anyway, you have done your duty."

I let that hot potato drop. Anna and Mum exchanged a look that said there would be further talk when the children weren't around, namely me.

On Tuesday morning, I was on time for my appointment with Mr. Monroe. He was pleased to see me and was excited about the movie's reception. He had forgiven me about the points. The studio wouldn't make a fortune, but it would make money.

I told him about donating half my share to the Shawnee Tribe for an educational fund. He thought that was great and asked if they could use it as publicity. I didn't see any reason why not, so I gave my permission.

After that, he explained the tax advantages that could be had for both the studio and me.

Then, he wanted to know what I wanted to speak about. He was receptive to working out a deal with Pinewood. Warner Brothers would offer to rent me out to Pinewood for a movie package deal, meaning two or more movies. Part of the deal would be that it wouldn't interfere with my schooling.

That sounded like a win for everyone. Pinewood could capitalize on my current fame; Warner Brothers would profit from my rent, and I could continue to do what I liked.

We had lunch in the canteen. As I was getting ready to leave, I ran into Susan Wallace, who was there on behalf of another of her clients. She had in tow her latest "star," a kid named Steve Martin. He was just getting started as a comedian, but she was shopping him around trying to find him a movie.

We were introduced, but you could see him restraining himself from some smart-aleck remark. If it had been about someone else it would have been funny, but since it would be about me, it was smart aleck.

I asked Susan if I could have a few minutes with her. Mr. Monroe was kind enough to take the kid off her hands.

When we were alone, I told her about my concern about her conflict of interest. She took it in good part and told me she wondered if it was going to work. I updated her about Pinewood Studios, and that made her decision easy. She would be my agent and a silent partner. In turn, she would find a replacement publicity agent. Also, she would put the screws to Pinewood. They would pay through the nose to have me.

Chapter 15

A day I hadn't been looking forward to finally arrived. Wednesday was the day of my business update meeting, followed by a meeting of my Board of Directors. Even though I owned it all, I felt inadequate to run things. I don't mean the day-to-day operation; I didn't touch those, as there was no way that I had the skill set or training to run those.

It was the high-level decision-making that scared the heck out of me. The better the business units did, the more people worked for the company, and the more families depended on me for their livelihoods. What if I made a terrible decision that destroyed everything?

As I did my morning run, these thoughts and many others went through my head. I tried to set them aside, but they kept coming back. I was out in the park, so there were many miles of trail. When I returned to the house, I realized I had run over fifteen miles.

My time wasn't good, but I could have gone on forever. Arriving back home, I had worked up a sweat but was far from exhausted. If I ever had to run for my life, I would have a chance; that is, if I had a head start.

I cleaned up and donned a suit and tie for the big event. Maybe I could fake it like I knew what I was doing. I went light on breakfast as I had some butterflies. Well, I started with the idea of going light, but when I started eating, I realized that my morning run had left me hungry.

Mum, Dad, and I rode together in one of the limos. We arrived at our office building right on time at nine o'clock.

The agenda allowed an hour each for Jackson Personal Products, Jackson Home Products, and the Entertainment Division. Jackson Transportation had a three-hour session in the afternoon.

First up was Personal Products, presented by Don Pearson. This was Don's first business update since he was brought on board with profit sharing. The meeting room was set up with a sideboard containing coffee, tea, orange juice, bagels, and donuts.

Considering I had just had a full breakfast, I did manage juice, coffee, a bagel with cream cheese, and a crème filled donut. Maybe I wasn't as nervous as I thought. Now the moment had arrived, I was as ready as I could be.

Don was upbeat in his presentation. New markets had been opened in Brazil, Argentina, Peru, Columbia, and Chile. That was South America. In Africa, hairdryer sales were great in South Africa. Market penetration was starting in Egypt and Southern Rhodesia. For some reason, we couldn't get a foothold in Liberia.

Don told us they were having problems finding anyone willing to talk to them in Liberia. I suggested they speak to the managing director of the Firestone Plantation. While not able to give them answers, he would be able to tell them who could.

He said he had no idea who that was and wouldn't know how to contact them. I told him that I knew Mr. Art Dawson, the managing director, and would call him for advice and arrange contacts for Don and his people. There, I could do something worthwhile for my people. I had the plantation number from the time I had played golf there.

Australia and the New Zealand markets had taken off. Europe was spotty. For some reason, the Mediterranean countries were slow adopters, while the Scandinavians couldn't buy enough dryers and curling irons.

The R&D department had just opened with the first personnel brought on board. I was asked if I could be available for a ribbon cutting on the new building sometime in October. I told him I could fly back from England, but it would have to be a quick in and out as it would in the middle of classes.

When I said classes, that took him back for a moment. He had forgotten that I was still in school.

The bottom line on the division was that it was going to earn over ten million dollars in profit this year. As Don had profit-sharing, you could tell he was a happy camper. At a quick break, he told me going out on his own was the best thing his parents could have forced him to do. He also let me know he thought he was the luckiest man alive to end up in his job. I told him I was the luckiest man alive by being surrounded by people like him. Hey, ten million makes everyone happy.

After Personal Products, it was Jackson Home Product's turn. This was Mark Downing and his new wife Sharon. They were professional in their demeanor, but you could see they were still in the honeymoon stage.

They relayed that the division was in the process of buying out a competitor for quick expansion. It was more for the production facility and its infrastructure than the product base. I liked this one because the workforce would be kept on.

Last year they made a profit of three million dollars. This year, it was on pace to make four million. I bet Mark's sister rued the day she insisted on him buying her out.

Sharon also let us know that her venture with Anna Romanov was going very well. Their using other stars to redo residences was a big hit, and there was talk of making a television show of the work being done.

They called this reality TV, but as she described how it would be edited, I thought of it as fake reality. Talk about a contradiction. Anna or Sharon would be present when the finished work was shown at the end. This would be the reveal. I blushed at my thoughts.

The last before lunch, we heard about the Jackson Entertainment Division. The accounting group gave us dry numbers from movies and music. This included money due from the failed Surfer movie and estimated revenues from *Over the Ohio*. OTO, as we started calling it, was doing fantastically. It was setting US box office records and was primed to do the same when released overseas.

On the movie front, it looked like fifty million dollars. What blew my mind was my music from all the songs was projected at five hundred thousand dollars. What was wrong with these people's ears?

Susan Wallace and Mr. Baxter were there to bring perspective to the dollars. It was all good from their point of view. Susan wanted to know if I would be going overseas shortly, as she would love to have me do an opening tour of Europe's capital cities.

I told her I had no plans to be in Europe shortly. There are different values for the near future. If she meant this afternoon, definitely not, leaving tomorrow, yes. She had to be clearer with her questions. I even felt a twinge at giving that answer; mind you, it was only a twinge.

I glanced at Mum and Dad, but they kept straight faces.

We had lunch brought in. It was only Mum, Dad, and me. I told them I hated giving Susan that answer, but I knew how she was. Dad thought it was a little funny how she asked the question to let me determine the time frame involved.

On a good note, for Susan, I had a contract to review from my entertainment lawyer Mr. Spiller, which set me up as a silent partner in her talent agency. It was generous support for five years. If she couldn't make it during that time, she probably should be pursuing something else. I had every confidence in her. She certainly had the goodwill of a long list of contacts.

If I had to make a phone call or two to help, I would.

After lunch, Jackson Transportation, the biggest group, arrived. It included Todd Goodson, President John Churchill of the Scottish Line, and Bob Wilson of Narrow Freight. Popeye was there, of course. As far as I knew, he didn't have a title unless it was Popeye.

We had allowed the entire afternoon for their presentations. Todd Goodson started with an overview of the entire operation. He had two points to bring up; one was that every group was performing above expectations but would need additional financing to grow.

The second item was about Freight Forwarding. It had grown so fast it was recommended that it be spun off to a new and separate part of Jackson Enterprises. It would be known as Freight Forwarding. I privately thought that name was bland. Why not something like Freight Express? It could be shortened to FreightEx. It never got to a point where I could bring it up, so I let it slide.

It turned out the additional financing being requested could be obtained in-house. It was a matter of shifting funds around. Since they were my funds, they thought it only fair that I approved. Frankly, the amounts being discussed were so large as to be meaningless to me. Sure, if you need another ocean-going freighter, just take thirty million out of petty cash.

At the last business meeting, the company was approaching one hundred million dollars in profit. The book value of the company was almost one billion dollars. This year's profits were estimated to be two hundred and twenty-five million dollars.

Putting it all together, I would make almost three hundred million dollars this year. As I said, it was so much it didn't seem real. During the presentations, everyone was upbeat the entire day, as they were all involved in profit sharing. My only worry now was that someone might decide to retire with their new fortune.

One last item brought up by the accountants was the royalty money coming in from the beer can pull tabs. This didn't fit neatly within any of our company divisions. They requested we set up a small group to track royalty income and ensure we received it from all sources. I questioned that. They used Mexicali Delight as an example. They sold and bottled beer all over the world. How would we know if they were paying from everywhere they used the pull tabs?

I could see the logic in that. I asked Jim Williamson, who was part of the accounting team, to develop an organizational chart. We would need agents to go out in the field to see what was being done. This also allowed me to have Jim head up the new group on a profit-sharing basis. He certainly had earned it.

He promised to have a draft available within the week.

After all had left except Mum, Dad, Popeye, and Sam Wingate the corporate attorney, we had a meeting of the compensation committee. As a group, they had all the numbers in advance.

I was informed that the board was going to increase my compensation. I had been making one and a half million dollars a year as president of the company. It was now going to be three million a year.

I think they were prepared for a battle. I didn't give them one. Last year I learned that my salary acted as a cap on the entire company. It wouldn't be fair to middle management if I didn't take a raise. The logic seemed suspicious to me, but as all American industry went with it, so would I.

I would be in a ninety-one percent marginal tax bracket, so my three million dollars became about a million, less state and local taxes. Poor me!

That didn't consider the net profit from the company. I would have to pay twenty-five percent if I held it long enough. Since I had no plans to buy Ecuador, I was good.

I was beginning to see why Dad didn't like President Eisenhower's taxes. However, I think it was more of a congress thing rather than a presidential idea. I know one thing. I wasn't going to bring any of it up with Ike.

As the last event of the day, we held a formal board meeting. This included shifting funds for Jackson Transportation's expansion and approving a new division called Freight Forwarding. I brought up the name Freight Express with FreightEx, but no one liked it.

I formally put forward that a new division called Jackson Licensing be created with Jim Williamson as its head and that he be included in the profits of said division, the same as the other division heads.

All items were approved unanimously on a voice vote.

Dad wanted to know my investment plans for my profits this year. I told him I would sit down with an investment firm and discuss my thoughts on the services to the airline industry. Not airline companies, but those who built, maintained, and serviced them.

I specifically thought it was time I had another investment group involved. It's not that I wasn't satisfied with the current one, Schwab; it just seemed prudent to spread it out.

Mr. Wingate said, "Hear, hear."

I think that meant he approved rather than that he was hard of hearing.

After that, we were joined by Popeye's wife, my Aunt Sybil, and went to dinner at the Brown Derby. We had a wonderful meal that was almost marred by one event. Mum and Aunt Sybil were returning from the restroom when they were accosted by a couple of drunks from the bar. I say almost marred because Dad and Popeye stood up, ready to do battle.

I didn't think Mr. Cobb could move so fast. He whispered something to the two guys. They turned and saw Dad and Popeye and decided they had somewhere else they needed to be.

Mr. Cobb was apologetic about the incident, but the ladies shrugged it off. On our way out, I asked him what he whispered to those guys.

"I just told them if they took on the Jackson clan I wasn't going to pay for their funerals."

"Oh, they know how Popeye is on the docks?"

"No, they saw you in the movie. It has half of Hollywood quaking in their boots every time they see you. They now think you are a psychopathic killer.

What can you say to that? We headed home, and I went to sleep thinking about getting out of town—what the heck, out of the country!

Chapter 16

If I had my way, I would have been on an airliner early Thursday morning. Unfortunately, the airlines have a thing called a schedule and a fixed number of seats they can sell. All seats to England were booked up on Thursday. It would be Friday evening before I could get a flight.

I complained to the family at breakfast, but they weren't too sympathetic. Instead, I went to the studio and brushed up on my various skills. I was there most of the day. At lunch, I ran into Susan Wallace.

When I saw her, I was overcome with guilt about yesterday. I asked for a few minutes. I came clean with her. You could tell she wasn't happy at first, but she came around. She had to laugh.

"Rick, if you were in court and were asked if you were doing something, you would answer I'm not doing that, meaning that you weren't doing that at that exact moment."

"Exactly."

"Words are dangerous, and you give a new meaning to what is, is."

"I'm glad you see the humor in it. I just couldn't go another month like last month. It was exhausting. At least here in the US, we know how things work. How would you arrange an opening event in Berlin or Paris?"

"That's a good point, but that is why the studio has representatives all over the world. They could and do make things like that happen. Now, are you sure you don't want to do a couple this month?"

Thank goodness I was on a studio lot. It only looked half weird when I turned and ran screaming down the street. I'm pretty sure she got the message.

After half a block, I slowed down, shut up, and walked along laughing. You read about running away screaming; I just did it. One guy walking towards me asked me what movie I was doing that in. I told him that it was a Susan Wallace production.

He replied that he hadn't heard of them but would check it out. I encouraged him to do so. After that, I returned home. I related my day to the family, including running down the street. Mary thought the scene would have gone better if I had been pulling on my hair. It would give it a more dramatic flair.

Who is this kid, and what did she do with my baby sister?

Friday morning was spent with an investment house recommended by Jim Williamson. They were more than eager to get their hands on two hundred million dollars.

I went into detail about my expectations and controls that would be in place to ensure that there would be no churning of my account. They didn't take that too well initially, but I didn't care. I wasn't there to make them money; they were there to make me money.

They backed down quickly. My first requirement was that they put together a model portfolio based on the air transportation sector. They were to provide it to Jim for his and then my review. The session was over by noon. We shook hands on the deal.

Jim and I discussed the meeting on the way back to the office. He agreed that we needed to closely watch them, but it would probably be okay.

After dropping him off, I returned home and packed for my flight to London. This required me to put a change of clothes in a carryall, along with several books to read. Believe it or not, one of the books was on geology, especially of Africa. I sensed that serious money could be made there if politics and corruption didn't get in the way.

One of our limos took me to LAX to catch a flight to London. The only flight available was TWA from Los Angeles (LAX) to

Dayton, Ohio (DAY), then to New York City (IDL), and then to London (LHR).

One saving grace was that the trip would be on the same plane all the way. At each stop, I could get off and wander for a bit, just remembering to take my boarding pass with me. I had also purchased two first-class seats so no one would be next to me.

I didn't know you could do this until I saw a seat occupied by a cello. I asked a stewardess about it and learned that you could buy as many seats as you wanted. Heck, if the seats weren't sold, I could have bought out the whole first-class section, though that would have been a bit much.

The flight from Los Angeles to Dayton was uneventful and only took five hours. We had a good tailwind. I got off to stretch my legs in the Dayton Airport. It wasn't that big and had no stores except for a newsstand. I had plenty of reading material, so I didn't bother to stop.

Returning to the boarding area, I saw a lot of passengers dressed in blue. Dayton is the home of the Wright-Patterson Air Force base. The guys in blue were an Air Force general and his six-person staff. Over in a corner, trying to look invisible, was a single airman.

The airman looked like he would rather be in any place in the world but around all those high-ranking officers. The lowest officer was a major. Taking pity, I went to the airman and sat in the empty seat beside him.

"You don't look pleased to be around all these officers."

"It never ends well when there are all chiefs and one Indian."

I had to laugh at that and agreed with him. I had a thought. I went over to the podium and talked to the ground attendant. I showed my two first-class boarding passes and explained I was going to ask the single airman to join me up-front.

Since first class was full, I knew the officers would all be in coach per policy. This would save the airman some misery. He was going all the way through to London to join his family there.

The gate attendant was more than pleased to assign the seat to the airman. I called him by his rank, airman, but he looked like a little kid. He most likely was older than me but didn't seem to have any real-world experience. It seems the attendant had been enlisted and had his fill of officers.

I collected my airman, and we were boarded early, even for first class. Airman Bill Nelson was effusive in his thanks.

When general boarding was announced, the brass came aboard. They didn't pay much attention as they filed past, except for the lone major in the group. He gave a hard look at Bill as he passed us.

The seatbelt light was barely off when the major appeared next to Bill.

"Airman, you will have to move to the back of the plane so the general can move up here."

That got my attention quickly. Using my most plummy British accent, I stated. "Major, the airman is my guest. I have bought and paid for the seat he is sitting in. Even if you could force him into the back, your general wouldn't be welcome here."

I didn't know it was possible to flounce down the aisle of an aircraft, but he managed. Bill was uncomfortable, to say the least. He even volunteered to move back so I could avoid trouble. I wouldn't hear of it.

Soon, the general himself came up to us.

"Major Johnson tells me you won't surrender this seat to me."

I answered, "That is correct, sir."

"Good for you. I have no idea how he could think such an overreach was allowed. Enjoy your flight, airman."

"Thank you, sir."

Well, that settled that. I was happy that all officers weren't like the major.

In New York, most passengers disembarked and left the area. A few stayed around as they were proceeding onward to London. The entire Air Force contingent was going to London for some reason.

Two officers were standing next to the major, and they were muttering just loud enough for Bill and me to hear that they thought the airman should be put in his place. The general was on a pay phone, so heard none of this. The other officers were more concerned with chatting up one of the stewardesses who would be coming aboard with the crew change.

Our overnight flight to London was long and uneventful. Upon landing, Bill and I went our separate ways. He had to get in line for foreign passengers while I was able to use the line for UK citizens. It was much shorter and quicker. Having a diplomatic passport certainly helped.

I grabbed a black cab and went to the Plaza on the Strand. The front desk was expecting me and had my key ready. I didn't have to sign in or anything like that. I took a shower and changed into a fresh suit.

I was hungry and took the penthouse elevator back to the ground floor. As I exited, I saw a flock of gentlemen in blue. Yes, my favorite US Air Force officers were waiting for an elevator.

When I exited mine, I heard the ever-helpful major ask why they couldn't go up in mine. The bellman with them first greeted me.

"Welcome back, Sir Richard."

"Thank you, Frank."

I heard Frank start to explain that the elevator only went to the top penthouse floor. I went to the grill and had a leisurely lunch. A limousine from the palace picked me up for my appointment with Mr. Norman.

When I arrived at palace security, I was welcomed back and walked around the line of people waiting. Like bad pennies, the Air Force group was in line. This was almost too funny for words.

I nodded to the general as I passed him. He didn't notice, as he was glaring at the major. I suspect they would be creating a command further away than Thule for the major.

Mr. Norman welcomed me back. They had missed my flying service. There was talk in the palace of creating a small fleet of planes to service Europe. He complimented me on my latest song and movie.

You could tell where his heart was when he asked if I would be doing anything else with Frank Sinatra. I told him that we were keeping an eye out for a song that would work for both of us. What I didn't say was that Frank was looking for one to sing. I was looking for one to run from.

Our meeting turned out to be much longer than I had thought. The Messenger Service had come up with new documentation and new uniforms. Previously, the only uniform was the tie with Greyhounds. Now they went all out with shirts, sweaters, blazers, and grey slacks. The whole ensemble looked pretty good.

Since my tailor had my sizes, they had ordered several complete sets for me. They were at the palace, and I had to try everything on. They had done a bang-up job, and there were no problems. Even the collars on the blazers set well. I hated it when they bunched up in the back.

We were given new identification cards, and our diplomatic passports were updated with additional pages bound into the spine.

Mr. Norman and I had lunch in one of the many dining rooms in the palace. It was a private room set off from the main dining room, well, the main dining room for those who had daily business at the palace.

As we entered, the US Air Force group was just being seated. Eyes were on us as we went to the private room.

After a long and leisurely lunch, we returned to Mr. Norman's office. He had a note on his desk. After he read it, he asked me where I was going next. When I told him I was flying back to Oxford to stay at The Meadows, he asked a question.

"We have a liaison general from the US Air Force who needs to go that way today. Could you take him and an aide with you?"

I was gobsmacked; talk about fate, or whatever.

"Certainly."

What was I going to do, say no?

"If you want to head out to Heathrow and get the Messenger Service aircraft ready, I will have him delivered to the private terminal."

"Do I have time for a quick stop at my hotel?"

"I would think so."

After that, I headed back to the palace exit. To continue the wild set of coincidences, I came across Queen Elizabeth at an intersection in one of the main halls. She and several of her ladies in waiting arrived at the intersection at the same time I did.

"Sir Richard, I didn't know you were back in England. Did you run away from your circus?"

"That is exactly what I did. It turned out to be more than I bargained for, so I came back to hide here until school starts."

"Did your Mum come with you?"

"No, but she told me to give you her regards if I saw you. Oh, and Dad wanted me to remind Prince Philip that Philip owes him ten quid from the Kentucky Derby."

"I will speak to the Chancellor of Exchequer to see if England has the funds."

"Yes, I know Ike is worried about the balance of payments. He made the same bet with Dad."

"Where are you going from here?"

"To The Meadows."

"My Mum is there with your Grandmum; tell her she has to return to London someday. She can't keep avoiding her duties forever."

"Will Your Majesty give me that in writing? Otherwise, she might have me beheaded."

"Write something like that to my Mum? I don't think so!"

We both had a good laugh, and she asked me for a longer visit the next time. I held my position in a half bow as she and her group turned and left. I was not about to turn my back on her.

When the queen had moved on, I turned to continue. There stood the general and his group of officers. I nodded my head and passed by them. A palace driver took me back to my hotel, where I changed clothes. The devil made me do it as I donned my RAF reserve uniform with its various bits and bobs.

From there, the driver who had kindly waited drove me to the airport.

This was going to be very interesting.

Chapter 17

After checking the fuel and doing the rest of the preflight on the Greyhound plane, I taxied to the private terminal. I don't know why it was called the private terminal. It was open to everyone and used by the general aviation crowd. When there is a true private terminal with extremely limited use, what do they call that?

At Heathrow, there is even a military terminal run by the RAF, but I had been instructed to meet the general here, probably because it was easier to drop him off here without going through any security.

Going inside, I spotted the general waiting with one aide, a captain. I approached them in a military style, stopped at attention, and saluted.

"Flight Officer Jackson reporting."

I kept my eyes straight but was aware of the general's look of surprise. To give him due credit, he recovered quickly. Upon standing, he eyed my insignia closely.

"I recognize the Legion of Honor and the CBE, but what is the first one?"

"Order of the Garter, sir!"

"And the greyhound above your flight wings."

"I am a Queen's Messenger, seconded to the RAF, sir!"

I was proud of those crisp sirs.

"You seem to be on intimate terms with Her Majesty."

"She is my godmother. Our families are quite close."

"I gathered that the Queen Mum is staying with your grandmother."

"Yes, sir! Part of my mission is to get the Queen Mum home before she and Grandmum drink all the sherry and decide to go pubbing."

Now, why did I just make that all up? It sounded good, anyway.

"And the Ike I heard referred to?"

"My godfather, President Eisenhower."

"I gather your family is also on intimate terms with him."

"Yes, sir. Well, it is dicey about him and Dad. They had a disagreement over a girl during the war, and Dad hates the tax policies."

The general looked like he was in the tenth round of a twelve-round match but kept slugging.

"I thought the taxes were heaviest on the very rich."

"Yes, sir!"

I think I won the match with a TKO at that point.

"Is the aircraft ready?"

"Yes, sir. This way.

I picked up the general's bag and led him and the captain to the aircraft. The captain had kept his mouth shut during the whole conversation, but his eyes were at the point of bulging.

I led them out to the grey aircraft with a greyhound painted in a white square.

"Nice paint job. Why did the RAF choose a Cessna?"

"They didn't. It is one of mine. I let Mr. Norman, head of the Messenger Service, choose the paint job."

"Of course, you did," I heard the General mutter.

Once we were in the air, the general, who turned out to be Major General James Sullivan, was pleasant. He apologized for the major's actions on our flight over. Upon return to Stateside, the major was being reassigned.

"Meanwhile, while we are here, I gave the rest of my staff the day off. They are going to that new movie, *Over the Ohio*. I hear it is very good and would like to see it myself."

It is a good thing I had the plane on autopilot.

"If you have time, I could arrange a private screening at our house."

The captain finally opened his mouth. "What, show it on bedsheets, and where would you get the film?"

"I always get a copy of my films."

The captain got it first; the fact that my name tag said R. Jackson hadn't meant anything.

"Are you Sir Richard Jackson, the actor?"

"Yes, sir."

"General, you know that Major Patterson had some very unkind things to say about Sir Richard here, even though he was in the wrong."

"Yes, your point?"

"That movie, *Over the Ohio*, has Sir Richard as one of the stars."

The general got red in the face but managed to hold himself in, well, almost. He exploded into laughter.

"That seems a fitting punishment. Maybe I won't send him to Greenland after all. Seriously though. I don't think he is ready to be on my staff. I will take care of that later. Maybe General Hawthorne has a slot open."

I asked, "Is that Lieutenant General Hawthorne?"

"Yes, do you know him?"

"I used to date his daughter."

"Let me guess, he called you Cowboy?"

"The Secret Service uses that for me. He agreed with them."

The general got a very serious look.

"I don't know any details, but I understand you did our nation a great service."

"I may have helped a little."

The general snorted and then said, "We had better change the subject."

"Agreed, the FBI is still mad at me about that."

The captain in the back seat must have been dying of curiosity, but he never said a word.

Our conversation became more general in scope. The general was most curious about my educational background and plans for the future. That brought out my business interests. To say that caught his attention is putting it mildly.

When we landed in Oxford, he asked if we could continue our talk in a more private area. I had my car at the airport, but it couldn't carry all of us, much less their luggage. As usual, I only had my carry-on.

I hadn't thought to call ahead for a pickup, so we had to wait awhile for Mr. Hamilton.

He brought the large old Bentley. I was glad he hadn't decided to hitch up the Queen's Coach, as we called it. Our conversation continued during the half-hour ride.

The general commented on that, so I told him that I had three identical wardrobes, one at Jackson House, another at The Meadows, and a third at the Plaza in London in my suite.

"Rick. can you tell me how much you are worth?"

"Somewhere north of half a billion dollars plus the value of my factory infrastructure and ships. I would guess almost a billion, but it changes daily."

I think I heard the captain in the back gulp.

"Does your Messenger work take up much of your time?"

"Not really, one or two days a month at the most."

"What about your RAF commitments?"

"Even less; if they have someone really important visiting, I may have to ferry them around. As I mentioned previously, it was a bit of a ruse to let me carry passengers."

"Everyone seems confident in your flying abilities. Why is that?"

That brought up brush fires and landing 707s.

"You have had your share of adventures, haven't you?"

"A few, some more fun than others."

The captain was sitting across from us in the limo, so he was in a position to join the conversation.

"Would that be your rescue of Bridget Bardot?"

"Well, that ranks right up there."

I then had to tell the long story that got cut short when we arrived at The Meadows. Mr. Hamilton's footman was at the door in his most formal attire. Putting on the dog, were we? Oh, that's right, the Queen Mum is here.

I inquired as to where my Grandmum and she were at.

"The last time they were sighted, they were in a pony trap chasing ducks around the large pond in the east meadow."

"That sounds a little dangerous for two old ladies."

"Oh, the Queen Mum's guards are following them on foot."

Some things are hard to picture. Two old ladies tearing around in a pony cart followed by two poor guards dressed for the city chasing them on foot. What a movie scene that would make. I had to remember that.

The general asked if he could share an idea that he had. Somehow, it didn't strike me that a general with an idea about me was a good thing. Trying to be gracious, I had coffee brought to us in the small reception room instead of the large room at the front of the house.

It didn't take the general long to get down to brass tacks.

"Rick, I'm at Oxford today for a meeting with the bursar to finalize arrangements for US Air Force officers to continue their education here. One of the last items I have to handle is to have an onsite officer act as a go-between if any problems arise with their presence. It occurs to me that you would be the perfect person."

Alarm bells were ringing in my head.

"I would think that you would need a US Air Force officer to do that.'

"Very true but having the RAF second you to the US Air Force would be easy."

Thinking fast, I thought of my out.

"I'm only a flight officer, the same as a first lieutenant. I think you would need someone of equal if not higher rank to the students for that position."

"Correct, it would have to be at least a major."

With an internal sigh of relief, I replied, "Well, as much as I would like to help, that leaves me out."

"I don't see a rank problem. As you said, your seconding to the RAF was to allow you to carry passengers. You have no command authority as such. The same would hold with the RAF seconding you to the USAF. It would allow you to act as an intermediary without our student officers overruling you. At most, they would have a recent promotion to major, and you would have the date of rank."

"What about uniforms? What would I wear?"

"Your RAF ones. You are seconded, not part of. I have wondered why you wear the RAF uniform since you are seconded from the Messenger Service."

"The Queen's Messengers until recently didn't have a uniform, and the new one is a blazer with the discreet tie we can wear, but that's it. There is nothing for fieldwork. We are usually in first class."

"Understandable. I can see why the RAF wouldn't want you in mufti all the time. Anyway, you won't have to buy new uniforms."

How can I gracefully get out of this?

"Rick, by being a student living near campus, you will have a greater appreciation of the problems faced by members of the armed forces here on campus. Most campuses aren't particularly soldier friendly, but Oxford has had hundreds of years to develop its attitude."

That gave me pause as I thought of Balliol College and my school Trinity, and the singing across the wall. Trinity would only be considered conservative when compared to those people at Balliol. I would hate to have to wear my uniform to class. I could do it and be damned to them, but it wouldn't be pleasant.

"As I see it, your job would be hearing students with complaints and reporting those that are valid to me, and I would address them with the university officials. Today, we get complaints like 'They don't like me,' and there's not much we can do about that. What we can address is discrimination in housing, grades, tutoring availability, and issues of that sort."

"Well, this would have to be approved by the Messenger Service and the RAF."

"Sooner started, the better. Who would you have to talk to in the Messenger Service?"

"That would be Mr. Norman at the palace. That was why I was at the palace yesterday. I had to check in for assignments since I'm back in England."

"Could you call him right now?"

Help, I could hear the train that was going to run me over or, more likely, the bulldozer that was plowing me down. This man didn't become a general in the USAF because he was shy or slow. My best hope was that Mr. Norman would shoot the idea down immediately.

I placed a call to London and was put through to Mr. Norman. My hopes were dashed in short order.

"That is a capital idea, Rick. We have several members whose relatives are in the service and have attended the universities, both Oxford and Cambridge. They all report the same prejudice. It has been talked about in the various ministries, but no plans have come forward. I'm certain both the queen and prime minister will approve. Whitehall's support will be a given."

"I have one concern; General Sullivan wants me to be seconded at a higher rank so that the officer students can't pull rank on me and make demands."

"Excellent point. Let me ask you a question. Has the Queen ever handed you personally a message to deliver?"

"Just some notes to my mother."

"But they were handed to you directly by the queen?"

"Yes, sir."

I had no idea where this was going.

"That makes you a Senior Queen's Messenger. We only have two ranks in the service. Queen's Messenger and Senior Queen's Messenger. By handing you a missive, the queen has declared you to be a Senior Messenger."

"What does that mean?"

"First of all, it means you have a top-secret security clearance in the UK. Second, your equivalent rank in the RAF is wing commander, the same as a lieutenant colonel in the USAF."

"What!"

"Now, as you Americans would say, don't get your panties in a twist. It is a courtesy rank. You would have no command authority, but by the same token, those of lesser rank couldn't order you around.

"Rick, this is very exciting, I will bring this up with the proper authorities immediately. May I speak to General Sullivan?"

Well, there went my hope of his not liking the idea. From the sounds of this end of the conversation, the general and Mr. Norman were getting along famously. My only hope now was that Whitehall would decide I was way too junior to hold this position and would appoint a serious officer to the job.

It was late enough that I invited the general to dinner. That went very well. Grandmum and the Queen Mum were in high spirits from their afternoon outing. I think a lot of spirits may have been involved.

When the Queen Mum asked General Sullivan why he was at Oxford, he shared the whole scenario. He had an appointment tomorrow and hoped to place me as the liaison with armed forces students.

The British Crown has always been a staunch supporter of her armed forces. I found out how staunch when I heard old words used in new ways that were not polite. Once she wound down, she told us she would be giving her daughter her marching orders in the morning.

Okay...Wing Commander Jackson, it is. This shouldn't be that big of a deal, should it?

Chapter 18

I was surprised in the morning when I found the general not only up but ready to join me on my daily run. He kept pace with me the whole way. I hadn't run with anyone else since the braves of the Shawnee Tribe, and it was nice.

We both had enough endurance that we could talk a little as we ran. The general explained that what he had in mind was that I was to be a communication conduit. I was not expected to correct problems on my own. I wouldn't have the authority to do so.

The idea was that students with problems would come to me. From there I would be either the chaplain, listening to their complaints and then telling them to bear with them, or bring it to the attention of the proper authority —that being the Oxford bursar's office or the appropriate military. The military could be any branch of the British or American armed forces that had students there.

That seemed simple enough. Since there were thought to be only about twenty students from all sources, it shouldn't be a burden. I thought I had heard this tune before.

After cleaning up and having breakfast, I flew us to London for a meeting at Whitehall. This was coming together very quickly. Someone at the palace had sent a rocket up. From a conversation I partially overheard at breakfast, I think the Queen Mum had wound up the queen and things were going to happen. Whoever said that the Crown was only a figurehead had never seen it in action.

The armed forces had the word royal in their name for a reason. So, instead of meeting with the Oxford bursar this morning, we were headed to London to meet with the mandarins of Whitehall.

The general was very enthused about the project. I think he had dreams of glory. This project could be the beginning of something big for him. He talked about how they should have a program like this at every major university in the world. Naturally, he would be the one in charge. I suspect visions of another star were in his dreams like sugar plums.

That thought was mean of me. The general saw a real problem and was trying to solve it.

We were both in our dress uniforms when we were escorted into the meeting room at Whitehall. I thought I had seen gold braid before. Never anything like this. From the wariness of the introductions, one could tell the brass felt like they had been blindsided.

Mr. Norman had joined us and introduced me as Senior Queen's Messenger Sir Richard Jackson, KG, OBE, LOH. I thought that was laying it on thick, but it certainly got their attention.

The Air Vice-Marshal Lord So-and-so, not his real name, but I forgot it as soon as I heard it, which could prove to be a problem later, asked me to describe the program I wanted.

Did I want this? I had been roped into this by the Air Force general, Sir Norman, and a slightly tipsy Queen Mum.

In for a penny, in for a pound. I did the manly thing and dumped it all into General Sullivan's lap. He gave a clear, concise overview of the proposed program. When he stated that he thought there might be as many as twenty students involved, you could see the looks around the room.

"General Sullivan, you don't appear to understand all the ramifications of this. Commonwealth Armed Forces students are attending. The closest estimate we have today is a little over one hundred with some of them having dependents along."

"That is many more than I thought. When this started, we were only looking at American officers."

"Understood. This is getting away from all of us. Sir Richard, what are your plans?"

What! When had this become my problem? I thought hard for a second. I could either whine or step up.

"I need to find out exactly how many people will be involved, survey the most urgent problems, and then make recommendations to my British and American contacts when they are appointed."

Find out what you are facing first. Any Boy Scout Senior Patrol Leader knows to do that.

"My question is, sir, what resources will I be provided with? Budgeted money, on and off-site cadre, infrastructure at Oxford."

This started some hemming and hawing.

The vice air marshal told me that the British would provide initial funding of ten thousand pounds. The general, not to be outdone, volunteered fifteen thousand from his budget.

Sir Norman spoke up, "One last point: Sir Richard will need a rank which will give him the necessary seniority to command respect and obedience in his position."

"I thought a Senior Queen's Messenger is brevetted to an RAF Wing Commander."

"Normally, that would be so, but two Lieutenant Colonels are attending, one from Hong Kong and a Canadian. The queen was most direct in wanting Sir Richard to rank all those attending."

"I suppose it doesn't matter what he wears on his shoulders, as he won't be giving orders."

"That's correct, but the real concern is his receiving orders from students."

"Excellent point. Sir Richard, do you have anything to add?"

"Sir, I hope you aren't planning on enrolling at Oxford shortly."

He got a befuddled look and then laughed, "Young man, I think you will do just fine. Now, Group Captain Carstairs here will set you up with your British budget and promotion orders, along with your official orders."

This took the better part of an hour, and it gave me some time to think.

I told the general I had to make a private call. Upon inquiry, I was escorted to an empty office. I placed a call to the White House using my code words. Ike was not available, but his chief of staff heard me out.

"Richard, we will look into this. On the surface, it seems like a good program, but when the Pentagon gets done with it, it could be a nightmare. Please keep me posted. Would it be too much to ask for a private report every other week?"

"I can do that. I would prefer it."

Another Boy Scout lesson, when on a camporee and other troops can affect your plans, keep the Scoutmaster up to date. Without his input, I got talked into taking a campsite infested with fire ants. Never again! What had started simply now had me ranked equal to a full colonel in the US Air Force.

The general told me that his call to the Pentagon had thrown the cat amongst the pigeons as this had become a project with high political visibility. Several people would be angling to shove us aside and take it over. Just the fact this had the direct approval of the queen had them wetting their pants.

I never figured that out. Almost all Americans were interested in British royalty and would give them undue respect. Who won the Revolution anyway? I tried to see both sides of the picture as I represented both sides, but it was still confusing at times.

I decided to come clean with General Sullivan; he had been straight with me.

"It has been arranged that I will submit a report to the White House chief of staff every two weeks. I will copy the queen and the prime minister if she directs it."

The general took a long, hard look at me, "You are much more than you seem. It is like you have been playing these games for years."

"A little."

At the same time, I thought about tossing the heads of KGB agents over their embassy fence.

"A little."

What was supposed to be a relaxing time before classes resumed turned into a whirlwind. On Tuesday, our first stop was the bursar's office, where I shared a copy of my orders. He thought them most irregular and not the way things were done at Oxford. They would have to form a committee, discuss the issue, and decide how to proceed. He was confident it could be concluded by the end of the next school year.

I asked him if there were any objections to me taking surveys to find out how many students were involved and what issues may arise. He didn't see a problem with that.

From there, I flew the general back to London. General Sullivan told me that now I had to be patient and let the system work. The USAF would send out surveys to all the students on their list. Would I please talk to my contact at Whitehall to do the same for all their enrollees?

The interesting part was that a contact at Whitehall had not been established. Whilst in London, I called Mr. Norman, who told me he would find out who I was to liaise with at Whitehall. On my flight home, I thought about what had been set in train. It would be next year between the university, the Pentagon, and Whitehall before anything could happen. That didn't sit well with me.

One thing that did move quickly was my promotion and written orders. They arrived on Wednesday at The Meadows, sent by special messenger. Neat, a message by a special messenger to a Senior Queen's Messenger. Typical bureaucratic idiotic solution. Someone should write a book about such things.

At least now I had something to show people that I was legitimate.

I drove down to my on-campus garage room and walked over to Mrs. Butler's door. She was home and had time for me. I told her I had to find a meeting room for about eighty people and asked if she could suggest anywhere. If anyone in Oxford knew, she would. I had to pay for my answers by sharing what was being thought of. Gossip was her stock in trade.

She had several suggestions. The one I liked the most was a large pub. It had a meeting room in the back. It was only several blocks away, so I walked over to the Ugly Cow. Who thinks of these names?

I arranged to rent the backroom for Saturday evening. There would be one hour of free beer from seven to eight o'clock. If free beer wouldn't get students to come, nothing would. This would be all out of my pocket unless I could get it reimbursed by one of the military groups. Fat chance of that.

I then stopped at a printer and had a rush job on a flier. It said free beer for one hour, 7 to 8, on Saturday night in the backroom of the Ugly Cow. Must show a military ID to enter.

With these in hand, I walked over to the Student Union at Trinity and loudly asked if anyone wanted to earn five quid for several hours of work. I had ten takers immediately.

Their mission would be to place the fliers on every billboard in town they could find. I sent them out in teams of two, thinking there would be less chance of the fliers being put in the trash bin. I paid ten pounds upfront.

I sat down with a cup of coffee and waited. Three cups later, they started coming in for their second payment. The only problem encountered was at Balliol. They didn't want anything with "military" on their bulletin board. I doubted if many military people would be at that school anyway.

I returned to the Ugly Cow and let the manager know what was up. For a fee, he agreed to provide two of his bouncers to check ID at the door. For another fee, he provided tables and chairs for eighty.

A little more and a sound system was included, and was I interested in serving any munchies? You get the picture.

I went all out. This would end up costing a bomb, but if I wanted it to start right, I had to bear the cost. If I waited on the bureaucracy, it would take forever.

Saturday night came around. I was at the Ugly Cow an hour ahead of time. I had brought clipboards, paper, and a pen. I even thought of name tags. When I entered the door, I noticed two pretty girls arriving at the bar. Before they could order a drink, I approached them.

The barman Jack who I was getting to know, arrived at the same time. I had him introduce me. I told them I would like to hire them for the next two hours for five quid to register people who came to the backroom.

One of them clarified, "You are going to pay us ten quid each to get the names and addresses of all these handsome military blokes?"

"Yes."

"If you had asked, I would have paid you!"

It was a little more complicated than that. They were to hand out the forms that wanted names, addresses, military or naval service, country, rank, occupation, and school. I also had a copy of my orders to go with the form.

At six-forty-five, the room started to fill up. There were going to be more than eighty people here, more like two hundred. By seven-fifteen, it was standing room only. The crowd was in a good mood—free beer!

I decided it had to be a very short meeting. I stood on the small stage and spoke into the microphone. It gave the usual squeal, which got everyone's attention.

"I am Group Captain Sir Richard Jackson, a Senior Queen's Messenger. I have been tasked to identify problems encountered by members of the military attending school at Oxford. There are considerably more of you than had been estimated. If you fill out the form, we will mail you information at the next meeting, which will be in a larger venue.

"At that meeting, you will be divided into groups and asked to list your problems and concerns. Please return the forms to the lovely young ladies who handed them out. Enjoy the beer for the next hour."

As was normal for this type of event, people came up to me at the podium. There were eight of them, not a group but eight individuals. They crowded around me to hear any answers I might have to their questions. One thing very noticeable, they were the mature people in the room.

Those who were talking and having fun looked like typical college-age kids. These guys were in their early twenties to their thirties. These were the people I needed to talk to. I signaled one of the girls over.

"Can you ask Jack the barman if he has a smaller room we could use?"

It only took a few minutes, and we were led to a room that would seat twenty comfortably. That is when the real business started.

Chapter 19

Once we were settled in the smaller room, we did a round of introductions. They were from different countries of the Commonwealth and the US. Their ranks were from first lieutenants to majors. I wondered if I was going to have a problem when the two majors started comparing their dates of ranks. The more senior date would outrank the other.

I interrupted them, saying that there would be time for that later. Neither of them had read the handout that described my orders. I was questioned as to my rank and on what authority I had called them together. You could tell that some people had read the orders as they looked down so they would not be involved in what would occur next.

"It is all described in the copy of the orders you were given."

"What military are you in?"

"None. I am a Senior Queen's Messenger who has been seconded to the RAF as a Group Captain. The US Pentagon and the United Kingdom and Commonwealth Armed Forces (UKCAF) have approved this program. It is a test program to try to improve the conditions of the US and UKCAF students at Oxford University and if it works, will be rolled out at many major schools worldwide."

It took a US army captain to ask, "What is the US equivalent rank of a group captain?"

One of the others tersely told him, "A full colonel."

I added to that, "I was given that rank to ensure that none of the students could derail my mission. From a practical standpoint, I have no authority over you.

"I'm supposed to survey you as a group and find out what issues you are facing to see if they can be rectified."

That unleashed the flood dam. I let them carry on for a while as they listed grievances. When they started to repeat themselves, I asked if I could recap what I had just heard. Heads nodded.

"First, the housing allowance provided does not match the cost of housing in Oxford, so you are forced to share too small of a space with too many people. This is even worse for those who have families, as it is hard to share.

"From the family point of view, you know no one else at the school, so unlike living on a military base, there is no support community."

"You are looked down upon by the socialists who dominate the colleges. You can handle that, but you can't handle the difficulty you have in arranging tutors because of this bias. There is also the cost of the tutors when you factor in the housing costs.

"Not as critical, but it would be nice to have a place where you could meet as a group and study or have a beer together."

They all agreed those were the high points of the problems faced.

"My job is to relay these findings to each of your services, and they will try to come up with solutions. From what I can see, you will all have graduated by then. I will be looking for other solutions."

We finished, and I paid off my two young ladies, who appeared to be having a good time with all the young men at their disposal. I asked if either of them typed. One, Susan, did, while the other girl was only interested in having a good time. Susan and I exchanged contact information, and she agreed to type up all the information we collected.

There would be a long list with individual cards for each person. Later, it would be broken down by rank, nationality, school, etc. I asked her how much she wanted, and she thought it would be worth twenty quid. I had no problem with that. I hoped she did a good job as I would need services like this in the future.

The eight men agreed to meet here again on Saturday afternoon so I could update them on progress.

The next morning, I stopped at a realtor's office. This one specialized in commercial projects. I described what I was looking for.

"It looks like you need to buy a college!"

"Are any for sale?"

"As a matter of fact, yes, there is Farmington Hall. It was going to be a for-fee college, one of those that people would pay a bomb for their children to attend so they could say that they went to Oxford. The scheme went bankrupt, and now the Bank of Scotland is stuck with the property."

"What size is it, and what shape is it in?"

"It was built to house three hundred students, two to a room. It has a kitchen, bar, study hall, and library with the usual porters' office setup. There is a nice yard in front and several outbuildings with a maze in the back garden."

"It sounds good. How long has it been empty?"

"It was never occupied but has been sitting for two years. The bank has a caretaker living on the property so it should be in decent shape."

"May I inquire as to the asking price?"

At that point, a door opened from the inner office.

"Price, must I tell you once more not to waste time on people who can't afford properties."

"Sir, he isn't wasting time," I said.

"Just who are you?"

"Sir Richard Jackson on a project for the Ministry of Defense."

"Oh, that's different. How may I help you?"

"Price here is doing a good job. I will stay with him."

"All right, but if there are problems, I can step in."

Price spoke up, "Yes, Dad."

Price was his first name, and I got back to business.

"The bank is asking five million for the entire property but would probably take less. They thought one of the real schools would snap it up, but they don't seem to be in the market this year or think the longer they wait, the lower the price."

"Let's go take a look."

It wasn't far so we walked over. The place was huge. I could see why it failed; someone had tried too hard and spent a fortune to make it fit in with the five-hundred-year-old buildings surrounding it. Both inside and out were fantastic.

Even with this ancient look, all the modern hookups were there. Unlike the true older buildings, electric lines and water pipes were built in behind the walls rather than attached to the exterior with iron brackets.

All the dorm rooms were set up for two students each. They were large, comfortable rooms that would be easy to live in. The common areas were furnished. This place was move-in ready. I met the caretaker, and he came across as solid and competent. I asked him if he was planning on staying on.

"If the new owners will have me, I would like. My wife and I live in a little cottage out back, which suits us just fine. She was going to be working in the porters' lodge when they opened. I don't know what will happen now."

"I'm going to make an offer on this place. If it is accepted, I would like both of you to stay."

He looked at me like I was crazy, a kid of my age, buying a place like this? No way. He didn't say anything, but his face showed it.

I asked Price if we could return to his office so I could make several phone calls. This was where being in the UK worked to my advantage. I was able to get through to Jackson Enterprises. Speaking to Jim Williamson, I told him to have whoever did our real estate deals buy the property known as Farmington Hall.

I gave him Price's office details and the contact information at the Royal Bank of Scotland.

"Also, they are asking five million pounds sterling."

Price kept looking at me like I had two heads. I gave in and told him that it helped to be filthy rich. We chatted for about fifteen minutes when his phone rang. Jackson Enterprises wanted to make a formal offer as per my instructions. They also got instructions from him as to where to wire the good-faith money. He made it simple by having sent it to the Royal Bank of Scotland.

He took down all the pertinent information, and from there we walked around the corner to the bank. Since he was well-known at the bank, we were able to get in immediately. The bank manager got a huge smile when he was told an offer was being made on Farmington Hall. It was an albatross hanging on the bank's books.

The manager asked what the plans were for the hall. I explained that it was to be used as housing for military students attending Oxford. The housing allowance they were given only let them live in hovels, and my orders were to arrange for better housing.

You could see wheels turning in his head.

"Do you mind if I ask how you see the finances working?"

"Not at all. Each student is allowed the equivalent of two hundred pounds a month for housing. The lowest cost of housing in Oxford is around a thousand pounds a month. That means five students have to share a room only meant for two."

"I know there are at least two hundred students from the military in attendance. Two hundred pounds from each of them equals forty thousand pounds a month."

To get him in the right frame of mind, I used the price of four million pounds for my math.

"Over thirty years at five percent interest, it would work out to about six million to be paid back or two hundred thousand a year. That leaves comfortable room for operating expenses."

"You realize that this will upset the housing market in town."

"Their problem, not mine. If they weren't gouging, I wouldn't have to do this."

"Exactly why do you have to do this?"

I shared a copy of my orders. They got his attention.

"According to this, you are working for the Crown, directly to the queen."

"I would hate to disappoint Her Majesty."

Hey, use every tool in the toolbox.

A young lady brought a note in and handed it to the bank manager.

"I see a deposit of two hundred thousand pounds has been made."

Price took the lead, saying, "As you can see, the offer is four million pounds."

"I don't have the authority to sell at that price. The best I could go to is four point eight."

"Who has the authority?"

"That would be the regional manager."

"Could you please inquire with him?"

"He may not be available, and these things take time."

At that point, I had to interject, "Time is one thing you do not have. I realize that this possible sale will upset the local housing market, and thus you have valuable information that you undoubtedly would like to capitalize on. I'm not giving you that time, as it will probably have ill effects on my fellow military."

I must say he had nerves of steel, as he didn't look like he was going to back down.

"May I use your phone?"

"Who would you be calling?"

"The Chancellor of the Exchequer to have him call your head office."

"That won't be necessary. I will see if I can reach the regional manager."

"Thank you."

I wondered who the Chancellor of the Exchequer is and how he fits into the banking scheme of things. You don't need nerves of steel when you are an actor. You just have to play the role.

It only took a few minutes for the manager to contact the regional office and get his manager online. The regional manager came in with a counteroffer of four point two million. I told them I would take it. As I had learned long ago, leave some meat on the bone.

"My part here is done. My head office in the US will handle the rest of the transaction."

From there, Price and I returned to his office, where I called my office, gave the terms of the deal, and told them to proceed.

He had a dazed look on his face. For a brief afternoon's work, he had made a five percent commission of two hundred ten thousand pounds. I suspected that it was equal to their entire office income for the year. His dad came out, took one look at his son, and asked what was wrong. Price told him what was right.

All his dad could say was, "I never; I never."

I started to stand up but had another thought.

"I need to buy at least a dozen houses, preferably in the same estate area. Would you know of any?"

I think Dad was in danger of a heart attack. He worked his mouth a couple of times, "Price, what about the Waterman Estates? It will have thirty units when completed, but they have finished fifteen of them."

"They would be good. They have all the modern cons. There are two and three-bedroom models, so they have something for most families."

"How far are they? Have any of them sold yet?" I asked.

"Only a fifteen-minute drive, and no, they are planning on opening sales next week."

"Fine, let's check them out."

This was moving like a freight train!

The houses were every bit as nice as I had been told. They were in the process of furnishing the demonstration/sales unit when we arrived. The pricing was such that the same thirty-year payout would hold. So, I called Jim Williamson back and told him to buy all the houses in the development.

This all seemed crazy on the surface, but I had now provided decent housing to all the military students and within their housing allowance. My orders had been to come up with a definition of the problems being faced and recommendations for solutions. I think I did that nicely.

After that crazy day, I left a father and son who were going out to celebrate with their families and headed back to The Meadows. There was a message from the Oxford bursar's office that the problems the military students were reporting were not within the purview of the university and that they couldn't help.

Tomorrow, I would arrange to get together with what I was beginning to think of as my cadre of officers to arrange another meeting of all military students to let them know of the new housing possibilities. My luck, they would say they would rather stay in their expensive pigsties.

I suspect when it all becomes public, my name will be mud with both town and gown.

Chapter 20

During my run the next morning, I was thinking about yesterday's events. I started to calculate the number of purchases and economics when it hit me: I would profit from the rental of Farmington Hall and the housing estate.

That wasn't what I set out to do, and I didn't think it would look good to any outsider. Even though the residents would be getting better conditions at a better price, I still could be accused of profiteering.

The more I thought about it, the more nervous I got. By lunchtime, I was a wreck. Because of the time difference, I couldn't get through to Jim Williamson until then.

I heaved a sigh of relief when he picked up his phone. I must have been hyperventilating a little because he told me to slow down.

"So, Rick, you don't want to be seen as taking advantage of the situation?"

"Not at all."

"Okay, let's do it this way, we will donate the properties to a trust fund. Jackson Enterprises will guarantee the loans, but all monies will go through the trust. Any profits will be disbursed at the direction of the board of trustees."

"Who would this board be?"

"There would be seven members consisting of officers attending Oxford and living on the properties. There would be two US, two UK, and three from other countries. The three groups would have a random lottery each year to select their representatives. That way, there would be no entrenched group taking control.

"This group would be responsible for setting policies in line with military practices. They would hire staff and ensure that the properties would be maintained and improved where needed. You would have no role in the operation under any circumstances."

"Jim, how the heck did you sort all that out just now."

"I didn't. When I saw what was going on yesterday, I contacted your parents. They have burned up the phone lines with the Pentagon and Whitehall to bail you out of this mess. Your heart was in the right place, and the fundamental idea was correct, but it would have been a public relations disaster for you."

"I guess I will have to call home and eat some crow."

"I'm afraid so. Your Dad mentioned that he thought you had learned your lesson about making an urgent decision immediately and thinking things through when you could."

"Ouch, I did step in it. Thanks for your help, Jim."

"No problem, boss, and don't lose sight of the fact that the result is a good thing."

Wanting to hide and lick my wounds sounded like a good idea, but I decided to get it over with. I did delay for fifteen minutes, trying to calm down. I then called home. I was glad of the delay. Jim had called Dad and let him know that I had seen the error of my ways before they had to point them out to me.

It still wasn't the most fun conversation I ever had. Not that Dad was mad. What bothered me most was how calm and nice he was. I thought he would be reading me my beads, but no, we walked through the whole event.

His only remark was, "The guys with stars on their shoulders would have liked some input so they could have shared the glory."

"I have a meeting set up with all the students, so maybe the "stars" could come and make the announcements?"

"That would smooth some feathers."

"How do you think I should handle it?"

"Call your contacts at the Puzzle Palaces and see when they want to do it. The sooner, the better."

"You mean The Pentagon and Whitehall?'

"That's what I said."

"Okay, should I keep you posted?"

"Not my circus, not my monkeys; all yours, son."

"Gee, thanks, Dad, but seriously, thank you, Mum and Dad."

"You are our circus and money combined, Rick."

"As I said, thanks, Dad."

At that, I got off the line. I was able to get through to General Sullivan. After a stilted conversation where I did my best not to say I screwed up, I let him know that I would appreciate it if he and the air vice-marshal could break the news to the military students.

He took it from there, contacted Air Vice Marshal Smyth, and called me back, letting me know that I should arrange a meeting on Friday with all concerned. He and Vice Air Marshal Smyth wanted to meet with me before the main meeting to make certain we were together on the project.

That was as close as the general came to say that I had been a Lone Ranger.

I arranged the meeting to be in the main dining room at Farmington Hall. I had some thoughts on renaming the hall after Oxford graduates who had distinguished themselves in the US and UK military. I told my cadre of officers as little as I could so as not to spoil the surprise.

Come Friday, I met Vice Air Marshal Smyth and General Sullivan at Farmington Hall in the morning and gave them a quick tour. They both liked what they saw. I felt like I wasn't in too much trouble when the general told me he now understood why I had grabbed the place.

"I knew you had money, Rick, but not this much."

Vice Air Marshal Smyth chuckled, "MI5 checked him out for a security clearance when he became a Queen's Messenger. Her Majesty may decree but the wheels must turn. He is worth more than many small countries."

"Maybe I should hit you up for a loan, Rick."

"You could, but the interest rates would be terrible, and I have a collection department."

I meant it as a joke. The vice air marshal didn't take it that way.

"I heard your family was friends with Mr. Lucky, but I didn't realize you are in business with him."

Opens mouth. Inserts foot. I was having some week.

"We aren't. I was thinking of my Uncle Popeye."

"Righto, he is much worse."

The general was looking back and forth at us, wondering what was being said.

The vice air marshal said, "Rick has an uncle by marriage who scares the Mafia."

Not much the wiser, the general let it pass. We wound up our tour and agreed on the governing terms of the new trust being formed. I told them about using prominent military graduates of Oxford as names for the hall and the estates.

I suggested Rowden-Hasting Hall and Rogers Estates. I had to explain about the First Marquis of Hastings, which had a more historical flavor for the hall, and both agreed that Bernard Rogers was a good man to name the estates after.

The General told me, "Rick, the other day I wondered if you were the Cowboy I first heard of, but now I see you have not brought us problems. You have brought solutions that are worthy of those group captain boards on your shoulders."

Vice Air Marshal Smyth agreed, "You need a lot of seasoning, son, but I think you are headed in the right direction."

"Thank you, sirs."

Thank you, Mum, and Dad.

At one o'clock, the dining hall had filled up. My superiors and I took the center stage which was equipped with a sound system. I introduced both of the general officers and left it to them. They explained that it was realized that military students at Oxford and other major universities faced many difficulties and that I had been given the task of identifying them.

The major one was the expense and quality of housing. Once I had reported it, action was quickly taken to rectify the problem. They went on to say that the now-renamed Rowden-Hasting Hall would have rooms for single students at less than their housing allowance, and the Rogers Estates would have the same deal for married students.

We had to allow fifteen minutes for the excited buzz to calm down. All were told to give thirty days' notice on current lodging. The first lot of trustees were named, selected by the generals from my cadre pool. When the trust was made official, there would be drawings for a position.

In the meantime, the current officers were to see that all residences were furnished and ready for occupation at the end of thirty days.

After that, the students were allowed to walk through the facility to see what was available. Married students and their spouses headed to the door to go and check out the houses. The generals and I sat having a cup of coffee.

General Sullivan brought up a new subject.

"Rick, would you object if we, the armed forces, bought you out on this project? We would return all the money you have put into this and take over the guarantee of the loans. It would look better for us if we did this, and if there was a default on this building, we would be stuck with it and not you."

"I don't see any problems with it. I wasn't interested in buying these properties as such, and you are right. I would have no idea what to do with them if I got them back."

"Fine, who should our people contact?"

I gave them Jim Williamson's phone number. I took the opportunity right then to go to the porters' lodge, which had the only working phone, and called him. He wasn't in, but the office took my message for him that told him he would be getting a call and why.

When I got back to the table, the vice air marshal had left. I didn't give it a thought.

"Rick, there is another issue that I have to address, and this one makes me feel lower than whale shit."

"What is that, General?"

"I came here with a problem, that of military students' discontent, but you identified the cause and solved it. In doing so, you gained the rank of Group Captain. My superiors do not feel it is appropriate for us to deal with a seventeen-year-old as a full Colonel. We have informed the RAF that we no longer need you to be seconded to the USAF."

Talk about a kick in the head. Thank you very much, and don't let the door hit you on the way out.

"I see, I really do, but at the same time, it is a real putdown."

"I understand, Rick, and wish it could have worked out differently."

"Do you have any idea what the RAF is going to do?"

"Not officially."

That told me all I needed to know. About that time, the students returned from their facility tour. They were happy and upbeat. They all wanted to thank me for my efforts. The married students also came back. I think several firstborns would be named after me.

I played my part down and left. The general was talking to a group telling them how the US wanted to take care of its officers and was always glad to put in such efforts.

I drove home slowly, paying attention to the traffic. I had enough on my mind that I didn't want to add an accident to my day.

At home, there was a message to call Mr. Norman. I figured I knew what it was. I was right. The RAF was rescinding my seconding as the rank was not appropriate for my age. I couldn't disagree with that; it was how it was handled after what I had done for them.

"Rick, you still are a Senior Messenger. We have amended our rules so that they have the same flying rights as you did in the RAF."

I was feeling cynical at this point.

"So, I can still haul people around for you. So glad to serve."

"Sir Richard, that is not an appropriate attitude. You should be proud to serve your Sovereign."

That put me in my place. I had better get my head on straight.

"You are correct, Mr. Norman."

"Well, one thing we are doing is coming up with some Messenger flight insignia. It will be some form of a greyhound with wings, like the Pegasus. Also, there will be rank insignia for each level.

As the first pilot flier, you will maintain your group captain status with us. While you will not be seconded to the RAF as a royal service, they and all other services in the world who recognize the RAF have to recognize your rank."

I could see that what had been done had not only upset me, it had stung the Messenger Service.

"The Army is also awarding you the Meritorious Service Medal. They have the most students at Oxford."

It also let the Army take a slap at the Air Force. Good old inter-service rivalry.

"Thank you, sir. So, what, if any, uniform shall I wear?"

"Good point. We will have some suggestions made up for your approval."

"My approval?"

"Certainly, you are going to earn that group captain rank. You are the head of the Flying Division of the Queen's Messenger Service."

"It seems like a lot has happened in a very short period."

"Her Majesty was not pleased. She also placed a call to your president, so you will be hearing something from the US."

Oh, boy, the can of worms was full and open today. I no sooner hung up than the phone started ringing. It was the White House.

"Richard, how are you today?"

"Feeling a little buffeted around, sir."

"I understand. I must say Elizabeth was not happy with the RAF and our Air Force when she called."

"I just heard that."

"I thought I would let you directly know that, first of all, I would never have approved you being seconded as a full Colonel. That makes no sense for someone your age and experience level. Also, it does not lead to good order and discipline within our ranks."

"The last person to have that sort of treatment was General Custer, and see where that got him."

I couldn't resist it. "At least I am considered a friend of the Indians."

"It would be our senior officers after your scalp."

"Oops, didn't think that through."

"And that is why you shouldn't be a colonel."

"Point taken."

"Now that that is out of the way, is there anything else in this affair that needs straightening out?"

"Not really, I would like to say that General Sullivan handled himself well during this mess."

"Thank you, I will pass that on. This will be getting him his third star, so he should at least be grateful to you."

"Thank you for the call, sir. I was feeling underappreciated earlier."

"Understood, Richard. Say 'hi' to your family for me and tell your Mum that I will let certain senior officers know they didn't handle this well at all."

I think Ike is afraid of my Mum. He probably should be.

Chapter 21

My weekend was quiet. I ran a lot, many miles. I also spent some time with several of the student officers I had met. It turns out several of them were into unarmed combat and met as a group to keep their reflexes up. I was a little rusty but not as bad as I thought.

I needed quiet time to reflect on the past week. I had gotten a lot thrown at me, done a lot, and experienced unexpected twists and turns. Upon reflection, I had done some good. As far as having the rank of colonel, so what? I didn't have it at the beginning of the week; now it was gone.

I wonder if *Guinness's Book of Records* had anything about time in grade.

The Messenger Service had allowed me to retain it, but I thought that was their politics as much as anything. The other services wouldn't push them around like a little brother.

When things died down a little, I would ask Mr. Norman if it was in the Service's best interest to keep my rank. It didn't mean that much. It isn't like I had a hundred men reporting to me.

I called home and updated Mum and Dad on everything. We talked for a while. They both agreed that I was taking the correct approach. Why get in a snit about something that didn't matter? Though Dad thought the Service should have stuck it to the other branches and given me a star.

I think my dad's a bit of a troublemaker.

My brothers and sister all said a quick "hello" to me. They were all busy. Denny was prepping for another beauty pageant shoot; Eddie was cleaning up from a camping trip. It seemed he had mice in his backpack when he got home. That went over well.

Mary was practicing for a PSA she had to film tomorrow. Also, she let me know her new fall collection was going to be neat. Even the big girls would like it. Big girls being twelve and up.

When talking to my parents, I told them that the military would give all my money back. This included the good faith money and the twenty percent down. Altogether, it was about a million dollars. Rather than take the cash, which might result in a tax hit as it had been moved in and out of the country, I wanted to leave it in the trust for the Hall.

Dad suggested I create a new trust under the control of the Hall's board of trustees rather than directly by the military. This way the money would only be spent on local issues. Otherwise, it would be treated as fungible and disappear on some idiotic scheme. That made sense to me. Dad told me he would handle it with Jim Williamson.

I asked how their projects were going. Mum was becoming a star attraction on the charity benefit circuit. Everyone wanted her there for her money. She didn't mind as long as it was a worthy cause that directed the money where it belonged. She had a list of some pretty big names she wouldn't give a farthing.

Dad's business front was going well. He was becoming a media mogul. His holdings in newspapers, TV, and radio were now so large he was considered an opinion shaper and not in a good way. Did I say my dad was a troublemaker?

On Monday, the Hall's board contacted me and invited me to a formal dinner where I should wear a dress uniform on Friday night. I was specifically requested to wear an RAF dress with group captain rank.

I got to add a ribbon to my bar when the postman dropped off a package. It was the Meritorious Service Medal and ribbon. I thought they had ceremonies for these awards. It was the Army version which I liked better than the RAF presentation.

Maybe I was still miffed at the RAF.

I spent the week running. I would run in the morning and then again in the late afternoon. I had no idea how many miles I ran. It seemed like I had to keep moving. I also gave some thought as to what I was going to do with the rest of my vacation. It was only the last week of August and I had all of September yet.

Maybe I would fly to Rome. I wondered if Sophia Loren would need a rescue.

When Saturday evening arrived, I dressed up in my RAF uniform for probably the last time. Hamilton made sure everything was in order. When I arrived at the Hall, there was an officer in uniform waiting for me. He held me back for a few minutes as the Hall filled. When it looked like all were there, he escorted me in.

As we broke the plane of the door I heard, "Attention on deck, Sir Richard Jackson arriving."

To have a room of over two hundred people stand at attention when you enter a room is an experience. I had enough wit about me to say, "As you were."

The evening was to celebrate the founding of the Hall and to thank me for my part.

It is embarrassing to hear praise like that piled on you. The highlight was when they read the text that would appear on a plaque that would be posted at the entrance inside the building.

It would be cast in bronze like a historical marker. They had written the true story of my actions in identifying the need for better housing and the acquisition of it. They even put in a line about how I was un-seconded from the USAF and RAF. That would go over well.

I wondered how long the plaque would remain. During a visit many years later, I saw it was still in place, starting to acquire a patina. At a place like Oxford, it could be there for another five hundred years.

People wanted to shake my hand left and right. I was asked to say a few words. I took the opportunity to tell them about the new trust that had been created earlier in the week. It was to be used at their discretion. Furniture, books for the library, and even the infamous class notes would be possibilities. These were suggestions, not orders.

Needless to say, that received an enthusiastic response. I closed by saying they should get to know their fellow officers in all branches and countries of service. Here was a new old boy's network in the making.

I was getting tired of shaking hands, but I couldn't turn away the last two young ladies who came up to me accompanied by their mothers. I expected to be thanked for their nice new bedrooms at their new house or something.

There were about six.

"Is it true that you are the brother of *the* Mary Jackson?"

Okay, I was getting a little big-headed, but come on.

"Yes, I am."

They proceeded to tell me how neat she was and that her clothes were "brilliant!".

This went on for a few minutes. I told them I would be certain to let Mary know she had fans in England. I got their names and addresses from their mothers. I told the Mums that I would make certain Mary sent something.

Later on, I got a note from Mary that she had sent them each an outfit from her collection, and an autographed Feed the Puppies t-shirt.

I'm glad that six-year-old girls know what is important in the world. I also wished that some seventeen-year-old girls knew what was important, namely me.

Chapter 22

Sunday I was at loose ends. I finally packed my golf clubs in the Aston Martin and went to see if I could play eighteen holes at the golf club. I had to wait an hour to get on, but I spent it practicing.

I was put in a threesome. They appeared to be nice people but the most I could figure out was that they were from Manchester. I couldn't understand them. I would catch about every third word. Talk about thick accents. I did understand "bloody hell" and "bollocks" when a ball went out of bounds.

I had a solid round, no records broken but it was good. They invited me for a drink afterward, but I figured if I couldn't understand them sober, it would be a waste of time with drinks.

I had dinner at home with Grandmum. The Queen Mum had left for some castle or the other. I thought I had a lot of places to live, but after Grandmum told me about all the residences supported by the royal family, I felt like a piker.

The next day my past caught up with me big time. I had put in place a program to track people I knew if something about them made the newspapers in a good way.

There were also anniversary cards to my now thousands of workers in Jackson Enterprises. I hadn't given them any thought, maybe thinking my US office would take care of the cards.

They took care of them all right, in the form of a large package addressed to me. I should never have given Jim Williamson the address of The Meadows.

I spent the entire day signing cards and writing notes. At least there were some preprinted ones for anniversaries, birthdays, and graduations.

After signing almost a thousand of those, my hands were numb. There would be a whole bunch of personal notes that I would have to write. This paying attention to people was a lot of work.

Moaning and groaning aside, it was still a good thing.

I also got a letter from Dick Wyman. He wanted to let me know that he had started his own company to perform stunts. He was going to specialize in high work, like multi-story building falls, jumping from aircraft, etc. Better him than me.

He asked that if in my work I saw a need for his services to bring his name up and let him know of the possibilities.

I certainly would as he and Jane had helped me out so much when I first came to California. They still lived in the house where our subbasement tunnel came out, so it was in the family's vested interest to take care of Dick.

I wrote him a note back congratulating him on his venture and told him that I would not only bring his name up but that he could count on me for backing if things moved too slowly.

One of the newspaper articles clipped for me was about Emily Weeks soloing. Even though I felt she treated me unfairly, I wrote a note. Let bygones be bygones. No sense in carrying any baggage around if I could avoid it.

Another newspaper article was about the trial of the sheriff who ran the cattle rustling ring. He had gotten ten years. I thought about sending him a note but decided that would be nasty. I had not forgiven that group and how they treated the tiger incident.

That reminded me that the tiger skin was in my room in Jackson House. Maybe I should have it shipped over here. It would be cool in my garage apartment.

That got me thinking about how my life had changed in the last two years. I had to laugh at myself when I remembered when we first started to fix up and rent out houses in Bellefontaine.

When asked how many we should do, I said, "Let's go for rich." I thought we had nailed that one.

While I was grinding through all my mail, the phone rang. Mr. Hamilton let me know it was for me.

It was a producer from the *Maverick* TV show. He wanted to know if I was interested in doing an episode next week. I would have to fly back to the States for two days of work. I would have to fly back to LA tomorrow and be ready to work on Thursday and Friday.

My first thought was no, but as we talked, it began to sound like fun. After my work with the military setting up housing in the last couple of weeks, I was ready for something different.

I asked why the notice was so short and was told there was a contract problem with one of the actors, and they had to change the episode. When I pursued that further, they said James Garner had the issues.

They hadn't contacted Susan Wallace yet. I told him until they did that, I couldn't give them an answer. This was a polite way of saying until my agent negotiates the fee, I'm not committing. I told him I would like to take the part if an agreement was reached.

I think they were trying to do an end-run to get me at the same rate as the last time. Now that *Over the Ohio* was such a hit, my value had gone up.

I wanted to do the part but also wanted to be paid fairly. This would also help force the issue with Susan about finding her replacement.

They would have to make it quick if I were to get a flight home to be at Warner Brothers on Thursday morning.

They did. Susan called me within the hour. She had doubled my fee for the one episode. That sounded good, and I told her to go ahead and commit me.

There was only one problem. When I called my travel agent, I was informed that on Wednesday, no seats were available in any class that would get me to LA.

That included such wild things as flying all night to Hong Kong and back to LA.

I was in a real quandary. I had accepted the role and didn't want to go back on my word.

I came up with a solution. It was a bad solution. I chartered a jet, a 707. I would lose several thousand dollars on this appearance, so much for worrying about getting my worth. At least I would keep my commitment.

I decided I wouldn't even mention it to anyone but Jim Williamson to pass on to my tax accountants so I could at least salvage some tax money from it.

Now, it seemed stupid to have that large of a plane to myself. I thought about how I could give some people a free ride. I could hardly stand outside Heathrow with a sign, though it would be interesting.

I thought of the military students at Oxford. They had a phone tree that could get the word out. I would have to make sure that they understood it would be a one-way ride as I wouldn't be chartering a flight back.

I called, stating that they would have to be at the Oxford airport at eight a.m. for an eight-thirty departure.

To my surprise, thirty people were waiting for me at the airport the next morning. There were no late arrivals. The nice thing about the military is if you aren't there fifteen minutes early, you are late.

The thirty people were from seven different families. They had all been waitlisted for two weeks on MATS flights back to the States. The MATS flights were full, and it was almost impossible for a group of three people to travel together, so a family of four or more had little chance.

They had been going to the airport every day for two weeks trying to get home and were always turned away because of higher-priority people. They were getting desperate, so my flight was a godsend.

Most of them were trying to get to the East Coast but were ready to take any flight that would get them back to the US. The student member of the family had graduated and was trying to get home for their next posting. They had thirty days' leave and burned up half of it waiting for a MATS flight.

Since it was my charter, I held it up for a few. I made a phone call from the private aviation lounge to my travel agent. I had each family head tell my travel agent their final destination.

She would be booking their flights while we were in transit. I got back on the line after she had all their information and told her to charge everything to my account. I could afford it, and these people had suffered enough.

The flight itself was uneventful. There was enough room for the little kids to run around and play in the back of the plane. It was certainly more comfortable than a C130 would have been.

The crew even invited me up front, and I was able to log a couple more hours in a 707. That was more of a vanity thing for me as I had no intention of being an airline pilot.

When we landed in LA, there was a list of all the connecting flights, times, and tickets waiting for us. I think a couple of children might be named after me.

It was early evening, so I was anxious to get home. Mum had arranged for one of our limos to pick me up. I got a big welcome at home as though I had been gone forever.

I was updated on family projects. Mum was really into the charity scene in the LA area. She had a party of one sort or another at Jackson House almost weekly. Dad had set himself up as chairman of the board of his business and was trying to step back from running the daily CEO operations.

He planned to look into expanding his growing media empire into other countries. He would do this by buying existing outlets.

Right now, Australia was looking like a good place to start. It was a growing market with little consolidation going on.

Denny's photography business was going well. The studio was getting a name for successful portfolios, so much so that the Ford Agency was starting to subcontract some of their work to them.

Eddie and Mary were in the doghouse. They had been caught calling stores and asking if they had Prince Albert in a can and, if so, to let him out.

I had to snicker, as Denny and I had never gotten caught. That gave me a thought. In private, I asked Denny if he remembered calling homes and asking if their refrigerator was running. When the homeowner said yes, we would tell them they had better catch it.

I knew that by reminding him of that, he would mention it to Eddie, who would tell Mary who would have to do it. I owed her a few. It also allowed me to practice my spy craft by using a cutout.

It wasn't as though the kids would get in much trouble. Right now, they had to help with dishes. A little humility wouldn't hurt Mary at all.

As a fail-safe, I told Dad about my nefarious plan. I knew that he would be okay with it. Mum, not so much. He thought it would be funny as he did things like that when he was a kid. Though their refrigerator was an icebox and didn't run.

Mum and Dad were both very interested in my experience with the military, both the ups and downs. Their only comment was that some things never seemed to change. My position with the USAF and RAF didn't fit into their rank structure, so I had to go after they had used me.

The next morning after my exercise and run, I went over to Warner Brothers for my *Maverick* stint. They were ready for me in makeup and costume. Ben Maverick rides again!

The storyline is Ben finds a lady and her beautiful daughter who have been cheated out of their savings and gets their money back for them, plus the store they had thought they had bought.

It opens with Ben coming out of a saloon where he has been in an all-night poker game. He had won most of the money earlier in the evening but couldn't leave without being robbed on the way out.

His simple solution was to outlast them all until daylight, when the town marshal would be patrolling, and then leave the game. That part worked.

As he was going back to his hotel, he finds the two women crying on a bench at the stage station. They had just found out the deed they had paid for by mail in answer to a newspaper ad is a fraud.

The deed of the dress shop they thought they had bought didn't have the owner's signature. One would have thought they would have been suspicious of buying a dress shop from a man, but they went ahead and did it.

They had shown their deed to the town marshal, and he told them there was nothing they could do.

Being the nice guy that he was, Ben gets them a room at his hotel.

He runs a game of his own by conning the fraudulent store owner into buying a played-out gold mine. He did this by buying gold ore from a prospector he knew and then claimed it was from an old mine in the mountains near town.

He bought the mine from the owner for a song as it was worthless.

Making sure the bad guy saw the assay, he listened to the guy's offer to buy it. He bargained him out of the store and the same amount of money as the ladies lost.

Making certain he had a good deed to the store, he returned the ladies' money to them and then sold them the store for one dollar. This transaction was performed in front of the town marshal and the leading banker.

The swindler was now dead broke, and the town marshal ran him out of town as a worthless bum.

It was a very weak plot, but what can you do in a short TV program?

What I thought was going to make the whole thing fun was that I got to kiss the girl at the end.

She and I had no personal chemistry during the filming, and it showed during our kiss. They had to do fourteen takes to get the kiss right. I think it had to do with the fact she smoked, and I didn't. Try to picture an ashtray forcing itself into your mouth.

That is when I found out that kissing the wrong person could be work. I think she learned the same lesson, as we both couldn't get off the set fast enough.

Chapter 23

The TV show took two days, Thursday and Friday. I was glad when it was done and told the producers that it was fun but that I wasn't in a hurry to do another one, and certainly not with that actress.

I took most of Saturday off but caught the early evening flight to London. That put me into Heathrow at nine o'clock Sunday morning. I went to my suite at the Plaza, cleaned up, and went out to my favorite fish and chips shop.

When I got back from lunch, the front desk had a message for me. I don't know how he tracked me down, but Mr. Norman asked if I could drop by Monday morning around nine.

It is some world going from owning houses in Bellefontaine to dropping in at Buckingham Palace.

The next morning, after my run down Rotten Row in Hyde Park, I went to the palace to see Mr. Norman.

While at the park, I kept an eye out for my young lady of the fickle finger of fate, but she wasn't to be seen.

Did she give everyone the finger or just me? If so, who could it be? The only one I could think of was the blonde Christine, but that wasn't her style. Running around like a madwoman, that is. Giving me the finger wasn't within her repertoire. At least, the running around like a madwoman wasn't.

At the palace, I was escorted immediately to Mr. Norman. I found that they had been looking for me everywhere. They had no idea that I had gone to the US for a TV appearance. It took a phone call to Jackson House to find out I was back in England.

I was asked, a little curtly, to keep them informed in the future if I was leaving the country. By the way, they had checked all the airline manifests. Did I travel under an assumed name?

You should have seen his look when I told him I chartered a 707 when I couldn't get a commercial seat.

I didn't bother to tell him about my hitchhikers. He had enough to mull over.

He got down to why they were hunting me.

They needed civilian transportation to take a Russian spy to Berlin for a prisoner exchange. I was to take delivery of a "package" and take it to the Glienicke Bridge and exchange it for another "package." There would be no record of the contents of these packages.

Two guards would accompany me. While not being told, I suspect these guards would be from MI6. This came about for several reasons.

First, we weren't allowed to use military aircraft for this trip for some reason stipulated by the Soviets.

Second, MI6 wanted an aircraft with some official capacity. The Queen's Messenger Service plane would be perfect as it also had diplomatic immunity when on a mission. The exchange was to be tomorrow; that is why they were desperate to find me.

Lastly, there was to be no record of who was exchanged. We had demanded that. I had to wonder who we were getting back and why we didn't want it known.

This incident would later cause the service to expand to a fleet of four planes and a group of pilots.

Mr. Norman made it clear there was some danger involved. If my plane were to go down in East Germany, I would be held as a spy, no matter my diplomatic status. I would be held prisoner for a long time. It usually took two years or more to get people back.

I told him I was willing to accept that risk and would do my best not to go down in East Germany.

I was given a ride to Oxford where my Greyhound plane was hangared. I went over it with a fine-toothed comb as it would be a long flight to Berlin.

In the morning, I arrived early and performed the preflight checks again. Who knew what may have changed overnight?

I had just finished when a plain black van pulled up to the plane with three people: my package and two escorts.

The prisoner looked tired but, other than that, in good health. His clothes were rather shabby looking. He looked like he should be riding the rails to get home.

He was thin, maybe in his mid-forties, with greying hair and a mild look. He was so nondescript it was amazing, a textbook spy.

He seemed disinterested in what was going on around him, just another day at the office.

The two escorts were big, beefy guys. Either one of them would have been more than I could handle. They wore suits and ties, but nothing could make them look like anything but guards or maybe bouncers at a nightclub.

They both had cloth bags with them, the type you would bring your groceries home in. Since they weren't closed at the top, I could see in.

The contents were chocolate, perfumes, and whiskey. I asked about them.

The lead, at least the guard who spoke, told me.

"This isn't our first exchange at this location. We found it helps keep things smooth if we bring some gifts for the permanent guards."

I asked, "How will this work at the bridge?"

"It will be dusk when we get there. We will be in a public works van. Traffic cones will have been set up earlier to keep the bridge clear. We will park on our side in the Wannsee District, which is American. The other side is Potsdam, and it is the only checkpoint controlled directly by the Soviets.

"We will escort our person to be exchanged to the center of the bridge. They will do the same from their side. There, you will sign a receipt showing packages were exchanged. We take our guy and fly back here."

"That sounds straightforward enough."

"We have been doing this for a couple of years, and it has gone smoothly every time. That is why we keep it such a secret. Once word gets out, someone will try to take advantage of it."

The guard spoke with a very educated upper-class accent. Unless it was for the palace, I had to revise my opinion about them being bouncers.

I had filed my flight plan. There was to be a refueling stop in Dortmund, and then we would land at Tempelhof Airport.

I was looking forward to seeing the airport, which had started life as land owned by the Knights Templars and ended up as a showpiece for the Nazis.

It reminded me of the story about the British Air pilot having trouble identifying the correct taxiway. The German ground controller in a very snide manner, asked if he had ever been to Tempelhof before.

The pilot replied, "Only five times in 1944, but I never landed."

We took off on time, and the flight was uneventful. There was little to no conversation. One of the guards asked the Russian if he was glad to be going home.

"Not really, but they have my family, so I have no choice."

That shut everyone up.

At Dortmund, we used the restrooms and grabbed a bite to eat while the plane was fueled. I may have been paranoid, but I insisted on sitting where I could see what was being done during the refueling. I even checked the fuel sumps to make certain no water had been introduced.

The lead guard, that is all I could think of him, as I wasn't given any names, told me, "You seem to have the right instincts for this game. You take after your mum."

"You know my mum?"

"I served with her in North Africa."

What was Mum doing in North Africa?

"Shall I tell her someone says hello?"

"Tell her James says hello."

No, it couldn't be, could it?

"I will do so, and the last name?"

"Stock, James Stock."

Now I know he was pulling my leg.

"Kidding aside, who should I say hello from?"

"Just tell her Jimmy from Morocco. She will know."

"Okay."

When we landed at Tempelhof, we were met by a van with Berlin Public Works on its side. Of course, it was in German.

We all got in the back. I was very surprised to see a gurney, along with a doctor and the most extensive array of first aid equipment I had ever seen.

My surprise must have shown on my face as Jimmy told me that the Soviets played rougher than we did.

Our timing was good, so we were taken directly to the Glienicke Bridge. At a roundabout a block from the bridge, traffic was redirected. The signs looked like those in America that said Construction Zone and Men at Work.

We went up to the start of the bridge and stopped. Our driver blinked his lights twice and was answered by two blinks on the other side.

The spy, the two guards, and I got out and headed to the center of the bridge. We could see a similar group approaching from the other side. The only difference was that our guy was walking alone, while ours was supported by two guards.

When they got closer, I realized the two guards wore full Red Army uniforms. Two others accompanied them, one who looked like a clerk, the other dressed as I thought a KGB type would be.

That is in a long black trench coat with a matching Homburg hat. How he looked and carried himself screamed arrogance, which could be backed up by terrible force. Not someone to meet in a dark alley or even at noon on Main Street.

The first thing that occurred was I had to sign for receiving and releasing packages. The clerk had to do the same for his side.

My two guards handed their cloth bags over to the Soviet guards. I was really surprised when the four guards shook hands. I guess they were used to doing this.

Mr. Arrogance just stood there and glowered at the proceedings.

My two guards took charge of our spy. He couldn't walk. He was barely conscious. With no further action, both groups returned to their side of the bridge. I was off the bridge when I realized not one word had been spoken during that entire transaction.

When we got to the van, the doctor was waiting. He took one look at our returned spy and said we had to go straight to the hospital.

I don't know if he really was a spy or just someone captured and treated as a spy so they could get theirs back from us. This was a nasty game being played.

When we got to the hospital, our man was taken in immediately. I wondered what would happen now. I still was signed for this guy and would have to stick around until someone else took responsibility.

This sort of thing had occurred before as a man from the British Embassy showed up. He had the proper ID, but, more importantly, he was known to my guards. He was a trade attaché, but I suspect he was MI6. He signed my paperwork and told me I could head back to England when I was ready.

It was late enough in the evening that I decided to stay the night. The embassy had a guest room I could use. It was more like a closet, but since it was only one night, I didn't care.

I was up early the next morning. After cleaning up, I found a canteen in the building. I had to pay out of pocket. It appeared to be for lower-level staff, and I received many an odd look as I was a newcomer.

I wore my Greyhound sport coat with the pin and tie, so it was evident I was a Queen's Messenger. Though I got plenty of looks, no one attempted to talk to me.

As I was leaving, a frantic young aide found me.

"Sir Richard, we have been looking all over for you. The ambassador wants to invite you to breakfast."

"I just ate."

"Please come with me. I'm sure he will want to talk to you."

If not before, I was now the center of attention. I looked around, gave a shrug, and told the aide to lead the way.

The ambassador was a nice gentleman; he invited me to have coffee with him since I had eaten. We did the usual small talk. He let me know that our returned spy, his words, not mine, was going to make it but had been tortured severely.

"This is one of the worst cases we have had this year. Usually, they knock them around a bit and send them home. They never tell me for certain, but I think this man was truly a spy. All the others were just pawned for trading."

"That's brutal."

"Yes, it is, and now we have to return the favor. We don't torture in the physically brutal sense, but the next one we pick up will go hungry, be cold, and not be allowed to sleep."

"This is like a war."

"Yes, a cold one. I have seen a hot one. This is much better, believe me."

"I do. I have heard enough stories."

"Ah yes, how is Lady Jackson?"

"She is fine. Shall I give her your regards?"

"Yes, tell her Dwarf says hello."

Now, the ambassador was almost as tall as me, and I wondered how he could have gotten that name.

He must have caught on to my confusion.

"Strange things happen in wartime, including names. We had the Nazis checking out every midget in Morocco."

I had to talk to Mum about Morocco. After talking a bit more, I was excused. I guess the ambassador just wanted to meet me because he didn't bring up anything specific.

I headed back to Tempelhof. I spent twice the time I normally did doing my preflight. Other than the normal flight line checks, the aircraft had sat without security. Someone could have tampered with it. I found no evidence that anyone had.

It was a busy airport, and it took me at least fifteen minutes to get into the air. My flight plan was to fly west to Hamburg to refuel, then straight to Oxford.

I was about halfway to the West German border when my plane was rocked by a huge gust of what I thought was the wind. The second time it happened, I realized a jet fighter was buzzing me.

Once he had my attention, he tried to slow down to match my speed. He couldn't go that slow, but he signaled that I was to follow him.

That was the last thing I was about to do. I remembered what that poor guy at the checkpoint looked like.

I slowed to just above stall speed and took a good look around. I was buffeted around again. This guy was serious.

Looking down, I saw a huge forest below me. There was a narrow road heading due west, so I decided to go for it and landed.

Chapter 24

Mr. McGarry would have been proud of that landing. I dove straight down, flared out, and landed in about half the distance I would normally take. An old logging trail to the right of the road looked wide enough for my plane.

I turned a quick right and taxied as far into the woods as I could. From the air, it would be hard to see the plane. From the ground, it would still be obvious.

Shutting it down, I grabbed my go-bag and exited the plane. The jet was trying to loiter over me, but its turning radius was so great that it had to leave my sight. That meant he couldn't see me.

As soon as he was out of sight, I ran across the road and into the woods on the other side.

I barely got under cover when two things happened. One, the jet came back, and two, I realized I didn't have a map. It was in my Jeppesen case.

I had to wait for another round of the jet, then ran back across the road, got the map of the local area from my case, and also took my flight log. That would be a bear to recreate.

Again, heart in hand, I waited for the jet to pass over and crossed the road. As I did, I heard a vehicle or vehicles coming near.

West Germany was exactly due west from where I was. That would be the first direction they would search. I headed south. I remembered from the maps that the area I was in bulged into West Germany. If I headed south, I would cross into West Germany, but it was maybe twice the distance.

My go-bag was a knapsack that I could wear. After tightening the straps, I was ready to go. I took off towards the south at a good running pace. I didn't push it because I had a long way to go and didn't want to twist an ankle.

I got my first luck of the day when I came across another logging road that headed south. I was able to pick up the pace following this road.

What I was hoping was that they would have no idea which direction I went. They would have to start a search radius. If they underestimated the distance I could cover, I could keep ahead of them.

It hadn't rained for a while, but there wasn't a lot of dust for me to leave tracks in. Maybe all those miles I had run the last several years would pay off.

After an hour, I felt like I had created enough of a head start to take a break. I didn't stop; I just slowed to a walk for ten minutes. I drank from my canteen. The water tasted metallic because I hadn't changed it out recently, but it was good.

I didn't make the full ten minutes when my nerves gave out, and I started running again.

I did take the opportunity to check the compass from my go bag to confirm I was heading south.

I had some trail mix in my bag. I regretted not having my pistol, but carrying one in the UK was too much of a hassle, so I didn't bother. I did have a hunting knife with a six-inch blade, not a Bowie knife, but it could do the job.

I had a small first aid kit and a change of socks and underwear. Those were the contents of my bag.

As I walked, I threaded the scabbard through my belt. I heard a sound approaching from behind. It seemed like a heavy truck. I got off the road. The sound stopped.

I went deeper into the woods and waited. The truck had stopped, so I crept back through the woods. I could see the road that I had just traveled. Around a bend, there was a military truck still unloading troops.

They were sent into the woods in a wide search line, going back towards the plane. I had gotten out of the first search zone. Staying in the woods, I headed south for another mile. I then went back to the road and started to run at a steady pace.

I think in the first hour, I had gone five miles. Every hour from here on would make their search pattern more than four times as large or were those eight times? Geometry was never my strong suit.

It didn't matter. I kept going. It wasn't yet noon, so I could get some serious miles in if nothing went wrong. As soon as I thought that, I wanted to kick myself– talk about asking Murphy to show up.

He must have been busy elsewhere that day because I was able to keep going for another six hours. I estimated I had covered thirty-five miles.

As dusk settled quickly in the deep forest, I started to look for a place to spend the night.

I saw a deadfall that hadn't fallen entirely to the ground. It was a dead tree leaning against another. There was a triangle formed under it.

Since it was a fir tree of some sort, the living tree had branches sticking out. I crawled under them and found myself in a cozy area under the branches. Well, cozy if you aren't picky.

At least I was out of the breeze, which had been picking up all afternoon. I checked the contents of my go-bag. There was water, trail mix, and a flashlight with good batteries. There was a light blanket like the airlines used, TWA in this case. I wonder how that got there....

I had put in a change of underwear and socks. I wish I had thought of a jacket. I ate the last of the trail mix, drank half my water, and settled in for the night.

I had camped out many times, but it was with a group. It sure was lonely being out in the middle of nowhere, knowing that East German army troops were searching for me.

I must have woken up a hundred times during the night. The rain had moved in and was starting to drain into my shelter. It was time to move on. I wished again I had a jacket.

I had worn my blazer, but it didn't cover me, and if there were a next time, I would include a cap. A baseball cap would be great right now.

I could moan all I wanted, but what is, is. I started a slow jog down the trail south. As I loosened up, it got easier, and I even warmed up a little.

After an hour, I had to stop and change my socks. They were damp, and that is an easy way to get a blister. I put the damp ones inside my shirt, hoping my body heat would dry them out before I had to wear them again.

I drank the last of my water from my canteen. I was now at the mercy of the local streams. This was not good, as I knew that parasites lived in them. In scouts, we had been taught about *Giardia* and the terrible diarrhea it could cause.

That is the last thing I need.

The road meandered south. For every mile south I went, I probably did another half mile east and west, but overall, I was heading south. So, even though I was moving south, it was taking me a long time to get there.

Lunchtime came and went; I was out of food and water. I could go without food, but I did need water. Supposedly, you could go without liquids for several days, but not when you were running like I was.

The sun was starting to set when I staggered to a stop. I was having trouble running in a straight line. I had to find water, food, and shelter for the night, or I was in big trouble.

It was in this state of mind that I rounded a particularly sharp bend in the road. I came almost face to face with a man.

We both stopped, startled by the presence of the other. He appeared to be in his mid-forties. His features were what I would call hard-bitten. His life had not been an easy one.

From his dress, I think he was a hunter, or more likely, a poacher judging by the time of day. From his weathered alpine hat to his frayed jacket and twill pants, he looked like someone who lived his life outdoors.

He was carrying a rifle. It looked like something from World War II. I wouldn't have been surprised if he had carried it in the Wehrmacht Heer.

I took this all in in an instant.

He reacted first, saying something in German. I replied, "Ich spreche kein Deutsch."

I don't speak German is one of the few phrases I know.

He replied, "Englander?"

"Yes."

"What are you doing here?"

"Trying to get back to West Germany. My plane went down, and I don't want to be captured by the Stasi."

"Yes, that would be bad."

"Do you have any spare food and drink, particularly water? I have some British pounds and American dollars."

"I do."

"How much?"

"How much do you have?"

I could see where this was going. I had no choice. I pulled my wallet out and handed him all the paper currency.

He took it with a grin and then raised his rifle.

"Hands up. You will be worth a reward."

Nice guy. I raised my hands in the air.

"Turn around."

I did so slowly, hoping he would poke me with the rifle to get me to move faster. He did, which was his undoing.

As soon as I felt the rifle, I spun around to my left, using my left arm to move the rifle barrel away from me. It mostly worked.

As I was turning, he discharged his weapon. It was no longer pointing straight at me, but I still felt a searing pain across my back.

As pain radiated from my back, I grabbed the rifle barrel with my left hand. I then swung my body into him. This is where size and weight count. He stumbled backward but kept his feet.

He wouldn't let go of his rifle, so I pulled him in close to me and stepped around behind him. I had momentum in my favor, so I let go of the rifle and took him in a neck-breaking hold. I twisted as hard as I could, and his neck snapped.

He voided himself in his death. Now that the immediate danger was over, pain washed over my back. I hadn't turned the gun quick enough, so I had a graze across my back.

Removing my blazer, shirt, and t-shirt, I was able to feel the wound. It was low enough on my body that I could touch it. I had lost the top layers of skin, but I was really lucky that it didn't touch my spine.

I opened the first aid kit. It contained some sterile wipes, a small tin of aspirin, and a roll of gauze. There were Band-Aids, and that was it. I felt smart when I put it in my bag. Now I wished I had a lot more.

As Mum said, "If wishes were horses, beggars would ride." I would have to make do.

It took some contortions, but I used the wipes, which stung like the devil, and then wrapped the gauze around me. Fortunately, it was long enough to go around me twice, and I could tie it off in the front.

I took four aspirin, hoping it would help with the burning pain.

All I could hope was that it would keep me from chafing the wound and prevent infection.

Once that was done, I checked out the dead poacher. I put his hat on first. Then I removed his jacket and shirt. They were a little tight, but I could wear them. No way was I going to try his stinky pants on. I removed his hunting knife, which was much better than mine. I put it in my backpack.

He also had a backpack. It was the best find of all. It contained a full canteen, two sandwiches, and two pairs of dry socks. He must have been a Hitler Youth. It looked like he planned on spending the night in the woods.

I dragged his body to the side of the road after retrieving the cash I had given him. His wallet was very thin and had no money. I could see why he would try to turn me in for a reward.

After a long drink of water and one of the sandwiches, I was ready to move again. I was refreshed, but my back was burning. I thought about taking the rifle with me but decided against it.

It weighed a lot to be running with, and if I were in a position to have to use it, I would be in more trouble than I could handle.

I ran south for about another hour and started to look for a place to spend the night. The area was becoming hilly. To my left was a steep bank, which would be a difficult climb; to my right, a small but fast-moving stream.

I was able to cross the stream on several rocks, keeping dry. I then followed the stream, hoping to find some shelter. Instead, I ran out of walking room. The hill was now steep to my right as well, so I was forced to keep moving downstream.

I even ran out of the bank to run on and had to run in the shallow depths of the stream. It had now widened out and slowed down. Near the shore, it was a shallow sand base, so other than getting my shoes wet, I was able to keep moving.

Several hundred yards along, another smaller stream joined the main one. Since it was in a cut in the bank, I used it to move out of the confining stream bed. I still had to run in the water, but it wasn't that deep. If it had been in the spring, it would have washed me away.

I finally came to a level area that was even with the road. The road was at least a hundred yards from me. I would probably have to backtrack in the morning.

A downed tree was nearby with a hollow where the stump had pulled up. I was able to get down in the hollow away from the light breeze that had come in with new rainfall.

After eating the last sandwich, taking the last of the aspirin, and putting on dry socks, I huddled down in my TWA blanket and fell asleep.

I woke sometime in the night to the sounds of a truck, men, and dogs. They made a large racket but didn't come near me. I thought it was the East German Army looking for me, but had no way of knowing, and even if I did, it wouldn't help, so after listening for a while, I went back to sleep.

Chapter 25

I woke up stiff and sore. My back felt like it was on fire. On top of all that I was running a fever. Things weren't looking too good. I forced myself up. I had half of last night's sandwich left so choked it down. That and a drink of water, and it was as good as it was going to get.

I thought about the sounds I had heard last night. The East Germans had figured out I had gotten out of their search zone, so they had expanded it. They probably had set up roadblocks on every road around here.

I had no choice except to go cross country. Establishing west with my compass, I headed out. One problem I faced was the density of the forest. It was hard to sight in on something far out, so I had to check the compass frequently.

It was not a case of going in a straight line. Unlike what I had read about German forests, these woods were unkempt. According to the books, a German forest would be like a park.

This was wilderness—like the Civil War campaign. Deadfall after deadfall, bramble bush after bramble bush kept me detouring and having to recheck my compass heading.

I tried to run for a while. I ended up staggering around, so slowed to a steady walk. Somewhere along the way, my watch had disappeared, so I had no idea of the time. I tried taking a break every fifteen minutes. Just a breather, but it helped.

I drank the last of my water. Feeling my forehead, I thought the fever had gone up.

I kept this up all day long. By evening, I was lightheaded. I ended up drinking from a small stream that appeared to be spring-fed. The immediate danger was dehydration. I would have to gamble with the rest.

I crawled under the skirt of a large fir tree and spent the night. In the night, I woke up shivering and then I was burning up.

At first daylight, I started west again. The forest opened up and looked like the parks I had read about. It made things a lot easier going. I could sight further ahead, so I didn't have to check my compass as much.

I tried to jog, but that wasn't in the cards. I just kept going, putting one foot in front of the other. It seemed like I had just started, and the sun was setting.

As I staggered along, I realized that I was on a well-used trail. I had to get off it. I turned to go into the brush and fell. I tried to get up but was having a problem.

I got as far as my knees and fell again. I heard someone say something, but I blacked out.

When I came to, I was in a bed. Opening my eyes, I realized it was a hospital bed. All that to end up captured. At least I had tried. I wondered what was next.

What was next was Mum coming into the room, followed by Dad. I did a double take; yes, it was my parents.

Mum came over and hugged me. That is when I found out that I had an IV in my arm. Her avoiding it was what brought it to my attention.

"We have been so worried ever since we heard that your plane went down due to bad fuel in East Germany. They were searching all over for you. Why did you leave the plane?"

Whoa!

"I didn't have bad fuel; a MiG jet was trying to force me to land at an airport. I didn't want to be a captive, so I deliberately landed and ran."

"That's not what the East Germans are reporting."

"What can I say? I know the fuel wasn't bad. They certainly were hunting me. They had troops with dogs after me."

"Another thing, Rick, how did you get shot?"

I told them about coming across the poacher and the outcome. It didn't seem to bother either of them that I killed him.

"That hasn't been mentioned anywhere. The body hasn't been found, or they are suppressing it."

"After I saw that guy at the Glienicke Bridge, I was not going to be captured. How did I get here anyway?"

"A couple of hikers found you and called the police."

"I mean, how did I get into West Germany?"

"You were ten miles inside the border when they found you. You were pretty much out of it. We have been concerned about you for the last two days."

"Two days?"

"You have been unconscious for the last two days. They loaded you up with penicillin to fight the infection."

Looking up at the glass bottle flowing into the IV in my arm, I asked, "What's in the bottle?"

"It is a glucose solution; you need nourishment."

"Oh."

The next thing I knew, I was waking up, and Mum was in a chair by the bed. I asked how long I had been out; it had been for another eight hours. I was more clear-headed than I was earlier.

A nurse came in and checked me out and left with a cheerful, "He'll live."

Mum told me that the West German government and the Crown wanted to interview me about what had happened. It wouldn't be until I was discharged from the hospital.

The nurse came back with a doctor. After examining me he told her to remove the IV. I could eat some food.

I was hungry so I was looking forward to a meal. Imagine my disappointment when a cup of chicken soup was brought in along with a gelatin dessert. It was green and wiggled, the only good thing you could say about it.

I tried to sleep, but I must have been getting better. I woke up during the night every time a nurse came into the room. Then, there was the early morning routine.

One good thing was that my bodily functions were working. Based on that, the doctor told me I could be released later in the day.

Mum and Dad were there when I was released. It was a good thing as it seemed like half the German government was there with questions.

We were led to a conference room in the hospital. I was still in a wheelchair as I had not left the grounds yet.

Dad took charge of the ground rules.

"Rick will tell you his story. Take notes of any questions you may have and wait until he finishes to ask them."

No one had issues with that approach.

I told my story, starting with the spy exchange. I left nothing out, including where I got shot and killed the poacher.

There wasn't any way out of telling them I killed a guy, as I had to explain the gunshot wound. One guy started to ask a question, but Dad shut him down.

"Make notes of later questions. Any more interruptions, and we are done."

I had never seen Dad come across so strong before.

I finished up, and then the questions started. I was taken through the whole sequence at least twice more. They were polite but thorough. I was so glad my parents were here; I don't know what it would have been like without them.

Finally, the questions died down to nothing. Dad wheeled me out to the door of the hospital, where I was allowed to get up and walk. I was a little shaky but could do it on my own.

We were driven to a small airport where a chartered plane waited for us. We flew back to London. From there, we went to my suite at the Plaza.

Mum and Dad didn't badger me with any more questions during the trip. It was late in the evening when we got there, so I went directly to bed and slept like a log.

I got out of bed with only a little discomfort, but I wouldn't be doing anything that required stretching. My back was stiff, and even though I had bandages around it, it burned if I twisted too much.

Even dressing was a problem as I put on a shirt. I could do it, but as I raised my arms, I got a reminder that skin had been torn off my back. I was fortunate that was all that happened.

The doctor told me it was a miracle that my spine wasn't hit. A fraction of an inch and I would have been dead or paralyzed.

Grim thoughts aside, I went out to the suite living room. Mum and Dad were there. Breakfast had been set up and kept warm with chafing dishes.

After I had some bacon, eggs, and potatoes, we talked over coffee.

"Rick, it seems the Soviets don't like you. You have gotten in their way too many times."

"Apparently."

"We aren't going to forbid you to do anything, but we think you would be wise not to go to Berlin anymore."

"Dad, that sounds like excellent advice."

"You have an appointment at the palace with Mr. Norman in two hours. He wants to hear from you about what went on."

"That will give me time to get cleaned up."

We went to the palace as a group. My parents weren't letting me out of their sight. Mr. Norman was ready for us.

"Rick, will you tell me what happened in your own words? I have read the West German police report and MI6's report, but I would like to hear it in your own words."

I told him the whole story once more. He kept coming back to my fight with the poacher. He questioned every detail several times over.

I finally asked him why he was focusing on that.

"Because the East Germans have asked that you be extradited to stand trial for murder."

"Not bloody likely," Mum exploded.

Mr. Norman replied, "Calm down Peg, I said they requested, not that we are going to comply. Though the Foreign Office thinks it might help relations if we did."

That statement made me wonder what the life expectancy of the foreign secretary had just become.

Mum got even more worked up at that comment.

"Tell the foreign secretary that—"

She shut down. I don't think she wanted to go on record as threatening him if he had an unfortunate run-in with a Sterling machine gun.

"Her Majesty has firmly told them this wouldn't happen. She will dissolve the government if they try."

That made me feel better to have her on my side.

"There is also the issue of your airplane. They have seized it as evidence in your crime."

"They are welcome to it. I wouldn't trust the plane ever again after it has been in their hands."

"Good decision. The Messenger Service will replace it. You lost it in the line of duty."

"How is our man that I helped get back?"

"I'm sorry to say he didn't make it."

"This is a Cold War, as Bernard Baruch stated."

"You do know your history, Rick."

"I just didn't know that war is the keyword. I thought it was cold as in relations."

"It is very much real."

"Anyway, I need to tell you that your days of flying over East Germany are over."

I chuckled as I told him, "I knew that, and Mum and Dad have reinforced it."

"There have been concerns voiced about your safety even here."

"I'm not going to run and hide."

Dad spoke up, "Peg and I have talked about it. We are going to have surveillance put on Rick for the next several months until this dies down."

"Rick, you do know the newspapers, especially the tabloids, want to have an interview."

I groaned at that.

"Do I have to?"

"It would be a good move on your part, showing you have nothing to hide."

I looked at my parents. They looked at each other and shrugged. Thanks, Mum and Dad!

"I will do it. The sooner the better."

I thought about calling Susan Wallace, but there wasn't much she could do about this, and she was changing jobs. On second thought, I decided to call her as soon as I could as a professional courtesy.

Our conversation wound down, so we got ready to leave. As we stood, the door opened, and Her Majesty was there.

"You certainly lead an interesting life, Sir Richard."

After the prerequisite polite bow, I replied, "I'm afraid so Your Majesty. It is getting to be painful."

"How is your back?"

"I'll live. I have to work it a bit so the scar tissue doesn't restrict my movement."

"Good. Don't worry about our government's response. You got shot by an East German. What were you to do but defend yourself?"

I liked this take on things, though you could make a case that I wouldn't have been shot or had to kill the guy if I had just surrendered to the Stasi.

Of course, then I could have ended up like the poor guy from the bridge. I bet he hadn't even killed any of their agents.

That made a shiver run down my back. This cold war was real, and I was a target.

"Thank you, Your Majesty."

"Just what I expect from a Garter Knight."

With that, she left us.

Upon returning to the hotel, I placed a call to the States. It was still early there, so I was able to talk to Susan. She took it calmly until I told her I had been shot.

After going through all that once more I asked her what I should do about a press conference.

"Do it, and get it behind you. Read a statement of the facts and then don't take any questions; otherwise, they will want to know how it feels to be a murderer on the run from the East Germans."

"Thanks, Susan. Are you sure you don't want to stay on as my press secretary?"

"No, Rick, I'm looking forward to this change. I'm still looking for a replacement."

"Okay, I support you either way. Thanks for the good advice.

I called the front desk and arranged a room for a press conference later today. I then called the Palace press room and asked them to announce the conference.

About fifteen minutes after I hung up the phone, I had a call from the foreign secretary. He had the nerve to ask me to surrender to the East Germans as a good relations gesture.

I told him to hang on. I quickly told Mum what he had asked, handed the phone to her, and walked out of hearing distance.

I never knew what was said, but the issue was never brought up again.

At the appointed hour, I went downstairs and read the statement I had given to MI6 and the West Germans and left the room to shouted questions. Susan had called it right on the questions.

Chapter 26

I spent the weekend doing stretches as much as my body would allow. I did take the time to write a letter to Don Palmer, my unarmed combat instructor, thanking him for his lessons which had probably saved my life.

I described the brief fight in great detail and asked him if I could have gone at it any differently. Like how to avoid getting shot!

Knowing Don, he would tell me to be quicker.

My parents headed back to the US as they had plenty going on there. They updated me on the family. It seems Mary and Eddie were in trouble again. Something about refrigerators running: Dad and I avoided eye contact.

Buster Brown shoes had approached Mary. They wanted to sponsor her footwear. She, Mum, that is, was considering it. Her concern was that Mary would burn out by the time she was seven.

My thought was the rest of the world would burn out before Mary.

This was a back-to-school week for me, so after dropping my parents off at Heathrow on Monday, I had a car take me to Oxford. I didn't have a car or plane in London and didn't feel like driving anyway.

I didn't let on, but my back still was a problem. Especially if I sat too long. At least in the back of a limo, I could move around.

When I arrived at The Meadows, the staff came out like I was a returning hero. Returning yes, hero no.

I went to pick up my bags, but Mr. Hamilton would have none of that. Grandmum was there to give me a big hug and had a few nasty words to say about the Huns. I let them pass by; the French and the Germans were two subjects you didn't want to get her going on.

Of the two, she liked the Germans the best. You only had to kick their behinds about twice a century. The French were never to be trusted. Not that she was opinionated or anything.

I took a long run, well jog, and walked around the area to keep loose. It was helping. Tuesday, I did as much of my morning routine as possible and then cleaned up and headed into Oxford to make certain I was registered correctly for all my classes and had the books I needed.

Usually, when on campus, I was just another person. Not today. I think everyone and their brother knew about my East German adventure.

Coming out of the bookstore, I ran into several of the military students. They looked like they had been running.

"We just heard you were back, Rick. We will be with you for the rest of the day. Some of us will be rotating in and out to make certain you are always accompanied."

That took me back in a very nice way.

"Do you think there will be problems?"

"Some of these students are right Bolsheviks; they could try to give you a hard time, and we aren't having it."

In fairness, I told them about my parents' concerns, which were more serious than some students.

"That makes it much more important to have an escort."

I thanked them for their concern.

"Rick, when your wife thinks something is a good idea, your friend agrees, then your commander calls with a suggestion, one can take a hint."

I had to laugh at that.

"I get it, and thanks again."

My first lecture told me a lot about how I was viewed on campus. Before starting his lecture, the don asked, pointing directly at me.

"Are you the Richard Jackson who was involved in East Germany?"

"Yes, sir, I am."

"I'm not comfortable with having a known murderer in my class. Get out."

"So, I'm convicted without a trial on the word of a communist regime?"

"Get out. This class will not proceed with you in it."

I got up to leave, and to my surprise, about three-quarters of the class left with me.

Outside, a crowd gathered around me with questions. I took the time to answer as many as made sense. No, I'm not going back to stand trial. I did kill that man in self-defense.

I learned unarmed combat at the movie studios to support my roles. This was a little misdirection from earlier problems.

I'm still a Queen's Messenger and will be continuing, just not to the Soviet Bloc.

After that, I returned to my garage hideaway with my volunteer escorts.

I had two other classes later in the day, but the dons in those ignored me. I did stop at the main office to see about getting a replacement class for the one I had been kicked out of.

No one there had heard of the incident, so I was quizzed in depth. I was taken to the bursar. His take on it was simple.

"You are worth more to us than that don. Do you want to continue in that class?"

"Not. As a matter of fact, I didn't want to take poets of the Regency period in the first place. The Wasp of Twickenham never did anything for me."

"Pope is not everyone's cup of coffee."

I had to smile at that. The bursar certainly knew his Alexander Pope, who was known for his love of coffee.

It was decided I would be enrolled in a class on Victorian poets. Out of the frying pan into the fire.

The bursar wanted to know if I wished to have any steps taken against the don as he had exceeded his bounds. I told the bursar, "To err is human; to forgive is divine."

He about fell out of his chair laughing.

"I can't wait to tell this story in the faculty lounge. What an ironic act of revenge."

That saying, first written by Pope and how I used it, followed that don for his entire career. I shouldn't have been, but I was very proud of using his field of expertise to get back at him. So, sue me.

The bursar also questioned me about the military students moving out of rented flats. I explained what had been done: the purchase of the failed college, which was now Rawden Hall, named after the First Marquis of Hastings, and Rogers Manor, named after a NATO commander, both graduates of Oxford.

He had mixed emotions about the whole thing as he confided that he owned several of the now vacant flats. I asked him if he had been in any of them recently, and he had not. I suggested he take a good look at them before letting them out.

He agreed, but I could see he wasn't thrilled about the loss to his pocketbook. Oh, well.

Two evenings later, I went to a meeting at Rawden Hall with the military students. They had come together as a community. Before, they were each person or family on their own. Now they were a group with common goals.

It had been decided to put up a stone wall around Rogers Manor, as the housing project was now named. They were also developing a park in the center of the area. It would have children's swings, etc., plus a pavilion for group events and picnics.

Even the single officers living in Rawden Hall got behind this.

I spent Thursday night at the Dog and Crown with Bill, Tom, and Steve. Of course, they wanted to know about my German adventure. As I told the tale, others listened.

I also learned about the saying, dining out on this story. I didn't have to buy a pint all night. The guys told me I was a regular James Bond.

Well, I was, if getting forced down, running for my life, then getting shot, and wandering in the woods in a fever made me a high-class agent. I don't think that was how Mr. Bond would have handled it.

Several of the girls were very flirty, but I wasn't interested. I had other plans for the weekend.

I had called Nina Monroe at her school in Switzerland. Her dad had made certain I had her phone number. Hmm, I wonder what Dad's agenda was? No matter, I liked both him and Nina.

I wondered what sort of young lady she had grown into at the high-class boarding school. My experiences with girls of that ilk weren't the greatest.

Using my civilian Cessna, I flew to Zurich Friday afternoon. I had hotel reservations at the Marktgasse Hotel. I told my travel agent I wanted an upscale address. She assured me this was as upscale as it got. The quoted price was certainly upscale.

I took a taxi from Zürich Flughafen to the hotel. I thought about a car and driver, but my trip was only for the weekend, and I didn't even know if it would be needed.

I met Nina in the hotel lounge before dinner on Friday evening. Two friends accompanied her. Nothing had been said about them.

Since they were dressed to the nines, I was glad I wore a suit and tie.

Nina had changed; man, she had changed. The California high school girl I knew had grown into a beautiful young lady. This is what Anna Romanov must have looked like in her late teens.

She came up to me and hugged me and did the kissy thing on the cheeks. I liked her kisses from our parking days better.

She introduced her friends. The whole girls' school was atwitter about my visit. They were along to confirm that Nina knew me and that I would show up.

At first, they came across as reserved and tried to act as though they were upper-class. That pose fell apart pretty quickly as I answered their questions about my recent German experience.

They would have grilled me all evening about my exciting life if I had allowed them. Instead, I redirected them to tell me about their school. It is much easier to listen than talk if what you're listening to is interesting.

It sounded like an all-girls school is a snake pit. It also sounded like it could be a lot of fun or a nightmare, depending on where you were in the pecking order.

These girls appeared to be in the middle.

As they talked, they relaxed and came across as high school girls of their age. They were all juniors.

Nina was the most interesting to me. She held back and let the other girls talk. You could tell she was checking me out every way she could. That was fair because I was doing the same.

I wanted to know if she was the same girl I knew in California, and I think she had the same question about me.

I concluded that her personality hadn't changed. It just had a more sophisticated veneer. It was only a veneer; with a smile, the California girl would appear.

I could see her beside me in the Court of St. James, at a movie premiere, or just goofing around in jeans and a t-shirt.

We finished dinner and talked a little longer, but the girls had to get back to school. They had a curfew on Friday at eight o'clock. On Saturday, it was ten o'clock and eight again on Sunday.

That made sense if you had custody of a bunch of teenage girls and wanted to return them to their families in the same condition you received them.

Nina and I agreed to spend Saturday together. Her friends were told to butt out by Nina when they wanted to join us.

She would meet me here at the hotel in the morning.

We did meet Saturday and had a wonderful day as she gave me a tour of Zurich. We stopped for coffee and tortes, had lunch at a sidewalk bistro, and dinner at a place that served hamburgers and French fries, American style.

At the end of the day, I walked her to the gate of her school. Before we arrived, she stopped around the corner from the school and gave me a scorching kiss.

Before this, I didn't know what she considered our relationship to be. I was happy to know she wanted to take up where we had left off in California.

I asked her why here on this corner.

"I would be in so much trouble if I were seen kissing you in front of the school. Now, when you take me to the gate, we can shake hands. Of course, I will spill the beans with all the girls."

"Well, if you are going to spill the beans, let's do it right."

At that, I kissed her, starting tenderly, and worked my way up to demand. She responded but finally pushed me away.

"Wow, wow, wow, you have learned how to kiss since we were together last."

"All those movie scenes, my dear."

"I bet."

We laughed, and I escorted her to the gate, where we very formally shook hands. She spoiled it a little when she held up her hand in the British V for victory, not Churchill's V but the proper one.

Our date for the weekend was done. She had classwork she had to do on Sunday. It was also best that I headed back to Oxford. I had schoolwork of my own to do.

I told her I would call her in the middle of the week and that I would be back in several weeks.

I used the plane to fly back to England, but I wasn't certain I needed it.

The first thing I did Monday morning was to go to a flower shop and send flowers to Nina.

After classes on Monday, I received a phone call at The Meadows. It was an international phone call from Mr. Monroe, Nina's dad.

My first thought was panic!

It turned out he didn't know I had seen Nina over the weekend. He acted happy to hear it.

What he called about was that Pinewood Studios wanted to do a screen test and see if they could use me in any of their upcoming films. I agreed to do the test. It is not as though I had to study for them. He gave me a contact to call to set things up.

I had the impression that Mr. Monroe had contacted them to try to keep me in the industry. I could understand that as I was a moneymaker for his studio.

It was too late in the business day to call, so I put it off until Tuesday.

Tuesday when I called, I was put right through to a Mr. Parker. He had been told that I was a student at Oxford, so he was willing to work with me and have the screen test this coming Saturday.

Chapter 27

I got the weirdest phone call on Monday. Before I left for class, the British Foreign Office called. These are the guys who wanted to turn me over to the East Germans.

Now they wanted me to play golf with some Arab prince. He was with the House of Saud who owned all the oil in Saudi Arabia.

He had gotten it into his head that he wanted to play golf with the winner of the US Open, namely me.

I was going to turn them down flat when I was told it would be at St. Andrews. Now, who would turn down a chance to play on a course like that?

Especially since they were picking up the travel and golfing expenses.

It would be this Wednesday. I would have to cut some classes, but priorities are priorities. I had to do it for England, my duty and all that. That would be my excuse, and I would stick to it.

I asked around if anyone knew of this prince. He seemed to be a big party guy. He was attending Cambridge but spent more time in the casinos and bars of London than at school.

I just didn't see him much as a competitive golfer. I flew up to Saint Andrew's the night before. A flunky from the Foreign Office was waiting for me. He took me to a third-rate hotel for the night. I wasn't too impressed with the Foreign Office, but I suspect I wasn't high on their list of people to care for.

In the morning we met the Saudi prince who had been staying at a five-star hotel. I knew this because the FO flunky seemed to delight in telling me.

The prince was everything I expected him to be, an overweight arrogant slob. He reeked of booze and cheap perfume.

I didn't think it would be much of a match.

As we walked to the first tee, the prince told me that we would have to make a bet. He understood I drove an Aston Martin. I confirmed it.

"I will bet my Ferrari against it."

"How many strokes do you want?"

"None," he replied.

I caught the eye of the Foreign Office guy. He was shaking his head *no*.

"What's the matter? Aren't you as good of a golfer as you are supposed to be?"

This guy was pushing my buttons. I held out my hand, and we shook on the bet.

It was a typical cloudy, windy day for St. Andrews, so no course records were set. I was shooting mostly pars and the prince double bogies.

We took a break at the ninth. When we were ready to start, he said something I found curious.

"Now you have saved your honor by showing how good you are, now is the time you fall apart, and I win."

The FO guy had joined us during our break but hadn't been on the course with us. Just the prince, our caddies, and his two bodyguards.

The bodyguards had been unobtrusive all day. I even remarked upon them. The prince let me know they didn't work for him; they were employed by his uncle the king.

As long as he wasn't attacked, they didn't care what happened.

The wind had died down and I had a better feel for the greens, so my score was much better on the back nine, still no record, but respectable.

The prince, if anything, got worse. You could see him physically tire as we went. His shots were terrible. At the same time, every time we went to tee off, he asked me if this was the hole I was going to collapse on.

I didn't collapse. When we got to 18, I had a 25-stroke lead on him. As we teed off, he told me this was going to be a disgrace the way I played this. No one would believe that I had beaten him.

"I'm thinking we have a bet, and I don't want to lose my Aston Martin."

I birdied the last hole, my first of the day. The prince quit after ten strokes.

The FO guy was waiting for us. The prince stormed past him trailed by his guards. One of the guards winked at me as he went by.

"Good job," he whispered.

The FO guy asked me how much I lost by. I looked at him like he was crazy. "I beat him by over thirty strokes."

I swear the guy got pale.

"But you were supposed to lose."

"There was no way I would lose to that clown."

"But we promised him you would!"

"No one told me that. I wouldn't have played."

"Oh lord, I don't know what I'm going to tell the minister."

"Just tell him I was my usual uncooperative self. And that next time ask me upfront. Better yet, tell him there will be no next time."

The FO guy took off. I ended up having to hire a car to take me back to the airport. I was going to offer him a plane ride back to London, but he could sod off.

On Thursday, the prince's Ferrari was delivered. It looked like someone had taken a sledgehammer to it. Every metal surface and window glass was damaged. The interior was cut up with all the seat stuffing pulled out.

The control panel had been hammered in. To say it was a mess was an understatement. My first impulse was to junk it; then had a better idea. A couple of phone calls and I talked to a Ferrari dealer in London.

They agreed to pick it up and restore it completely. It would cost almost as much as a new one, but it would be worth it. I intended to have pictures taken with me in it and send them to the jerk. Petty, I know, but sometimes it is fun to be petty.

On Friday morning I had just finished breakfast after my morning routine when Mr. Hamilton informed me I had a visitor waiting in the front hall.

The young man, maybe twenty-five, was dressed in a suit and tie. He had a satchel, which he made a big deal of opening and giving me an envelope.

I had now been hand-delivered an official missive from the foreign secretary. I knew it was official from all the seals hanging from the large red envelope. That and the fact it was hand-delivered.

The messenger, a different FO flunky than the last one turned to leave. I asked him to wait one moment as I might have a reply.

He impatiently nodded his head; he had better things to do. He did wince when I ripped the end of the envelope instead of using a letter opener like any civilized person.

The letter, when you took all the bumf out of it boiled down to "some things do not need to be said, you should just know."

I told him there would be a brief reply. Mr. Hamilton, who was hovering nearby retrieved a sheet of paper and an envelope both with The Meadows letterhead, and a pen from a drawer in the table. This table had a bowl to receive calling cards, which probably hadn't happened in fifty years. I noted a letter opener in the drawer, good to know if I wanted to fake civilized.

My reply was "Since I have no idea what you are talking about, maybe it should be said." Of course, I knew he was talking about losing the car, but I wanted to be a pain about this.

Sealing it in an envelope which had The Meadows embossed on the front, I had a bright idea and ran to my room retrieving my signet ring. The ever-resourceful Mr. Hamilton came up with sealing wax. Must do things properly you know.

I wondered how long the foreign secretary and I could play this game. The prince had probably cried to Daddy who cried to the foreign secretary. I wondered if the secretary played golf and what he drove.

That was my excitement for the day. I did see the don who didn't want a known murderer in his lecture crossing the quad.

I also heard "to forgive is divine" in a sotto voice.

It wasn't me.

Friday night I went to the Dog and Crown with the guys. They wanted to know what I had been up to lately. I described the golf match at St. Andrews. They all agreed the prince was a prat.

They thought that when I had the picture taken of the repaired Ferrari I should have a pretty girl next to me. That sounded like a plan.

Saturday morning, I was up early to get my workout in before I drove to Pinewood Studios. It was an easy one-hour drive in my Aston Martin.

It was cool driving my car to where the James Bond films were produced. I wondered if anything was in production at the moment.

I daydreamed about movie parts during my drive. I had never done a real comedy or better yet a romantic comedy. That would be neat. Some nice young actress kissing me. Yes, I could go for that. Well, if she was interested, not like that one on *Maverick*.

It would be cool if Sean Connery saw me in this car. It was not to be; there was no sign of the actor my entire stay.

My name had been left at the gate, which was a small relief as it showed nothing had fallen through the cracks. It would have been terrible to arrive at the front gate and be denied.

I was shocked when I was escorted into a conference room and Susan Wallace and a young man were waiting for me.

"You looked surprised, Rick. Do you think we would let you get away with work without getting our cut?"

This was said in good humor and I took it that way. She introduced me to the young man. Not so young really, about thirty-five. Interesting how I viewed people these days from my decrepit old age of seventeen.

Edward Thomas was being interviewed to be my publicist. Susan had brought him along to see how we would relate.

I was willing to give it a try. We shook hands and chatted for a few minutes. Ed, as he called himself, had been at a large agency and wanted to get out on his own.

He was presentable as far as his looks, well, clean-shaven, hair combed, and in a suit. I sneaked a look and even his shoes were shined. He was several up on me.

I wore my Oxford blazer with a blue button-down shirt, no tie, and grey slacks, but my shoes were shined.

I asked him who he had been handling at his previous employer. He had two names that I recognized that I would call B-listers. Since I was a B-lister, and now maybe an A-minus-lister, that told me his employer thought well of him.

It turned out he had not given notice yet; he wanted to be certain of a job before giving notice. I asked him how long he would have to work after handing in his notice, and he chuckled.

"They escort you directly out of the building. They will mail your items. So, practice is to remove anything you want and then give notice."

This guy seemed pretty levelheaded to me, and I was inclined to give him a chance. Let's see how he does when the Pinewood people come in.

We didn't have to wait more than another two minutes when a party of five came in. Why five I don't know, unless we had to be outnumbered.

Introductions were made all around. Mr. Donald Butler was the lead for Pinewood.

"Sir Richard, we are pleased to meet you and welcome you to Pinewood. He also nodded to Ed and Sharon. I have been given to understand that you would be interested in doing some work while attending school at Oxford."

"I certainly would like to explore the possibility. My concern is that scheduling might not work out due to my classes."

"That would depend on the movie and the role. What sort of movie vehicle do you have in mind?"

I could feel Ed's and Susan's eyes on me as we hadn't had a chance to discuss this. I told Mr. Butler that I hadn't discussed this with Susan or Ed, so this was news to them. This was a form of apology for springing it on them.

"I have done Westerns and dramas; I think I would like to try something lighter such as a romantic comedy."

"A teen scene sort of movie, we have plans for several. They are B-Listers or even lower."

"That doesn't concern me so much. I don't have a driven desire to be a major star. I just find it fun to make movies. I love the teamwork and all the ingenuity it takes to bring one together."

"That is a different attitude than we are used to. We would want you to do some readings. Comedy depends on timing. Some people have it, some don't."

"I will be glad to try out. I think I have the timing to be funny, but that is my opinion, not the camera's."

"I'm glad you understand about the camera, Rick. Some of the funniest people I know just don't work out in front of the camera."

"When do you want me to do the readings?"

"Today if you have the time. We set it up assuming you would."

Susan cleared her throat. I turned to her and told her let's see how the readings turn out before we talk about any business. You could tell she would rather start in right away, but I figured it would be best to find out if I could do it before making demands.

We went back to a small studio set up for auditions. I found this to be a little bit funny. This was the first time in my career I had to audition for a part.

I was given several stapled sheets. They were pretty worn so you could tell they were standard audition fare. I read it through several times and figured out where the pauses in delivery were to make it funny.

It did help that these were marked Pause in Delivery. I then read them out loud several times to try out the timing. It was amazing how much difference there was if you missed it by half a second.

There was also the tone of voice used. Dropping or raising your voice wrong would throw it off. Then there was the speed of delivery, plus how loud you did it. This was a lot more complicated than I thought. Fortunately, this test just depended on a slight delay in the line.

I waved to the guys in the sound booth that I was ready. My agents and the studio executives were watching through another window.

When the green light went on, I read my lines. At the pause point, I did it. I then ran through it another three times. I think I hit the pause correctly both in time and length for each run-through.

I was then given another audition set of lines. In this one, I had to bring an element of surprise, as in, "You what?"

Now timing and voice control came into play. Also, how I appeared to the camera. I not only had to sound surprised, but I also had to appear surprised.

I was drawing a blank on how to do that when I remembered what Mary had done to me. All I had to do was give the same reaction as when she told me she was expecting a finder's fee when she found my car keys, which I had left on the kitchen counter at Jackson House.

The memory brought a smile to my face as I read through the lines. The lines were simple, so I memorized them and then did the shot.

I had to repeat it three times.

After that, we took a lunch break while the film was developed. After lunch, we went into a small theater and watched my audition. I thought it went well but then I did have a bias. My people said good words, but the ones that counted were from the Pinewood people.

Chapter 28

It didn't take long to get the studio's reaction.

"Rick, I think we have a winner. The camera likes you. Considering it was your first run-through of that material, you did an amazing job. The fact that you did the second shot without having paper in your hands is a real plus. You will be easy to work with."

I thanked him and then said, "Ed, it is your turn. Don't give the farm away but I would like to do this. The important thing here is that any shooting schedule allows for my classes."

"Do you have any financial goals in mind?"

"Nope, I don't care. I just want the fun of making a movie."

I think Don Butler had such a coughing fit I thought he was going to choke on his cigarette.

When he finished, he was speaking so fast he was almost stuttering.

"You don't care about money? Who are you?"

"An extremely rich young man who can afford to do what he wants in life. That doesn't mean you can insult my intelligence, but money isn't number one."

At that, I left the room to allow Ed, with Susan's oversight, to work his magic. I was given a tour of the studio while they discussed what I may do for them and how I would be paid. I bet Ed was frustrated right now as I had pretty much tied his hands.

I was impressed with the studio. It was not as big as Warner Brothers, but it had everything you would expect in a studio. I spent time in the stunt yard.

They had a nice archery range, so I asked if I could shoot some. They set me up, and while I was rusty, it was not as bad as I thought. I collected an audience before I finished. They all seemed to know of me.

Before I could start to answer some of the questions that were being thrown out, a runner hunted me and my guide down.

When I got back to the conference room, it was to smiles all around. Maybe my name with Ed wasn't going to be Mudd.

What they had decided was that I was to be paid straight scale and a signing bonus based on my role in any film I appeared in. Any scenes would be scheduled around my schooling.

A surprise was the new image they wanted to craft. In any movie, I was to be well-dressed, well-spoken, and well-off. I wasn't to be a clown, though funny events could happen.

Depending on the role, I might get the girl or be the one that was wrong for her. Even if I wasn't the right one, I was always to be a gentleman. Sort of a young Cary Grant, I guess.

This was much better than I thought I would get. I dreaded the thought of doing slapstick like Jerry Lewis. He was the master at it, but it wasn't my bottle of Coke.

I was given a script to take with me to see if I was interested in the part. It would have to be pretty bad before I said no.

Outside, I apologized to Ed for blindsiding him on the money issue. He took it well. Based on that and the way he handled himself, I told Susan I would like to give him a chance. Would she see about getting a contract set up? I know fox and henhouse, but she had earned my trust.

People were waiting by my car. They were very disappointed that it wasn't Sean Connery's. I headed back to Oxford. I felt the day had gone well.

Sunday was a quiet day. I ran a few extra miles. After my East German experience, I wasn't going to let it slide.

While I ran, I gave some thought to how far I had come in life. For some reason, my mind got stuck on my tryout for the play in high school. The teacher told me to forget about it.

I wonder what she thought now. There was the girl who dumped me because I didn't get the lead. I couldn't even think of her name at the moment.

I spent the afternoon reading up on what my next lectures would be about. I had gotten behind with my prisoner exchange adventure but was now back on track.

Monday was a normal day up until lunchtime. I went to my usual lunch place, a small restaurant on campus. I usually sat at a table in the corner by the kitchen; it was almost always the last one taken.

Today it was taken. I had to do a second look at the person sitting there. The last time I had seen her was behind the counter at a Chinese laundry in Los Angeles.

She gave me a small wave, so I joined her. I had never been given a name, and it wasn't offered now. That saved her from having to tell me a lie.

"This is a surprise. What can I do for the government of China today?"

It didn't take a great intellect to figure out she wasn't here for a vacation or that the Chinese government would be doing anything for me. I may have been wrong on the last thought.

"Rick, always straight to the point. You wouldn't do well in business in China."

"I seem to be doing okay. I see the reports on the Chinese, Indonesian, and Australian exchanges."

"True, but we have to hide you as you are too blunt for our businesspeople."

I had to laugh at that. "Point to you. I don't have a lot of patience for small talk."

"That's why we like you, this is too serious for small talk. We need your help largely."

"What sort of help?"

"China is facing a great famine, and we have to import food, or our people will starve. We can't let it be known on the world stage or the government will lose face."

"If I understand, the government will let people starve rather than lose face."

"Sadly, that is the way it must be."

"What can I do?"

"We need to import as much rice and wheat as we can using your connections. We would like to pay in the same way, so we are not seen to be buying on the world market."

"I do know that the rubber market worldwide is getting to be saturated, so we would have to introduce something else into the mix."

"Rick, we also know this. We would like to use gold and rare earth ores."

"Gold, I understand; the market for rare earths not so much."

"They will be needed for advanced transistors and what are being called chips, which are many transistors on a single chip of silicon. We know Texas Instruments and Bell Laboratories are already looking for new sources of those materials."

"I will have to talk to my company and the heads of my governments."

"Ah yes, you are a dual citizen. It can be hard having two masters."

"Not so far, but you never know. I would have hated being caught between the British and the US over the Suez Canal."

She gave me a funny look.

"That has to have been the most egotistical remark I have ever heard a young man of your age ever make, except you probably would have been involved."

Talk about shot down in flames; at least she let me eject.

"Please make this a priority; many lives depend on it."

"I will act today."

"I will be back here each day until I hear from you."

At that, she left.

I went back to The Meadows as fast as I could. The first phone call I made was to Mum and Dad. It was still early morning there, so I caught both at home.

When they were both on the line, I explained the situation. They agreed that we should try to help but that the British and US governments should be made aware and express support upfront. Also, I should start at the top. So much for dumping the problem on my parents.

We talked a little bit more. I told them about Pinewood Studios and their plans for me. They were both excited about the fact that Pinewood wanted to keep my image "upscale".

They thought it neat that I used Mary's "Do I get a finder's fee?" as my inspiration for my audition. I found out that she did get a finder's fee for bringing Buster Brown shoes into her line of products. She would end up worth more than all of us.

After talking to my parents, I called the palace and asked for the queen. I wasn't put directly through. A secretary asked what I needed her for. I explained it was for guidance from the head of state on whom to approach within the government with an international situation.

That put the cat amongst the pigeons. Elizabeth was on the phone in minutes. I gave her a quick rundown of the situation. She thanked me and told me not to contact anyone else in the government. She would be able to use this to the Crown's advantage.

I hung up just now realizing that the thousand years of tension between the Crown and government had not gone away, just underground.

Next, I called the White House. Ike wasn't available and I had to explain to his chief of staff the reason for the call. Again, this caught immediate attention.

I wondered what was going on that mention of China and famine were magic words today. I even asked the chief of staff why it was so important. He reminded me that the Four Horsemen of the Apocalypse rode together. Famine was next to War and Pestilence, and they all rode with Death.

If you wanted a war, have a famine, especially since they knew the Soviets were having their hard times and buying wheat on the international market.

When Ike was on the phone, I explained the whole problem and solution as explained to me.

"Rick, you did the right thing in calling us in on this. I need to talk to my staff, but I think keeping this quiet is the right thing to do. The War Hawks would love to use this as an excuse for a foreign adventure."

I didn't ask, but I had to find out who the War Hawks were. Later I found out that they were the same people as the military-industrial complex that the president had warned the nation about. They wanted war, as they made money from it.

It reminded me of the book I had read, *The Merchants of Death*.

I spent the rest of the morning on the phone with Jim Williamson. He would be my contact for this project within Jackson Enterprises. His first duty was to have our shipping people find as many dry bottom ships as they could.

He was also to invest in the Baltic Dry Index fund as the rates were about to rocket upwards.

We would be shipping wheat from the US and Canada through Canadian ports. They were already handling wheat for Russia so it should go out without creating a lot of notice.

Rice would go from Australia, Indonesia, and the Philippines, using the Australian-Indonesian connection we already had.

Incoming ores would be smelted in Australia but sold on the US commodities market. This was to avoid upsetting the Australian market from a huge influx. That was a shame as we could have sold short on prices going down. Oh well, a million here, a million there. Jackson, you ass.

This all went down before lunchtime, so I was able to meet the Lady from China, as I thought of her, at the small restaurant.

When I told her the results of my calls, she heaved a visible sigh of relief.

"There were calls for war in Peking or the more proper Beijing."

"Who would they declare war on to get food?"

"Not to get food, my young friend, to distract the people. They were debating having the North Koreans invade South Korea or fighting the Soviets by invading Siberia. Supporting the Vietnamese against the French was also a possibility. If one wants war, there are many ways. Even Tibet and India were discussed."

She seemed to know a lot about the inner workings of the Chinese Communist Party.

She asked me to meet her here in two days for more details on my proposal. Her words, not mine. I felt that I was but a mere messenger in this mess.

After lunch, I attended a lecture on World Politics. Our lecturer assured us we were in an unprecedented time of peace. There were no possibilities of war anywhere in the world.

Amazing, and I was paying to learn this.

I heard back from the British government, as opposed to the Crown. It was the foreign secretary himself, the one who wanted to give me to the Stasi and lose my car to a Saudi prince.

He acted as though butter wouldn't melt in his mouth as he informed me that Her Majesty's government approved of my plans to feed the Chinese people.

I shouldn't have but told him I was glad to help, though it would have been hard to help from an East German prison. He ignored that comment. I guess I wasn't cut out to be a diplomat.

He did make one comment that showed a crack in his diplomatic armor.

"Sir Richard, I didn't know you had such a close connection with Her Majesty."

"She is my godmother, for what it is worth."

"I see, that explains the call we received. She was not pleased with us for not knowing about the Chinese problem and our opportunity to open relations. She suggested we use your contact."

"I will explore that."

"No, you will introduce our people, and we will take it from there."

Ah, here appears the foreign secretary I have grown to know and love.

"I respectfully decline."

"Now see here young man."

"Good day," I said and hung up. Interesting, I wonder when I would be deported.

To be safe, I called the palace and explained to the person who took calls for the queen how I was on the outs with the foreign secretary.

"Brilliant, he will now overstep his bounds, and we will have him."

Not wanting to be a part of whatever that was about, I gave my farewells and got off the line.

I wonder if it had anything to do with the sudden resignation of the foreign secretary for reasons of health the next day.

When asked, the queen replied that she saw no reason to dissolve the government at this time. Talk about a warning shot!

I woke up the next day worrying about China and feeding all those people. When I came down for breakfast, I had a surprise waiting. It was my eighteenth birthday today. The staff was all there to give me best wishes. My parents called along with my brothers and sister.

I was told my present was waiting for me at the airport, a brand-new Cessna in Jackson colors. There was a cake with candles. I blew them all out. My secret wish was that the Chinese wouldn't starve. I wonder what I will be wishing for when I am fifty.

Chapter 29

The next day The Lady from China met me and told me the peace portion of the Politburo was very pleased and wanted to proceed as outlined.

The War Hawks, as she called them, not so much, but they had to go along with it. What upset them was the military budget would be cut to feed the people.

What an ugly place was behind the scenes of our world, which had no possibility of war.

I told her the foundations had been laid and that all they had to do was inform Jackson Enterprises in Australia what they needed, and we would tell them the cost and delivery dates.

It seemed strange that I was going to make money by helping to stave off this disaster, but it is what it is. I made a mental note to donate money to some international relief fund. First, I had to know if the funds would make it where they needed to go. I didn't want to support a corrupt regime.

On Friday I received a formal letter from Buckingham Palace. I thought it might have something to do with the China situation.

I couldn't have been more wrong. There was to be a charity ball sponsored by Prince Phillip. My services were required as an escort. I would be escorting a Lady Pamela Norfolk, daughter of the Duke of Suttonham. It contained the contact details. I was to call her with a formal invitation and work out the details for attending the ball, which would be held at Windsor Castle.

Rather than put it off, I made the call since I had little choice in the matter. I suppose I could flee the country.

When I talked to her, she seemed disinterested in the whole process. She gave me my orders: I was to pick her up on the day in question, the following Saturday, in a hired Bentley. I was to be wearing a white tie and accessories.

The way she gave me my orders was as if I had no idea of what was proper. I could tell I would like this girl.

Just to spite her I wouldn't hire a Bentley; I would borrow Grandmum's. When I talked to my grandmother, she told me she had heard about this duke; she couldn't remember much, but she would make some phone calls to see what she could learn about the family.

That was before I left for school in the morning. When I got back in the afternoon, she had some information.

"The Duke of Suttonham has had quite a life. He is my age. He got married late in life. He was a rotter when he was young. Gambling, booze, wild women; you name it, and he did it. He went into the army in the War and had a spectacular career including the Victoria Cross."

"He came out a changed man. He worked hard to settle his debts and those his father had left him. When he was about fifty, he met the love of his life, Matilda. They had a daughter, the Pamela you are escorting to the ball.

"Tragedy hit the family when Matilda died in a car crash, another driver's fault. It devastated the duke, but he kept on raising young Pamela.

"He supervised his estates but then another disaster hit. A fund he was heavily invested in collapsed, and he lost everything.

"He didn't give up and is still working to pay everything off; unfortunately, he has loans coming due at the end of the year.

"This is where it gets really bad. His English estates are entailed and can only be inherited by a male. His father had borrowed on them to the hilt and no further monies were available.

"He has property in Spain, but it has tax liens on it and the Spanish government will not let him sell the property until the liens are paid. No one will loan him money on the property as they feel the government is trying to steal the property from him."

"Wow, Grandmum, you must have done a lot of digging."

"Not really, this is very common knowledge. So common the bookies in London are betting two to one that he will commit suicide before the end of the year."

"Why would he do that?"

"The English entailed property would go to some distant male relative, who I don't know, so Pamela would be relieved of that debt. He is known to have a long-standing insurance policy that will pay off even for suicide."

"This would give Pamela enough money to pay off the liens and sell the Spanish property, leaving enough to live a middle-class life without having to work."

"Why wouldn't she work?"

"She has been raised as a lady of the upper class. She would have no idea on how to do anything other than watercolors and serve tea."

"She could learn."

"Yes, she could, but she has been raised with no money and no mother. The only thing she has is the protection of her class. "She will be a total snob because that is all she has to define her."

Talk about a tough situation, and here I thought it would be all roses and chocolates for someone in her position.

A thought crossed my mind.

"Grandmum, who did you call?"

"Mary."

I knew this was not my sister Mary, but the Queen Mum. That answer consolidated my thoughts. This man had earned a Victoria Cross, and he was working hard to do the right thing, even if it cost him his life.

Then the Palace had sent an invitation for me to escort his daughter. I can take a hint.

I made a phone call of my own to the Palace and asked for the number of the Duke of Suttonham. They readily had it available for me, so readily I wondered if my call was expected.

It wasn't the same number as the one for Pamela. I guess hard-up doesn't mean only one phone line in the castle.

The duke was brought to the line. I introduced myself and asked if I could have an appointment tomorrow. We set it for 10 a.m., I asked that Pamela did not know I would be there, or that I was even there.

He asked why, and I told him that I didn't want anything to influence our going to the ball. He agreed, though acted puzzled. He should have been. I still wasn't sure if my idea would work.

On Saturday I was at his house on time. His house was remarkably similar to Ludlow Castle. In other words, it was not a house at all but a fortress that could be lived in.

It was a mammoth building on over a thousand acres of the beautiful English countryside. I could see why he fought to retain it.

He welcomed me with a solemn reserve. I didn't blame him. I hoped I had read everything correctly.

He was a ramrod-straight, thin man with iron-grey hair. He looked to be in his early seventies, which would be right since he was fifty when he had his daughter.

His looks were those of a colonel of the infantry, which he had been. I could see him charging tanks, which he had done during the War. I would have to look up his citation for the Victoria Cross.

After we settled down in a reception room that had probably seen Henry VIII, and a coffee order placed, he asked: "What can I do for you, Sir Richard?"

"I think it is what I can do for you."

"Let me tell you what I think has happened. You have some very powerful people who wish you well, but they cannot be seen to be involved."

"I don't understand."

"Let me share with you what I think I know about your situation."

I then proceeded to tell him everything my Grandmum had told me."

"That is all true, but I don't see your part in this."

"I'm about to make you a very large loan with no conditions."

You could see the hope flair in his eyes, then die.

"You can't have that much money."

"I have enough."

"It would take over ten million pounds to settle my problems."

"I have that."

"A child of your age."

"If it were a hundred million pounds, I have it."

"Unbelievable."

"Bear with me and assume I have it. You can check with my banker after you hear me out."

"All right, but this is mind-blowing."

"I would like to loan the money to pay off the liens the Spanish government has on your properties. As soon as the liens are settled you sell me the properties for enough to settle your encumbered debt.

"The sale price of the Spanish properties will cover the debt and leave operating money for the next five years. That should be enough time to get things completely turned around."

"Why would you do such a thing? The Spanish properties aren't worth that much. Nine million at the most."

"To put it simply, I could use the tax loss and it helps me support people who I admire greatly."

"Who is that?"

"I received an invitation to escort your daughter Pamela to a ball. It came from the Palace. When I called your daughter, she wasn't rude, she was dismissive."

He looked uncomfortable at that statement.

"I decided to find out what I was getting into. When I asked my Grandmum to borrow her Bentley, she wanted all the details. She then called Queen Mary and asked about you.

"Queen Mary gave her all the information, but she emphasized your Victoria Cross and how you turned your life around despite tragedy.

"I think I can take a hint the Royal family knew how I would react to this, so they started the process by sending the invitation, which was a royal command."

"I know about those," he grumped.

I wonder what ones he had received.

"Frankly, I wasn't impressed with my interaction with your daughter. I understand her position in society is all that she has, but I felt like a piece of furniture being moved around. I don't want her to have a sudden change and think of me as the one with money who will solve all her problems.

"You don't appear to know anything about my background, but I am a relatively famous actor and have had many unpleasant experiences with women. I don't care for another."

"Now I have to do my homework. Would I know of any of your movies?"

"*Sir Nickalous, Bandits of Sherwood*, and most recently, *Over the Ohio.*

"You're that Richard Jackson?"

"Yes, Your Grace."

"This is richer than you know. Pamela thinks you are some puffed-up knight pulled in for duty at the ball. She has one of your movie posters in her bedroom."

"Let's surprise her."

"I'm going to love this. You are right about her attitude, but with so much going wrong in our lives, I haven't had the heart to try to change her.

"Now, Sir Richard, this is awkward, but may we place a call to my bank?"

I gave him the bank's and my personal banker's name. It was Saturday, but the number I had given was supposed to be manned every day at all hours.

In short order, he was talking to my banker, who was at his home. When the duke identified himself and told him the amounts requested, I had to get on the line and give the codes to prove I wasn't under duress.

The duke was told that I could write a personal check for that amount. The duke, as an afterthought, asked if I was good for a hundred million. He was told it would take time, but they would advance me up to one billion pounds.

When the Duke told me that, it was the first time I knew I was in the billionaire ranks. There were very few of us in the world.

"No wonder the Crown wasn't afraid to ask you to help with my problems."

I was a little bit in shock still about being a billionaire. I did write him a personal check for one million pounds to take care of the property lien in Spain. We both then made nice, and I left as his daughter was expected in at any time.

His parting words in the driveway, were, "Are you certain I can't marry you off?"

Since he was smiling, I just shook my head and left as quickly as I could.

On the way home I wondered about where my new properties in Spain were. When time permitted, I would have to check them out.

When I got home, I shared all with Grandmum. She asked if she could update Queen Mary. I saw no reason why not.

After dinner, she gave the results of her phone call with Queen Mum. I was in good order at the Palace, not for what I had given, but for being able to take a hint.

Then Grandmum about floored me.

"Mary told me he is a very nice-looking chap and that I should meet him."

Grandmum! Too much information!

On Sunday I made my weekly call back to Jackson House. All was well. I told Mum about the duke and his daughter and what I had done.

"Rick, that is the sort of thing you will be expected to do from behind the scenes going forward. We are loyal to the Crown and the Crown is loyal to us."

"Will it always cost me a bunch of money?"

"No, sometimes it will bring you a bunch of money. For example, this trade deal with China could result in you having almost a monopoly between the UK and China. That would be worth many millions."

"Don't get me wrong, I just want to know what I've gotten into."

"It will be fine."

"What about Grandmum and the duke?"

"She deserves some fun in life. Just like your dad and me."

Mum! Too much information!

The kids were all fine. After the call, I went for my second run of the day. I had to clear some pictures out of my head.

Chapter 30

Monday was a school day like any other. I had settled into attending the lectures, doing my readings, and working with tutors.

Everywhere I went on the Oxford campus, I was accompanied by at least one of the many military personnel. One thing had changed; they now wore their uniforms. Before, they tried to hide in the crowd.

It was enjoyable walking with them. I learned about the different branches of services in many countries. I got insights into the cultures of the same countries.

Most of all, it was fun and relaxing to talk to my peer group. We would have lunch together. It was an ever-changing group, so we all got to know each other. I wondered how that would work out in years to come as these students gained in rank and had international duties.

The contacts made here would pay off in many ways. Very much like the rest of the students attending a prestigious school.

On Tuesday, I received by messenger two scripts from Pinewood Studios. Both were romantic comedies. We called them Rom-Coms.

The first, with a working name of *Edgware*, takes place in an upscale neighborhood on the north side of London.

James Fletcher, the owner of a dilapidated bookstore, looks up as the bell on the door rings one day and the most famous movie actress in the world walks in.

I'm proposed for the role of James Fletcher if I'm interested. The actress hadn't been cast at this time.

She is in Edgware, as a movie is going to be filmed there. During her downtime, she enjoys browsing through eclectic bookstores. She and James take a look at each other and there is obvious interest on both sides, but nothing happens at that point.

Later the same day in a tea shop next door, they run into each other again. Run into each other, he spilling his tea all over her. It is summertime, and she is lightly dressed in a polo-type shirt and jeans.

Since he got her wet, he invites her to clean up in his room above his shop which is just next door. They continue their interest in each other, and on impulse, she kisses him as she leaves.

He is stunned as she walks out.

Two days later she walks back into his store and a relationship is started. All scenes meet the censor's requirements, including one of them keeping one foot on the floor if they are in bed together.

Since she is so famous, the news people are all over their relationship. It is a lot for James to handle. Some people may not buy into this part of the script, but I had lived through it with Judy King. I wonder how she is these days.

Anyway, the famous actress finishes up her movie and goes back to Hollywood, and James resumes his reclusive bookstore life. That is, until one day the famous actress walks back into the store and they immediately hug and kiss. Happy ending.

The other script didn't even have a working name assigned. It features me as a very young prime minister of England. A serving maid is new to the office at 10 Downing.

She is very pretty, of course, and has been chosen for her intelligence and flair for languages. She serves tea for high-level visitors, among other things.

There is a growing attraction, always growing, all these attractions, between the two. A visiting US president tries to bully the prime minister into yielding on various policies. The PM is about to do so when he walks in on the president making some very untoward advances against the maid.

In a speech the next day, he takes a very firm stand against the president's policies, which gains him enormous favor with the British Public and the young lady.

The president leaves in a huff.

The young lady thinks she has to leave her job. I don't quite understand why. She leaves him a note on Christmas Eve.

The PM gets the note and immediately sets out to find the young lady at her parent's house. He knows the street name but not the house number.

Comedic scenes of people answering their door to the prime minister ensue. He finally finds the right house.

The whole family is going to a Christmas play at their children's school. The PM and maid end up backstage and kiss, just to have the curtain open.

He teaches her on the spot how to do the queen's wave and grin and bear it. Happily-ever-after ending. The only part of the script I worried about was where I had to do a dance scene coming down a set of stairs.

Both scripts sounded interesting, and I called my agents and told them to proceed with negotiations.

I called Nina in Switzerland just to talk. We were on the line for a long time. She wanted to know all the details of the two movie scripts. I did tell her I had to be an escort at a formal ball on Saturday, so I couldn't fly over.

That started an inquisition about who I was escorting. I told her about being given my marching orders. I didn't think she needed to know that she was a pretty young lady who was a fan of the actor Ricky Jackson.

I had learned this from Dad when he described interactions with other women to Mum. They just didn't need to know irrelevant details which could cause unwarranted stress. Especially to the male.

Oxford has a bus line and like most buses, they have huge advertisements on their sides. You can imagine my surprise when I saw one with a picture of my sister Mary, extolling her latest clothing line.

I wonder if I have had my picture on a bus. I have never seen it, if so. No, I wasn't jealous, just worried that the little kid might get overexposed.

Well, maybe a little.

On Thursday I met the duke, his lawyers, and my lawyers at my bank as soon as the bank opened.

Altogether it was going to take seven people to put this deal together. Extra lawyers were needed because of their knowledge of Spanish and British property law.

There was also a Spanish law firm specializing in property on standby for a phone call in Madrid.

The duke greeted me as though I was his long-lost son. Well, he nodded to me as he said, "Sir Richard."

I think that was as demonstrative as he ever got. He and Bob back at the ranch would have got along just fine.

I asked him why the Spanish government was holding so hard onto the property liens.

"It's the land value, Sir Richard; whoever owns it stands to make a fortune."

"Is there a gold mine to be developed?"

"Better yet, two major highways meet on a corner of the land and the area has not been developed."

"You mean this is all over a truck stop?"

"You Americans are so blunt, but in a word, yes. I had hoped to develop it to recoup my fortune. I got behind on the taxes, and the wolves started to circle. They paid off someone in the tax department, so I'm not allowed any extensions or settlements.

"Furthermore, no Spanish bank will lend money against the land. The only offer is from the people who want it cheap; they are offering shillings on the pound."

The lead lawyer recapped what we were to accomplish today.

First, I, Sir Richard, would loan the duke the funds to pay off his tax liens. These funds were to be transferred immediately to the law firm in Spain, which was standing by to receive a cashier's check from the duke. They would immediately go to the tax office and pay off all money owed.

This started the ball rolling. It took an hour for that to take place. Once that occurred, the second step started.

The duke sold the land and all buildings to Jackson Enterprises, free and clear. I wrote a check for twelve million pounds. The duke thought it was to be for eleven, ten for the land to pay off his English debts and an additional million for operating capital.

When he inquired why I was paying more than I was asked, I replied that girls were expensive to raise. I think I became a legend in banking and legal circles at that statement.

"Besides, I think our mutual friends would think it was the right thing to do."

My check was immediately deposited in the duke's account, where he then wrote a series of checks to clear his debts.

The duke was not a demonstrative man, so I said nothing about the tears running down his cheeks. The lawyers were so busy with their arcane paperwork that I don't think they noticed.

I was now a landholder in Spain. Did that make me a Grandee? I doubted it; I wasn't even sure what that was.

The duke handed me a folio of pictures taken of what I had just bought sight unseen. The first ones were of two major roads intersecting with the new style of cloverleaves.

I had to give some thought to what to do about that. One thing for certain, the guys trying to buy it now didn't have a snowball's chance.

Other pictures were of a hacienda and outbuildings. It was stupendous. I could see how the package was worth the money.

There were a thousand hectares or almost twenty-five hundred acres. That was large by any standard.

The land was used mostly for cattle grazing. I could play cowboy there all I wanted!

After all was wrapped up, the banker brought out a bottle of champagne and we had a toast to the successes of the day. Everyone but me made a direct profit on the day, and I suspected if I were patient and investigated things, I could also.

The duke and I had a short conversation about the ball and my picking up Pamela on Friday. He still wanted to surprise her, and I agreed to go along with it.

"Sir Richard, my title and estates are one of the few peerages that the daughter may inherit. Thank goodness I only have the one or we would have the abeyance situation."

"I have heard of it but don't understand."

"Male inheritance is through the oldest. If there are only daughters, they have equal rights to the title, but the title can only be awarded if the claimants agree on one of them having the title, and there can be no coercion."

"That sounds like the beginning of a murder mystery."

"I've not heard of it happening, but it could. However, a motive like that would lead to the surviving sister. Anyway, what I want to share is that I'm going to accelerate Pamela's estate management education, and I don't think she will be seeing anyone for some time to come."

"I understand, Your Grace."

I understand that I may have dodged a bullet. How do you tell a father you feel no attraction for his daughter? As a matter of fact, you are slightly repelled by her.

We finished up the transactions. I was determined to get to Spain before the year's end to see what I had just bought.

Saturday came quicker than I wished. I dressed up in my best white tie outfit. Mr. Hamilton fussed over me until I wanted to scream. Then Grand Mum had her turn. I think she polished every one of my miniature medals.

I must say, when I looked in the mirror with a topcoat, white tie, medals, top hat, and cane, I did look spiffy. With strict orders from Mum, the camera came out to record my appearance for posterity.

At least I wouldn't have pictures of Pamela and me. I thought that until I saw Mr. Hamilton putting a camera bag in the front seat next to him.

He was dressed in a full chauffeur rig for the drive.

When we arrived at the duke's estate, I found out what the rich do for pictures. They hire a professional photographer.

Pamela looked very nice in her ballgown. I suspect this was the first and only time she would ever wear it.

As soon as she came into sight, the two photographers and Mr. Hamilton started snapping away.

They both caught her look when she recognized me as Ricky Jackson the actor. Young duchesses do not squeal, but it sure sounded like it.

"Why didn't you tell me you're Ricky Jackson? I thought you were some stuffy knight, Sir Richard."

"You didn't ask."

This was my way of reminding her how she had treated me. Alas, she hadn't learned.

"I see you hired a Bentley as I ordered."

"Yes, Your Ladyship."

"Where is my corsage?"

"You didn't tell me to purchase one."

In the military, this was called dumb disobedience and frowned upon. She didn't have experience with this, so she was a little flustered but moved on.

We posed for pictures. Mr. Hamilton was very helpful in adjusting her gown, so it fell right. Pamela informed me that I should tip him well. Behind her back, he rolled his eyes but then held out his hand.

I just about lost it but kept a straight face.

"I will do that, Your Ladyship, if he serves well for the rest of the evening. Now it was his turn to keep a straight face.

While this byplay was going on, the duke was watching, and I could tell he didn't like his daughter to be mocked, even if she deserved it.

Discretion being the better part of valor, I got us into the Bentley and moved on.

The ball went as I expected. At least I had a better understanding of why she was like she was. This didn't mean I liked her, just understood her. For only one evening, I could put up with this.

She introduced me to her friends as Ricky Jackson, the actor. It was done in such a way as though I were a party favor.

The icing on the cake was when one of her friends asked if she would be dating me. Her reply was priceless.

"He is a sweet boy and certainly good-looking, but I think I want a husband with real money. Having to pinch and scrape is such a bore."

No, living off the extra board in Bellefontaine, Ohio is pinching and scraping. Then I amended that thought; deliberately getting detention after school to stay warm and dry is pinching and scraping.

On the ride back to the castle we were prim and proper. She did ask who the car was hired from. They certainly took care of their vehicles. I told the truth that it was borrowed from my grandmum.

She wanted to know her title.

"None that I know of; she was in service as a young lady."

Oh, and that killed that line of questioning. I did think about telling her that she was a drinking pal of Queen Mary but let it go.

When I dropped her off, she kissed me on the cheek and murmured, "It is a shame you are only a knight and an actor. If you were rich and titled, you would be very interesting."

Silence is a good tactic. On the way home, I thought about her and her life. Being a noble didn't necessarily mean that life was a bowl of cherries.

In Lady Pamela's case, I thought she was all fur and no knickers.

Chapter 31

Sunday was an easy day. Easy in the sense I had nowhere to go and nothing in particular to do. After my morning workout and breakfast, Grandmum inquired about my date last night.

I tried to convince her that it wasn't a date but a duty being performed. She didn't see it like that. When she saw that I hadn't any interest in Pamela, she changed her line of questioning.

Was the duke there when I picked Pamela up? What did he have to say? How was he dressed? The more she talked about the duke, the more concerned I got. Did Grandmum have her sights set on being a duchess?

I wouldn't be surprised if her new best friend hadn't put her up to it.

When I made my Sunday call home, it was almost a repeat of my conversation with Grandmum, except it was Mum doing the grilling. Dad didn't even get on the line. I knew he was a smart man.

Eddie updated me on his Scouting. He had just made First Class and already had enough merit badges for Star. He just needed his time in grade. He loved the camping part.

He related how he was allowed to go on a snipe hunt, but they didn't have any luck. I told him maybe next time; don't give up.

Denny was excited as he had just got his learner's permit and was taking driving lessons at school. How fast they grow up.

I spent the rest of the day reading ahead for my classes. I was holding my own. The end-of-term exams would tell me if I was doing okay. From the difficulty of the work, I thought I would end up with high marks.

Monday was a normal school day, for whatever normal was anymore. I attended all my lectures, accompanied by my military escorts.

In the evening I had a phone call, I was to attend a meeting of the queen's Messengers at Buck House on Tuesday. Darn, I would have to cut classes again.

This was to be all the Messengers in the country, both those who worked for Her Majesty and those who carried diplomatic pouches for the government.

This type of summons hadn't occurred since I was involved, so I was very curious. I drove down to London as it was a nice day, and there was no hurry.

There were about fifty messengers there. I noticed that a few families were present. What got my attention was that my family was there. What was going on?

They were seated in a separate area, and the meeting was about to start, so I couldn't go over to them.

Mr. Norman took the stage and started things moving. He began with several banal announcements. Such things as one drink with dinner is acceptable on the expense account, but a dozen won't be reimbursed. Wow, that is some heavy drinking.

The next was more interesting. Due to an incident where a Messenger had come into physical danger, it was felt that more protection had to be given to each Messenger.

All Messengers were to become members of the armed force's active reserve. Those who had previous military units would go back into those units at their highest rank. This was most of the Messengers present.

It was felt if each were a member of the military, foreign interests would think twice about causing trouble.

I wondered what would happen to me, as the RAF had disowned me.

The queen entered the room, and all rose. This was the start of an awards presentation ceremony. The Messengers weren't brought together very often, so they were taking advantage of this gathering.

I was the fifth person called to the front for an award. Families joined the awardees on stage. That explained the presence of mine.

I was awarded the Queen's Commendation for Brave Conduct. This was considered a minor award for both military and civilian use. The citation spoke of my being forced down in East Germany and escaping to the West.

It sounded like the award was a stick in the eye of the Communists, rather than for my actions. All I did was run and fight as forced. It wasn't as though I made any brave decisions and followed through at danger to myself.

The queen had an additional announcement.

"Sir Richard is in an odd position. He is very young for what he is doing. As a Senior Queen's Messenger, he is the equivalent rank of Colonel in the armed forces."

"The RAF does not need his services, so he is currently the odd man out. Fortunately, Coldstream Regiment has agreed to carry him on their rolls, though he will not be an active officer in the regiment.

"As we all know, young men will get up to mischief if they are left on their own, so I have appointed him as an aide-de-camp to the commander-in-chief.

"He will be robbing dogs for me."

This brought laughter from the crowd. In the US this would be called a gofer.

My thoughts were centered around the fact I would need a whole new military wardrobe.

My mum had pinned my new award on my suitcoat. I would have to look up how it was to be worn.

It was great to see the family. The queen graciously stayed for a while and greeted people. When Mary was presented, she told her that she needed to stop and see Princess Ann, as the princess had some clothing questions for her.

Mary never blinked an eye as she replied, "My pleasure, Your Majesty. Could this result in a Royal Warrant as a Purveyor to the Crown?"

Even the queen was startled by this request. Who had put Mary up to this?

"It might be possible, but as a mother, I will have final approval of any clothing. As to a warrant, we will see."

I translated this as a Mum's maybe, which meant no way. I was proven wrong after Princess Ann chose outfits that were designed and manufactured in England by a new division of the company that made the clothing in Mary's collection.

As to where she got the request, it was from the manufacturing company. They and Mary were going to make a mint. I saw their building on Carnaby Street. It had a very modern storefront.

I had to laugh, as they featured those funny-looking trousers that Denny and Eddie wore in that fashion shoot.

Later, a general from Coldstream approached me and introduced himself. He informed me that I would have to attend an orientation on being an officer in Coldstream.

This was a proud regiment, Second to None, and there would be no mucking around with their reputation. I had the feeling there had been some arm-twisting to find me a home in the military.

As a reserve officer, I would have no active duty, and if called up, I would directly serve the queen. I privately sighed in relief; I could not picture myself in a bearskin hat standing guard in front of Buckingham Palace.

I would probably crack up when the tourists got up to their antics. That or clobber one of them.

The general did say, "Good show," on my escape from the Communists, so I wasn't to be a leper, I think.

After the ceremony, Mum, Dad, and the kids bundled into a Bentley and followed me back to The Meadows. Grandmum hadn't come down to London for the presentation.

She had her good days and her bad days. This must have been a bad one because I knew she loved the pomp and circumstance that surrounded any royal event.

It was fun the next few days having my family nearby. I still had to go to classes, but the evenings were nice. Mum and Dad went to London one evening to see a play.

They were going to stay for Guy Fawkes fireworks on Saturday and head home on Monday.

I had a date in Switzerland on Saturday night but at Dad's suggestion, I called her and asked if she wanted to come to England and spend the weekend with us.

She jumped at the idea. I would fly over and pick her up on Friday and return her on Sunday.

All went well until the fireworks. Mum had used some influence to get us a box on the Thames to watch the huge London show.

Somewhere during the display, Mary disappeared. We thought she had gotten lost in the crowd, and we knew she was smart enough to let a bobbie know that she had been separated from her family.

As a group, we went to the nearest policeman to report her missing. I would certainly tease her when she was returned to us.

As we were walking along, a man grabbed me by the shoulder and handed me a note, then disappeared into the crowd.

The note said, "We have your sister. Do not tell anyone. Bring one person with you at 8 a.m. tomorrow to the Glienicke Bridge. We will free her in exchange for you."

I started to panic and then thought, this is Mary. You have to do this.

I turned to Nina, "A change of plans, we need to get to the airport at once."

Without notifying my parents, we drifted back into the crowd. Since the show was still going on, we were able to catch a cab to Heathrow.

I had a new Greyhound Cessna in a private hangar, so it was easy to get in the plane and leave after all the checks. It took most of the night to get to Tempelhof after stopping for fuel.

Nina understandably wanted to know what was going on. She had been a real trooper in going along with me so far without questions.

I explained that Mary had been kidnapped, showing her the note.

"It has to be the Stasi, East Germany secret police. They want revenge for my previous escape from them."

"Rick, you can't let them take you as a prisoner. What will they do to you?"

"I can't let them keep Mary; besides, they will just lock me up until they can exchange me for one of their spies."

I didn't mention the condition or fate of the last prisoner they had returned.

The plan we came up with was simple. We took a taxi to the bridge. I paid the driver a small fortune to wait. He was to take Nina and Mary to the British Embassy as fast as he could.

During the exchange, Nina was to pick Mary up and run to the taxi. I had a bright idea as we were going to the bridge. There was a camera shop open. I had the taxi driver stop and I bought a Hasselblad camera with a telephoto lens.

I asked the driver to take as many pictures of the exchange as he could. He was then to give the film to Nina. He could keep the camera.

My heart was in my throat as we crossed to the center of that bridge at the appointed time.

Three men met us in the center. They had Mary. She looked a little worse for the wear. More like grumpy for not getting her sleep.

The man holding Mary put her down. She ran to me, but I redirected her to Nina, who scooped her up and took off running.

This quick action caused some confusion among the men, who hadn't expected it. I took the opportunity to give the one to my right a left hook that took him off his feet.

Rather than fight the three, I ran to the bridge and jumped into the middle of the river. I had enough wits about me to go feet first and cup my privates as taught in lifeguard school.

I hit the water with a tremendous splash. It turned out the river wasn't very deep, but it was deep enough that I didn't break a leg.

As I bounced off the bottom of the river, I kicked my shoes off. Then, rather than surface immediately I let the current carry me. I didn't have enough air to go very far, but I wanted to be certain I was oriented so if I made it out of the water it would be on the West German side.

The river was fast enough that I got a good sense of which direction to go. I surfaced as quickly as I could and drew a breath then went down again. As I submerged, I heard gunshots, but they missed.

This time, I turned and went towards the center of the river before surfacing. I hoped this would throw their aim off as they would be looking toward my previous path.

My gamble paid off; I was able to get a deep breath before diving again. The best part was that a bend in the river was coming up and it would put me out of their sight if I moved fast enough.

It worked. As soon as I surfaced the next time, I was out of sight of those on the bridge. I dashed to land and made it safely.

I didn't take any chances but kept running deeper into Berlin. I got about a block, and West German police, who had been called because of the sound of shots fired, picked me up.

My water-soaked diplomatic passport was enough to get me a ride to the British Embassy, where I was reunited with Nina and Mary.

A quick explanation to the ambassador about what happened allowed me a phone call to The Meadows. Mr. Hamilton answered. I quickly told him I had Mary, we were safe and in Berlin, oh, may I talk to Mum or Dad?

To say my parents were upset was an understatement. You could tell they were relieved that Mary, Nina, and I were safe. They were also mad as hell at me for taking off on my own.

I was glad I was far away. I hoped they would cool down by the time I got back home.

The embassy arranged a flight back to Switzerland for Nina. Before she left, I had a short conversation with her. I figured another girlfriend was down the drain.

To my surprise, she asked if every date could be this exciting.

"I hope not, or at least in different ways."

She blushed like crazy when I said that. Then I realized that could be taken several ways. I tried to explain but the more I said the worse it got. I was a stuttering, stammering mess before my brain caught up with my mouth and I shut up.

Again, she surprised me.

"You are so cute when you get flustered. I will have to remember that."

She then laid a kiss on me to remember.

"Call me, Rick, when you are home safe."

She took off with a jaunty wave, telling me the girls would eat their hearts out.

I wasn't allowed to fly my plane home. Mary and I were put on a US Air Force C130 and taken back to London.

There I was debriefed by MI6. I told them everything but 'forgot' to mention I had a roll of film of the whole incident at the bridge. I wanted to know who those men were, especially the leader who had Mary.

Chapter 32

As far as I was concerned the Cold War had just gone hot. This had become personal. Not only were they after me, they had once again brought Mary into it.

You would think they would learn. I realized the first time it had been the KGB, and now it was the Stasi. Maybe they didn't share lessons learned.

My parents and I had a long discussion about the events. I gave Mum the film. She would use her backchannels to try to identify the main man in the pictures.

If I got the other two, they would be counted as bonuses. I had decided I was going after them.

This was on Monday. By Tuesday, Mum had a name and address for the man who had been holding Mary.

He was a Walter Konig, head of the East German unit assigned to Berlin. He lived on a small farm just outside of Berlin.

The best of the information was that he was a man of habit. He was picked up for work Monday through Friday at 8:30 in the morning. There was a guard and driver.

I explained my plan to my parents. They approved of it because of its sheer simplicity. No James Bond gadgets required here, or fancy sports cars, or parachute dives.

I intended to walk to his house, wait for him to come out, put an arrow through him, and walk back to West Germany.

Mum and Dad weren't thrilled with the whole plan but agreed this couldn't go unanswered.

The Communists had to be shown that I was a power within my rights, and they messed with me and mine at their own dire risk.

I would fly into Wolfsburg, Germany, and then walk the one hundred miles to Potsdam. Leaving tomorrow morning, I would arrive at Potsdam on Saturday, get the lay of the land on Sunday, and take my shot on Monday morning.

Herr Konig was about to have a very bad start to his week.

Trying to avoid any flags, Mr. Hamilton chartered a light aircraft to fly me to Leipzig. I would have the flight plan changed in route. By doing this, no one in Germany would know I was there until I had to show my passport.

This should give me enough time to get out of the area.

I should have known that Mum wouldn't let the plan stand that way. She presented me with a Spanish passport with a different name, Jose Hernandez. It had my picture, the same as my other passports.

"Don't get in trouble; it will only stand up to so much scrutiny. The Germans should never know you have entered the country until it is time to leave. Then use your diplomatic one."

"Yes, ma'am, no littering.

"Smartass."

I then thanked her profusely and gave her and Dad a hug. The kids were off playing somewhere, and we didn't want to alarm them.

I had packed my Trapper Nelson backpack with basic gear. There was a more complete first aid kit, flashlight, compass, map, fire starters, flint, five pairs of dry socks and a pair of tennis shoes, two pairs of pants and two shirts, two t-shirts, a waterproof poncho, and a jacket.

I also included dried camping food for a week, two canteens of water, and a ground cloth along with a sleeping bag and ten-power binoculars. There was a hunting knife, a hand hatchet, and a new Hasselblad camera with a telephoto lens.

These, along with my six-foot war bow and yard-long arrows came to forty pounds. Not the lightest weight but very doable for me.

I flew to London, where my charter was waiting. The pilot was completely uncurious about what I was up to. I don't know if he didn't care or had been warned off.

We arrived at Wolfsburg in the late afternoon. I would have two hours to find shelter in the woods. Customs was no problem; I only spoke Spanish. They had to call another official over to talk to me.

He took one look at my passport, stamped it, and said, *"Buenas Noches."*

I thanked him and left, and then took a cab to a park just outside of town. The cabbie was very talkative. It didn't help him because I was still in Spanish-only mode while he only spoke German, or at least that was the only language he used.

I gave him a modest tip, trying not to be remembered. As a last-minute thought, as I got out of the cab, I pointed towards France and said, "Paris?"

"Ja."

That was my big effort at misdirection. When the cab was out of sight, I followed a trail into the woods.

I estimated that I was only a couple of miles from East Germany and that I wouldn't get much more distance tonight, so I bedded down under one of the many fir trees, staying safely in West Germany.

In the morning after my morning ritual, I made a cup of instant coffee, ate some dry cereal, and headed out due east.

I kept off the paths and had no idea when I crossed the border. It is surprising what good time you can make when you aren't tired, hungry, wet, and wounded.

I planned to follow a railroad mainline to Stendal, then cut southeast to Premnitz. I found the mainline with no problem.

When I came to the top of a small hill, I saw a wonderful sight, a slow freight going uphill on its way through Stendal.

Any kid from Bellefontaine, Ohio knows how to hop a freight car. They may call them wagon-lits here, but a boxcar is a boxcar.

If there was a caboose with a conductor on board, it was out of sight around a bend. I slid down the hill as fast as I could, hopped into a car with an open door, and had a nice ride for the next three hours.

I jumped off as the train started to slow as it came into Stendal. I made certain to check for any watchers before getting off. The doors on both sides of the car were open so I was able to get out on the south side and book it over to the woods.

I was now over a day ahead of schedule and still had half a day left. The only downside to the trip was the smell. It was like a load of cabbage had gone bad.

That must have been why the doors were open. The Europeans closed the car doors all the time, whereas in America if they were empty, they were open. I wondered if that was a legacy of the Great Depression.

All those thoughts aside, I checked my compass and headed toward Premnitz. I had 70 miles down on my 100-mile trip and almost half a day to go.

I had a couple of close encounters with other hikers in the woods. I heard the first group before I could see them, so I was able to move further away and never did see them.

I stayed off the marked trail from then on. The next group I met was when I topped a rise. We came face to face.

It was a family: mother, father, and two children, a boy, and a girl, both under six. They had backpacks, even the little ones. We stopped and checked each other out.

On a hunch, I got out my map and compass. I pointed out the shortest direction to the West German border. The father shook his head and thanked me in German. I replied in Spanish. We looked at each other and laughed.

I thought as they moved on, the family was fleeing to West Germany. I hoped they made it.

This was Thursday. I thought about trying to push through to Potsdam and doing the deed tomorrow morning.

After thinking about it, I decided to stick to my original plan. I needed time to scope out the area. Taking advantage of the ride was good, but I couldn't let it weaken my overall plan. I had the time.

Based on that, I walked another ten miles and started to hunt for a place to spend the night. I was tempted by an abandoned farmhouse, but who knew what went on during the night?

Instead, I picked a spot under one of the dependable fir trees. I decided this far in to keep a cold camp, no fire. I would miss the coffee in the morning, but I didn't want any wood smoke in the area.

It was a good thing, as during the night I heard vehicles moving. They were unloading something at that abandoned farmhouse. Guards were patrolling the area, but they stuck close to the trucks and building.

They left, and in about an hour, another group showed up and collected whatever had been unloaded.

I was then able to get to sleep until daybreak. After taking a good look around, I checked out the farmhouse to see if I could get an idea of what had been going on.

There was a carton of Lucky Strikes on the ground. This was an exchange point for a cigarette smuggling organization. I made a note of my location as best as I could. I would have it passed on to MI6. They may be able to use this information.

It was an easy walk to the edge of Potsdam. From there I worked my way around to Herr Konig's farmhouse.

I found a good hiding place to set up camp about a mile away. I then crept closer to the house to spy out what I could. Nothing was happening until six o'clock right on schedule Herr Konig arrived home.

He had a driver and a guard. They were the other two guys from the bridge. What luck! I then retreated to my hidden camp and spent the night.

On Saturday there were people coming and going all day. It was a catering service doing a setup on the lawn. They were pitching tents and setting up chairs. A small bandstand was erected. He must be having a party Saturday night.

I watched from a distance that evening as his guests arrived. With them were guards with Doberman pinchers. They set out on a patrol around the house.

They only came out about twenty-five yards from the house. I was the better part of two hundred yards away, so I felt safe. The wind was blowing toward me so the dogs shouldn't get my scent.

It was still daylight as the guests arrived, so I got some pictures. If it were dark, I wouldn't have been able to take any pictures, even with flashbulbs, as I was too far away for them to be useful. They wouldn't have needed dogs to spot me then. The guests congregated and talked.

Just before dark, a speech was made by a fat guy and then an award was presented to Herr Konig. After that, a small band played polka music. All in all, it looked like a fun party.

One note that all wasn't right in Herr Konig's world was a side meeting between him and the fat guy. They had moved away from the party but still were in my camera range, so I snapped away.

Herr Konig told the fat guy something, and the fat guy went ballistic. Konig held his hands out as though he was trying to placate him, but the fat guy wasn't having it.

I have no idea what it was about, but I don't think it was career-enhancing for Konig.

I retreated to my hideout and had a good night's sleep. Sunday, Konig left his house. It appeared no one was home. I waited for several hours and then walked up to the house. I then paced off the distance from where the car would pick him up to my shooting spot.

I was shooting from a slight rise. It had enough of a drop behind it that I could be out of sight in seconds. I intended to take my shot, duck back out of sight, wait a few moments, then check on my targets.

I then went deeper into the woods until I came across an open field. I paced off the same distance as my shot, then left a large branch as a target. I then proceeded to spend half an hour practicing at the exact distance.

I had another cold camp and settled in for the night. At daybreak on Monday, I was awake and ready to go. Of course, I had to wait another two hours until I heard his transportation show up.

My last thought as I was getting ready was that some would look at this as first-degree murder. I certainly had shown up with a plan to kill Herr Konig.

I viewed myself as a soldier in a war I hadn't started. I hadn't started it, but I was trying to finish it. Would these guys ever take a hint?

These thoughts flew through my mind as I drew my bow. The yard-long arrow had a war point, designed to penetrate and kill.

My shot was true, taking Herr Konig in the center of his chest. I ducked back and nocked another arrow. I counted to five then raised back up.

The guard was out of the car and bending to Konig's body. I let loose and hit him square in the back. This time I stayed up and nocked another arrow.

The driver was halfway around the front of the car and frantically looking around. I took him down with another center mass shot.

There were no other sounds and no one else present. I thought about retrieving my arrows but decided I wanted them to see what could be done. Also, why take a chance of someone coming up on me.

Instead, I returned to camp, tried to leave no sign of my presence, picked up my pack, and headed west.

I took a slightly different route on the way back to West Germany. I thought about Stendal and a train ride but why push my luck? Three days later I crossed the border back into West Germany.

I had kept an eye out for the family I had met on the way but never saw them. I walked into some little town. I caught a cab back to Wolfsburg and met my charter pilot. Before we left, I called The Meadows and told Mr. Hamilton that the mission was a success.

My charter pilot dropped me off at Heathrow where I collected my plane after passing through customs. He never asked the first question. I wondered who he worked for.

At customs, they were a little puzzled by the fact I had no new stamps on my passport but didn't hold me up.

After that, I flew back to Oxford where my family was waiting. There were hugs all about. Mary told me she worried the whole time I was gone. I asked her why she should be worried. I only went to London.

"Pull the other one, Ricky. I hope they are dead."

What do you say to that?

"They are."

"Thank you, now quit getting in trouble with those guys so they will stop kidnapping me. It is getting tiresome."

"I hear you."

At that, Mum, Dad, and I retreated to the library where I was debriefed by them. I was given high marks on my execution of the mission. Was that a double entendre?

Mum took my film so that MI6 could look at it. The cigarette smugglers were interesting, but the interaction between the fat guy and the late Herr Konig could give some insight into the leadership of the Stasi.

With that, I took a long shower and thought about what work I had to catch up on for school.

Chapter 33

While I was on my mission in East Germany, I missed several events.

The first was the US presidential election on Tuesday, November 8th. John F. Kennedy beat Richard Nixon, 303 electoral votes to 219.

There was speculation that late vote counts in Mayor Richard Daley's Chicago sealed the deal. I had a hard time believing that a US election could be that dishonest, but a lot of my beliefs had been challenged in the last several years.

The other event I missed was Remembrance Day. This was on November 11th, the 11th day of the 11th month, the 11th hour, and the 11th minute. This was the time of the cease-fire to end World War I.

It was recognized, but not celebrated in the US, as it was in England. This was due to the loss of life in the respective countries.

The US, with twice the population of Great Britain, lost 53,000 men; Great Britain lost 774,000 men. The impact on Great Britain is still felt to this day as they lost their greatest and brightest to the slaughter.

That is why the whole country comes to a stop at the appointed minute. Big Ben chimes, BBC plays the *Ode of Remembrance*, followed by *Flowers of the Forest, O Valiant Hearts, I Vow to Thee My Country*, and *Jerusalem*. They end with both the *Last Post* and *The Rouse*.

The United States shows its patriotism on the Fourth of July, but it is nothing like the heartfelt sadness that sweeps Great Britain for the human loss. It was effectively the end of the British Empire.

The loss of the Empire pales to the loss of the people. One other time I was in England on that day. I wanted to see if the shivers I felt then would repeat.

Mum had taken the film I had given her to MI6. They were most interested in the photos. It completed a circle.

It was learned from a spy present at the late Herr Konig's party that he had been congratulated on my capture. It appears Herr Konig hadn't told of my escape during the exchange.

He was surprised at his party by the congratulations he received. He had to tell the truth at that point. That must have been when the fat guy went ballistic.

I bet the fat guy wet his pants on Monday when he heard about Konig's fate. What I wasn't certain about—was the plan started with Konig, fat guy, or higher up?

If it was the fat guy or above, I still had some work to do. I just didn't know how I would figure it out.

It turned out that I didn't have to figure it out. I received a written invitation to a reception at the Soviet Embassy in London. After checking with my superiors, Mum and Dad, Mr. Norman, and General Heartly of Coldstream, all agreed I should attend to see what was up.

It was on Wednesday night in London, so I flew up there after class. The dress was a suit and tie or first-class military. Since I didn't have my Coldstream uniforms yet, I went with the suit and tie.

Mr. Hamilton had placed an order with my tailor for a full set. Since they had my measurements, I didn't have to go in. At the rate I was collecting uniforms, I could start my museum.

Dang, I should have worn my 6th Ohio Volunteer Infantry uniform. It was too late to have it shipped from the US. I didn't even know if it would fit anymore, but it would have been a hoot.

It was a little weird going into the Soviet Embassy. I kept wondering if they were going to return my bowling bag.

It was nothing of the sort. I barely had time to get a Coke on ice when I was asked to join the Soviet Ambassador.

He gave me a cold fish handshake and wouldn't look me in the eye when introduced.

"Sir Richard, I have been instructed to let you know that the recent unpleasantness in East Germany has been resolved. The regional Stasi leader has had a sudden heart attack and has died. A hunting accident claimed the life of the Potsdam Stasi head and two of his guards.

"They were the only ones involved in the plot to kidnap your sister and exchange her for you. I am to assure you there will never be an attempt on your life through your family again. I think you have made it clear you take a dim view of those actions."

Dim view, my butt. After making that statement he turned and left. I went out and looked around at the audience. There was one young lady there who looked familiar, but I couldn't place her. I didn't care enough to try to meet her. I decided I had enough and turned to leave.

As I was turning, I saw her start a hand gesture. I thought she was going to wave. Instead of waving, I would recognize that finger anywhere.

I continued to turn and left. I didn't feel up to any scenes tonight.

As I drove home, I thought about what had transpired. They were going to leave my family alone, so my hot war was over and back to the cold war.

Wait a minute; they promised not to attack my family but said nothing about a direct attack on me. Maybe it was a lukewarm war. To top it all, why should I believe anything they told me?

I would pass on to MI6 and others the events of the evening. Everything except the young lady with the rude finger. That was personal. Though I guess trying to kill me could be considered personal.

I managed to get back into a real school routine for the next three weeks. Then it was time for exams. It seemed strange how they were administered.

The colleges taught or lectured but the university gave the exams. In America, there was only one institution that taught and gave exams. Here they were split. I'm not certain why it was, but that was the way they did it.

Anyway, I studied hard for the exams. Despite all the extra-curricular things that had happened this term, I managed to keep up with everything.

The results of my work were demonstrated by top marks in everything. I was very confident going into the exams, but when I walked out, I hoped that I had scraped by.

I learned to hate those blue books for essay-type questions.

I hadn't had a chance to get back to Switzerland to see Nina, as school was all-consuming. Now it was December 13th and the end of the Michaelmas term. Because of exam schedules, the term ended on Tuesday.

My Coldstream officer uniforms had been delivered, two sets, one to The Meadows and one to Jackson House. I was looking forward to wearing one at Christmas parties back in the US.

On Friday, I flew to Switzerland to spend Friday evening and Saturday with Nina. At her request, I took along a dress uniform with all my medals. She wanted to show me off to her girlfriends. I guess I was considered trophy material.

I didn't mind it with her. She was doing it for fun, not as a one-upmanship I'm better than everyone. She tried to be serious about it but kept giggling, thinking of her friends seeing me pick her up at the gate.

It went as she planned. You could hear the buzz as she got into the rented car. Yes, I got a Roller to put on the dog.

At dinner, we had a more serious conversation. She opened it with, "Rick you were a very good archer in *Bandits of Sherwood*. Did you keep it up?"

"Yes, I enjoy it very much."

"Apropos of nothing I read an article of some curious deaths in East Germany. Three Stasi officers were killed by an English longbow."

"That is curious."

"If they were who I think they were, they deserved it!"

"I'm sure they did."

"How is Mary?"

"She wanted to know when I was going to get those guys."

"What did you tell her?"

"Someone had got them."

"Are you going back to the US for Christmas?"

"Yes, it will be nice to spend time at home with the family."

"We should see each other at some parties. Are you taking your uniform with you?"

"Now that would be vain, wouldn't it?"

"That never occurred to me. We girls think nothing of taking our best."

"That's why we men have it better, we aren't slaves to fashion...besides, I ordered two sets, one is already at Jackson House.

For some reason, she reached across the dinner table and punched me.

I took her back to her school before curfew on Friday and Saturday. Why be late when you have a hotel room for the afternoon, and no I'm not going to tell you what went on.

Saturday evening was show-off Rick to the girlfriends, as we attended an informal gathering at a restaurant. We had a side room to ourselves. There were ten couples.

I must be becoming a snob because most of the guys seemed like Euro-trash to me. Minor titles, nothing to do in life except drive fast cars, gamble, chase women, and drink.

Well, at least I didn't gamble or drink. The biggest difference was they were a bunch of sponges. I had earned my money. Also, I was in the military, by a roundabout way, but there.

There were a couple of snide remarks about jumped-up Americans, but I let them live.

It may not sound like it, but it was a pleasant evening. Nina was happy, so I was happy.

Sunday, I returned to England with plans to fly back to LA on Monday for several weeks.

Monday's flight was uneventful except for one guy sitting behind me complaining about the recent US election. He was convinced that since Kennedy was Catholic, the Pope would be giving him orders.

From what I knew of Kennedy, not only was he not a strict practicing Catholic, but if anyone were giving orders, it would be him.

The Christmas season at Jackson House was a whirlwind. It is a good thing that Mum had a staff and a good caterer because something was scheduled for almost every day.

One night there was a Jackson Enterprises get-together for upper management. I got to hand out the bonus checks for the year.

We had seven new millionaires that night. The others present were just adding to their fortune. Jim Williamson took me aside and told me that I now had surpassed two billion in my fortune.

That was so unreal.

Nina accompanied me to every function, and I attended several of hers. At hers, I had to be in uniform, my red coat and white belt with all my medals. Even my official sword. I felt like I had snuck off the Warner Brothers set.

She was proud of her guy. We even talked about the future.

Neither of us was ready to commit to anything yet but felt we were past the high school stage of going steady. Somehow without me realizing it, a girlfriend had snuck up on me.

What was nice was that both sets of parents approved. There was good and bad in that. As Mary pointed out so gleefully, I was outnumbered by the women in my life.

For Christmas, we exchanged small presents, and even though we could afford it, no one went overboard.

Finished for now.

Back Matter

To be continued in Book 10 of The Richard Jackson Saga.
https://www.enelsonauthor.com/

For information on hiring Janet E. Rupert to edit your fiction project, email:
<u>janeteditorrupert@gmail.com</u>

Other books by Ed Nelson

The Richard Jackson Saga

Book 1: The Beginning
Book 2: Schooldays
Book 3: Hollywood
Book 4: In the Movies
Book 5: Star to Deckhand
Book 6: Surfing Dude
Book 7: Third Time is a Charm
Book 8: Oxford University
Book 9: Cold War
Book 10: Taking Care of Business
Book 11: Interesting Times
Book 12: Escape from Siberia
Book 13: Regicide
Book 14: What's Under, Down Under?
Book 15: The Lunar Kingdom
Book 16: First Steps

In the Richard Jackson World

Mary, Mary

Stand-Alone Story

Ever and Always

The Cast in Time series

Book 1: Baron
Book 2: Baron of the Middle Counties
Book 3: Count
Book 4: Earl
Book 5: Earl of the Marches

Did you love *Cold War*? Then you should read *Taking Care of Business* by Ed Nelson!

The **Richard Jackson Saga** ⑩

Taking Care of Business

A Coming of Age story in an Alternate History.

Ed Nelson

In Taking Care of Business in the early 1960s, Rick has to start paying attention to his businesses. Starting with a challenge from an Oxford Don and ending with a serious look at his business empire, he finds he has to be involved. If he doesn't pay attention millions of people could starve due to the untimely death of Chairman Mao. He learns that being sent down from Oxford is not the end of the world. It is also reaffirmed that broken arms and bullet wounds hurt. This tongue-in-cheek saga is all true, give or take a lie or two.